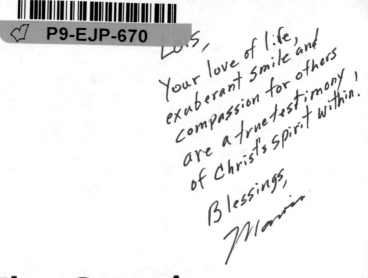

# The Guard

## By Marvin Breshears

xulon
PRESS

I want to extend a special thank you to my wife Kathy for her love and support during this entire process.

I also would like to thank to Rev. Larry Meeks for his encouragement and help with this project.

# Section 1

# 1

Stan and Julie awoke later than usual. Neither one had any particular reason to be up early. Stan, waking earlier than Julie, began kissing and caressing her to get her to wake up so that he could continue with his fantasies. Julie feigned sleep hoping to put off the inevitable that she knew would come soon enough. Stan had made sport of her until late in the night and she didn't want any more of it.

"Julie, baby" said Stan pleadingly, "let's have a little more fun before I have to leave."

"I have had enough, Stan daddy!" Julie replied as she shoved him away.

That settled it! Stan had had enough. He got up, took a shower and got dressed. Returning to the room, he said, "Get up and get dressed, we're leaving!"

"Leaving? Where are we going," Julie asked?

"I'm sick and tired of your antics! I have provided you with a place to stay, food and companionship and how do you repay me? You have been acting like a whining, nagging wife! How long have you been here Julie," shouted Stan?

"I don't know! I lost track of the days a long time ago!" Julie replied.

"It has been 4 months Julie. 4 months! And I am getting tired of it. I think I need someone that will appreciate me!" said Stan.

"No, Stan daddy! No! What are you going to do? What about the baby," sobbed Julie as she began to cry?

"That's another thing! The baby just complicates the situation! You weren't supposed to get pregnant!" said Stan.

"I couldn't help it! You wouldn't get me any birth control and you kept forcing yourself on me! What did you expect," babbled Julie, now sobbing uncontrollably?

"Hurry up and get dressed or I'll take you like that!" shouted Stan.

Reluctantly Julie got up and threw some clothes on and shuffled off to the bathroom to freshen up a bit and try to calm down. She didn't know what was happening or what she should or even could do. Had it really been 4 months since she came here? In some ways it seemed so much longer, but in other ways it seemed like it had only been a week, maybe two since she had been abducted by Stan and brought here. And where was here? She wasn't exactly sure about that. She knew that she was in a forest somewhere. She could see trees out of the one little port hole of a window in this place. And it seemed like she was suspended up in the air somehow from what she could see and the way that it bounced up and down when there was a lot of movement inside. Then there was home; more like prison where she had lived for 4 months. It appeared to be some kind of a ball or sphere. It was well insulated as she could not hear any sounds from the outside and it didn't take much heat to keep it warm inside. She did have to admit, that it would have been a cozy little place if she hadn't been a prisoner here. She had a bathroom with a shower, a small kitchen, electricity (if she used it sparingly, Stan said that it was power from solar cells) and a gas stove and heater.

Julie had always wondered about that fateful night that had earned her ticket to this place. It seemed like her life was like that. Always attracting the LOSERS! She couldn't remember how many boyfriends that she had gone through before she married Angelo. Then Angelo was no catch. Angelo the gang member. Angelo the drug dealer and user. Angelo the inmate. Angelo the LOSER! Now Stan daddy. She wasn't sure why it was Stan daddy, but it was what he had insisted that she call him when he first brought her here. He wasn't her daddy and she wondered if Stan was his real name or not. He never would talk about himself to her. Maybe it was daddy because he saw himself as her provider and protector-a daddy figure. Or, his childhood was so messed up that he didn't have a proper dad or mom or both. She wasn't a psychologist; she just knew that he was sick. And Stan daddy was a LOSER! One of the biggest losers in her life so far.

What Julie did remember about that fateful night was she had gone to The Turf Club there in Crescent City to relax with a drink or two and had been talking to this guy. And the next thing she knew she was there in this ball and the guy was having his way with her. He must have slipped something in her drink when she hadn't noticed. She always had tried to be so careful before. She just couldn't figure out how or when he did it.

"Julie, hurry up in there or I will come in and drag you out of there," bellowed Stan!

Reluctantly Julie finished up and came out to face her fate, whatever that might hold. Stan bound her hands with a cable tie and asked her, "Do I need to put duct tape over your mouth or will you be quiet?"

"No need for the duct tape," Julie said resignedly.

Stan unlocked and opened the door to the sphere and there was a small platform attached to a tree that he pushed her out on to. For the first time Julie saw that she was probably 25 or 30 feet up in the air. The sphere that she had been living in for the last four months was suspended between two trees and it was connected in such a way that it could be slid on the cable that suspended it. Sort of like those zip lines that she had seen on TV. That's why it felt like it moved every time Stan came to visit and every time when he left. She could also see that the tree branches hid the sphere from view at any angle unless you were right underneath of it. She had to admit that even though Stan was a sick, sick man, he was rather ingenious to have designed and built this little hideaway.

Stan put a harness on his self and Julie and then attached the both of them together to a cable that went up the tree to some box like contraption above them. They were joined together facing each other and Julie had to look into Stan's face and eyes. It was not a pretty sight looking into those eyes. In fact it was downright creepy. She had never seen before what she saw in those eyes right then.

A whirring noise started and Stan stepped off the platform with Julie. Julie gave a little scream at the brief sensation of falling off the platform and Stan gave a little sadistic laugh. Reaching the ground, Stan unhooked them from the cable and removed their harnesses. He then led them down an almost perceptible path. Soon, Julie recognized the sound of the waves beating on the shore. And it was not that much farther down the path when they emerged from the trees into a secluded little bay with a small boat dock tucked in under some overhanging branches and a decent size boat moored to it.

Stan pushed Julie onto the dock and out towards the boat where he helped her onboard. They were soon underway out into the ocean. Julie had a faint recollection that she had been here before. It must have been when she was brought here, but that is all that she could remember. After they had been sailing for about 15 minutes, Stan cut the engine and they started to bob there like a cork. Julie thought she might get sick and throw up. Stan retrieved some kind of weights out of a cupboard and Julie began to scream when it dawned on her what his intentions were for her.

All of Julie's screaming and struggling was to no avail. After he had attached the weights to her, Stan said goodbye and pushed Julie over the side of the boat. Julie sank quickly out of sight into the cold, dark waters of the Pacific Ocean. One of Julie's last lucid thoughts was wondering if anyone would miss her or even know that she was gone. Her husband, Angelo, sitting there in prison was probably expecting to receive the divorce papers any day that she should have filed and sent long before this; he had always sweet talked his way out of her not filing and she hated herself for it. Well, he can just keep wondering. And then her struggles with life were over and the depths of the ocean and the creatures that lived there claimed what had been Julie and the unborn, unnamed life that was growing inside of her.

"She was a liability and I was getting bored with her anyway. Besides she was starting to annoy me," said Stan to no one in particular as he restarted the engine. "I am just going to have to find me a new one. There are plenty of them out there and I love this part of the game. I think this must be what big game hunters feel like when they are stalking their prey. Except that mine is more fun; at least for a while until I get tired of them."

And with that Stan headed back to town. No remorse, no guilt, only anticipation of the hunt to come.

# 2

Billie Jean, that is Billie Jean Monroe or as her friends called her BJ, awoke where she left off when she had fallen asleep the night before. She had been ruminating. What a funny word, ruminating. Yes, she was ruminating. Just like Bertha their old milk cow did after she had eaten a pitchfork full of alfalfa or the half a coffee can (could she use "can" anymore, since coffee didn't come in cans anymore, but those awful plastic things that just cluttered up the landfill because no one around here recycled) of grain she gave Bertha every morning while her husband, Ralph, milked her. Yes indeed, ruminating. She brought up these questions that she supposed that everyone "ruminated" over from time to time. However, unlike Bertha, there was no real conclusion or digestion to the matter. The questions kept returning in one form or another to ruminate on them some more, only to set them aside to bring them up again another time when she could roll them around in her mind like a tasty morsel that you want to savor for a while longer.

This morning, those morsels were still there. Rolling around and around. But it wasn't a tasty morsel. It was a nagging, pregnant notion that was like the cheat grass in your sock or the small, sharp, jagged stone in your shoe that you didn't have time to stop and remove. But today, today was her day of rest. Not exactly the Sabbath, but at least she didn't have to go into work; not that she didn't have work to do. There was always plenty to do around the house and outside when you lived on a small acreage. Ralph did most of the chores and work around the place, but on her day off BJ liked to help him if she could – that is if she was all caught up on the household chores and/or didn't have any errands to run, like to the grocery store, the courthouse or who knows where else. But today nothing was on her agenda, at least so far. She was sure that Ralph would think of something before too long, he usually did. BJ almost never slept in. Not like most people would think of sleeping in. The last time she remembered sleeping in was three years ago when she got the flu. And that really isn't the same as sleeping in. Since she didn't have to go to work today and it would probably be another hour before Ralph would come in from doing the chores and insinuate that his stomach needed filling, BJ could just lay there being lazy for a bit longer.

So, BJ lay there in her warm, cozy bed ruminating on the questions of the night before; the questions with seemingly no concrete answers. The one question that seemed to rise above the others, like cream rises to the top of the milk in a cream separator or if it is left to stand undisturbed for a period of time, was "Where is my life going?" And with that question inevitably came the reflections on what was going on with her life presently and of course the twists and turns that her life had taken to get to where she was presently. Not that she had had a particularly bad or eventful life, but a life that she could never have mapped out ahead of time when she was young and just starting on this journey called life. She supposed that if she were to really "map" her life like a road on some roadmap that you picked up at the gas station (at least you used to be able to do that, but things change, even free gas station maps weren't free anymore) it would look more like California highway 101 or worse yet highway 1 instead of Interstate 5 in California.

Billie Jean was a hard worker; always had been. And, unless some physical ailment slowed her down, she supposed that she always would be. Although she would turn 65 this year and the government said she could collect her Social Security retirement next year in full, she didn't think that there would be any chance of that happening, retirement that is. And who knew about Social Security, what with all the talk of the system running out of money and all. But what did she know about any of that anyway. BJ just knew that her check was less every week because of something they took out called FICA. And every year now for as long as she could remember she would get a statement shortly before her birthday rolled around showing a breakdown of how much she had contributed each year that she had worked, since she had turned 16 and could legally work, and how much she could expect to collect by drawing at different ages if she kept working and contributing to the pot at a similar rate.

She had always surmised that they would probably have to carry her out of the Chart Room Restaurant where she was a waitress when the time came for her to check out of this place. Though she wasn't planning or even wishing that that would happen any time soon, but one had no guarantees about tomorrow or even the next minute for that matter. Already this year two of her and her husband's good friends were no longer with them. Both of them were young, at least to her way of thinking, too. One was 58 and the other was 59. Both had died suddenly of heart attacks. You just never know.

They did alright for themselves though; financially anyway. They were not rich, but they always had plenty of good food to eat, even if they raised a lot of it themselves and canned and froze what they could when it was in season. Ralph hadn't had a "real" job for what 10, no 20 years. My time whizzes by! Ever since the logging industry around Crescent City had gone into the toilet. He used to make good money as a logger. But when that started drying up and then the mill closed, there just wasn't much demand for a logger. The state employment people had offered to "retrain" him to do another job, but Ralph politely declined. Said he was "too old to teach an old dog new tricks." So, he collected the unemployment checks until they ran out and then started doing handyman jobs for various people around town. Ralph is very good with his hands and very mechanical too, so he can repair just about anything if there is a chance that it can be repaired. Plus, he manages our little acreage, which is almost 10 acres and is situated just outside of the city. That is enough to have our milk cow Bertha, a calf or two that we raise for beef, a couple dozen chickens that give us eggs and an occasional Sunday fried chicken dinner plus a good sized garden every summer that provided them with fresh veggies and they were even Organic; although they didn't go through the certification process, they knew themselves what had been put on them. That gave them some peace and satisfaction. Since Ralph was a logger, he always went out every year and cut and chopped up wood for their wood stove to heat the house with. That saved them from having a huge oil, gas or electric bill like she heard some people talking about. She didn't know how they would manage to pay a huge heating bill like that. Ralph might have been able to get on as a commercial fisherman, but he had a very real problem with seasickness. In fact, he could hardly stand on the beach and look out at the ocean without getting seasick; strange for someone who had lived all his life next to the Pacific Ocean. Besides, the fishing economy now was not much better than the timber. Yes, Ralph was a good man! A good provider! She couldn't have asked for anyone better.

So, even though Ralph didn't go off to an office or a factory on a set schedule, he wasn't a slacker either. He contributed to the finances and the welfare of the family as much as she did with her steady job. And there were times when she wondered how "steady" her job was. But God was good and He was always faithful to provide. She and Ralph had raised four kids on their meager incomes. They had turned out OK. They were good kids and now had lovely families of their own. She wished she could see them more often, but such was life. They had to go where the jobs were. They had had three girls and a boy. The boy was the youngest and he thought that he was pretty special to have three beautiful older sisters to pay attention to him and "mother" him. Now they were all grown up, married and all but the one girl had given her at least one grandchild. How blest she was. Two of them were talking about coming home for Christmas this year. She was so excited about that. But that was a few months away and anything could happen between now and then. Still, she couldn't help but have goose bumps just thinking about it.

BJ thought about growing up in Crescent City. She had never lived anywhere else. She hadn't even traveled very far away. Bill Story, BJ's paternal grandfather and namesake (BJ was supposed to have been a boy) moved to Crescent City with his wife and

BJ's grandmother, Maude, from Missouri when times were really tough and there was no money and no jobs to be had anywhere. They moved west to Los Angeles with a lot of other families on the promise of work and a golden future. However, once there, jobs were not as plentiful as everyone had talked about so Bill signed up with a timber company that was in town recruiting workers to go to Crescent City. Bill knew nothing about logging, but he was used to hard work, he was young and strong, and he figured that it couldn't be too difficult to learn how to be a logger.

And how right he was! It was hard work, but he made a decent living. He even made enough to raise his family on and buy a few acres to call his own; those same acres that BJ and Ralph were living on. BJ's dad, Robert (or as most people called him "Bobbie") Story, had been a logger like his dad, but he was tired of being a farmer. He and BJ's mom, Nancy, lived across town in a cute little bungalow by the ocean. BJ was always kidding them about their little romantic getaway next to the sea that most people would give anything to have, but even though it was cozy they didn't think their place was anything special or that there would be anyone out there that would envy the place. Both Bill and Bobbie had come to the end of their logging careers by the time the timber industry had gone into the toilet; a result of the soft demand for lumber and the pressures from foreign imported products. But Ralph had not been as fortunate, his career in the logging industry was in mid stride when it hit and it was a difficult transition for him.

Bill and Maude were now gone. They passed away within a year of each other. BJ still missed them and thought about them quite often even though it had been close to 20 years since they died. They had been a close family; did a lot of things together, especially outdoor things; activities that didn't take much money, because they didn't have a lot of money. They lived close to the Redwoods and the ocean so they had a big playground to play in. They particularly liked camping together in the summer months; one big happy family. BJ missed those times too. Now everyone did their own things and they didn't get together that much anymore; especially since grandma and grandpa were gone, and her kids had all moved away. Better opportunities elsewhere they said; nothing going on in Crescent City. They wanted to see and experience the world. She just looked forward to those times when they came home for a visit; which wasn't often enough to suit her.

Yes, indeed, ruminating! Thought ruminating!

"Oh, No! There's the door! Ralph's back in from doing the chores and he is probably hungry."

"BJ! It's already 7:30! Are you going to sleep all day? We have a big day ahead of us and you are thinking that this is a holiday!"

BJ thought, big day? What big day? Then she remembered the BIG DAY! She leapt out of bed, setting aside the ruminating, and scurried around like one of the mice that lived in the barn to get ready for the big day.

# 3

"Good Morning! Two for breakfast?"

"Yes, please. And, can you bring us some coffee right away? We're not morning people and need some help to get going!"

"Certainly, sir! Is this booth by the window all right? You get a good view of the harbor and the fishing boats going out. If you watch close enough you might see some seals looking for their breakfast. Would you like cream with that coffee?"

"No, thank you. We need it straight!"

Tricia Noyes had worked as a waitress since she was in high school. It wasn't all that long ago, but at times it seemed like an eternity. However she had only been working here at the Chart Room Restaurant for about 3 weeks. Tricia thought that she was fortunate to have found a job so quickly after moving here to Crescent City. Or maybe she shouldn't give fortune so much credit. Maybe God was really interested in her life after all and He was providing for her. She didn't pretend to know much about those things, but she was truly grateful for the job and the other assistance that she had gotten.

"Are you two ready to order?"

"Yes, I believe we are. We have a big day ahead of us and we're going to need a lot of fuel."

"Are you traveling?"

"Yes, we are. We want to go thru the Trees of Mystery and see some of the Redwood forests and then make it to Portland, Oregon by tonight."

"That will be a big day! A lot of driving! Ma'am, what can I get for you?"

"I would like the 'Lite Eater' #1, please."

"And how would you like your egg?"

"Over medium"

"What kind of toast would you like?"

"Whole wheat"

"Sir, what can I get for you?"

"I want the Dungeness crab, shrimp and cheese omelet with sourdough toast."

"Excellent choice sir! That omelet is famous. It was listed in the Coastal Living magazine not too long ago."

"I'm looking forward to trying it."

Although Tricia had not been working that long at the Chart Room, she had picked up that much since she started. She enjoyed working with BJ and was looking forward to getting to know her better. Even though she was older, much older than Tricia, she had sensed a kindred spirit between them from the first time they had met. BJ was almost like the mother that Tricia had never known when she was growing up. Her mother could never be counted on for anything. She was either in trouble with the law, or high on whatever drug was handy at the time or just plain missing; God only knew where she was or what she was doing. Tricia was shuffled off from one place to another and was watched by anyone that was old enough to dress and feed themselves.

"Here you go! And here is some jam for your toast. Can I get you anything else? Ketchup? Tabasco?"

"Some ketchup, please."

"And I could use some extra napkins."

"Here they are! Enjoy!"

It was not totally by choice that Tricia had moved to Crescent City. She would have preferred to have stayed in Sacramento. She loved living there. All of her friends were there and there was so much to do there. She knew no one here and this place was dead.

She didn't know if she would ever get used to the fishy smell all of the time.

"More coffee?"

"None for me, thank you."

"I'll take a half a cup, please. And can you bring us our check? We really need to get going."

"Certainly, sir."

"Do you take the money? Or do I pay at the cash register?"

"It doesn't matter. I will end up running the register either way. I can take it for you while you finish your coffee sir."

Tricia was not used to operating the register. Where she had worked before was a large establishment and they had a host or hostess that handled all of the money and all she had to do was make the customers happy. And she was good at it. She knew how to please them. And she was rewarded for it; both in praise from her managers and the tips that the customers left her. She had learned how to operate the cash register here quickly enough and even though math was not her strong suit (actually, school in general was not her strong suit) Tricia was pretty proficient at counting money and making change. She was a little worried about working here though. She wasn't sure if there would be enough customers and consequentially enough tip money to survive on. In fact, so far it had been rather meager and she had started to worry. She knew that she wasn't sleeping well and the financial stress was part of the reason. She kept telling herself to trust God. Trust God! But, that was easier said than putting it into practice. Just how was she going to make it? And how would she feed and clothe her two children, Timmy, 11, and Candy who was 7?

"Thank you, sir, ma'am! Stop in and see us again when you are in the area!

"And thank you! That omelet was marvelous!"

As Tricia, began to clear the table that the two had just been sitting at, it was then that she noticed the bill. The tip! It was not an ordinary bill. She was used to seeing a few ones, fives and tens, the occasional twenty, but this wasn't any of those. She had so infrequently had one of these in her possession that she thought it must be a mistake-it must be! As she picked it up, she noticed that there was not one, but two of these bills. Two one hundred dollar bills! Her tip! For her! There must be some mistake. She ran to the door to catch the couple and return it to them or at least to thank them, but their car was already going down the street. Two hundred dollars! How could she ever not trust God again?

The rest of the day was a blur. She was so pumped from the morning. She had also worried about being short-handed with BJ being gone for a few days and her still learning the system here and all, but that too had melted away. What good did it do to worry anyway? That didn't help either. She still did though, but there would always be some little answer like the two hundred dollars that would make her worries look silly. Trust! If she could only do that up front!

Tricia hated leaving Timmy and Candy home alone, but she didn't know what other choice she had. Timmy had insisted that he was old enough to care of himself and his sister, but Tricia worried about that as well. She wished that she didn't have to. There was always some news about a weirdo doing some awful thing to kids these days-abducting them, molesting them-just awful, unthinkable, unspeakable things; things that kids-and moms-shouldn't have to worry about. But the weirdoes did, and she did.

When she got home that night Tricia was tired and relieved to see that the kids had managed just fine by themselves, just like they had since she had started working at the Chart Room. And the house was reasonably fine as well. Not so bad that she had to fuss at them like she did some times.

"Timmy, Candy!" Tricia said. "I am going to visit daddy tomorrow after work. I shouldn't be too late, since I'm supposed to be off a little earlier."

Timmy, "I wish I could go visit him too! I miss him, mommy!"

"I know dear. We all miss him and wish that he were with us. Maybe soon. We are working on it."

"I have been praying for him!" Timmy said.

"Me Too," Candy piped up, not wanting to be left out.

"We just have to trust God! Trust that He is working things out-in our lives and in daddy's life," responded Tricia.

# 4

✤

Driving due North out of San Francisco across the Golden Gate Bridge one continues on one of California's most infamous state highways, highway 101. It remains inland as it travels north; as opposed to the more scenic and more arduous Highway 1 that hugs the rugged coastline as it twists and turns where the ocean is relentlessly and violently making incursions into the land; succeeding in some places, but not so successful in others.

As highway 101 leaves the Golden Gate Bridge, the magnificent skyline of San Francisco (if it's not foggy; which happens quite often), through the haute suburb of Sausalito and eventually into one of California's major wine producing regions, the Sonoma valley. Going past Geyserville through the valley formed by the Russian River in the coastal mountain range the terrain begins to get more rugged, covered with more vegetation and more sparsely populated.

The highway does return to the coastline close to Eureka -famous for its role in the California gold rush days and the inspiration for the California State Motto which means in Greek, exuberantly, "I have found it!" Another hour and half of driving North from Eureka puts you into Crescent City. All together it is 350 miles from the Golden Gate Bridge to Crescent City; a long six and a half hours of driving if not many stops are made.

Like Eureka, Crescent City is along the coast and has a history of timber and fish harvesting. However, Crescent City never did have to contend with the gold fever that inflicted and affected Eureka during those wild, gold mining days.

Crescent City, the county seat and the only incorporated city in all of Del Norte County, is not very large-both in population numbers and total area covered. The city takes up 2.1 square miles and three tenths of that is made of up water. Population numbers are almost that dismal-about 8,500 people which includes 3,500 inmates at the Pelican Bay State Prison that's located within the city limits.

The climate in Crescent City is Oceanic and therefore generally mild even in the winter, although it is one of the wettest places in California. In November of 1973 they recorded 31.25 inches of rain, the most ever recorded for any month. The record for the most rainfall ever recorded in a single 24 hour period belongs to January 9, 1995 with 7.73 inches falling in that time period.

Since the timber and fishing industries had fallen on hard economic times the city and the area were in a depressed economic state. And although they couldn't support the big box stores, the town did have a nice selection of grocery, variety/department, and hardware stores to shop in. They have the usual fast food chains as well as the mom and pop local restaurants to choose from for dining selections. They also have several banks, motels and even a cinema.

The one bright spot in their economy and the one employer that has probably kept the city afloat is the Pelican Bay State Prison. But they have their detractors too. In 1989, the California Department of Corrections came in and built one of the newest, meanest super-max prisons in their penal system. Pelican Bay is now an international model of sensory deprivation and isolation. Half of the prison is of the normal variety, but the other half is the X-shaped Super-Max variety where the inmates that are deemed incorrigible are locked in their cells 23 hours a day and only let out for an hour into a small exercise area by themselves.

Pelican Bay is the city's largest employer, which was good news for the city when they built there because the unemployment rate had reached the 20 percent mark. The flip side to that though, is the prison uses that economic leverage to coerce and intimidate the leaders of the city and to quell dissent among the townspeople.

Although the Pelican Bay Prison brought economic growth, there have been charges of another kind of growth. A conspiracy of the judges and prosecutors and even the jurors that are heavily loaded with prison guards and their families to keep prisoners locked up for longer periods of time on charges not deserving as harsh a penalty. As a result, the Pelican Bay inmates become permanently trapped in the system and even sent into the Super-Max facility just to keep the prison population at its highest possible levels, therefore insuring their jobs well into the future.

Those guards who have tried to play by the rule book and have tried to call attention to the abuses in the system have been threatened; their families threatened and have been forced to resign.

Besides Pelican Bay State Prison, the other ominous, foreboding, dark shadow that constantly hangs over the city is the ever present threat of tsunamis. Within a period of 51 years, the city has experienced tsunami conditions 17 times. That is 1 event every 3 years. Although most of these events were barely perceptible, one tsunami in 1964 damaged the city extensively. The damage included the destruction of 289 buildings and businesses; 1000 cars and 25 large fishing vessels were crushed; 12 people were confirmed dead, over 100 people were injured and numbers were missing; 60 blocks had been inundated with 30 city blocks destroyed. Most of the reported missing persons were later accounted for, not all of the missing was found.

And as is usually the case after some natural disaster such as this has occurred once, those left are always wondering when the next time will come. Crescent City did rebuild the buildings and the infrastructure. They also put into place an early tsunami warning system so that the loss of life would be minimized when that next time does come. But the trouble with time is that the farther away from the event that you get, the less likely that the young and the newcomers to the area will have been impacted by the devastation and so have a cavalier attitude to the 'next-time'.

The recent publication in the local media about the convergence of three major tectonic plates just off shore of Crescent City did nothing to allay the fears of the residents of the city that a major tsunami would overtake them since earthquakes were the major contributing factor to generating the devastating waves of a tsunami. Although, most experts feel that a locally generated earthquake would not cause a significant tsunami, but the next big one would come from a distant earthquake such as the one in the Alaskan Aleutian Island chain in the devastating 1964 earthquake and subsequent tsunami. And so the talk was not if, but when.

# 5

It was a big day for BJ. They were going to pick up their grandson, Rod Wilson, who was coming to spend the summer with his grandparents. Rod had just finished school for the summer and was looking forward to being on the farm and helping his grandpa with the chores. Rod would be turning 14 at the end of the summer and this may be the last summer that he would be able to do this or even want to do this. His parents, Ted and Alicia Wilson (BJ and Ralph's second oldest daughter), would be traveling a lot for their work over the summer and thought it might be best if Rod could spend some quality time with his grandparents. They lived in Seattle, Washington, which is not all that far from Crescent City, but they always seemed to be too busy to get down that way. And besides, the same line that they heard from everyone was that Crescent City is not really on the way to anywhere in particular unless you want to visit the Redwoods.

So, Ted and Alicia were putting Rod on the train, the Amtrak Coast Starlight in Seattle and BJ and Ralph were going to pick him up in Klamath Falls. BJ was worried that Rod might be too young to be traveling by himself, especially since there seemed to be so many weird, perverts out there these days. But, Rod had insisted that he was old enough and his parents agreed with him.

The train didn't come through Crescent City and the closest stops were either Klamath Falls, Oregon or Redding, California. Klamath Falls and Redding are about equidistance from Crescent

City, but in opposite directions of each other. Klamath Falls is to the Northeast and Redding is to the Southeast. BJ had been to Redding a dozen times or so over her lifetime, but she had never been to Klamath Falls, although she had always wanted to go there. She had heard how beautiful Crater Lake, which is near Klamath Falls, is and she had wanted to see for herself. Then, probably the clincher in the decision as to which city to pick him up at was the train schedule. The Coast Starlight left Seattle at 9:45 AM, which would be easy for Rod's parents to get him on the train, and it arrived in Klamath Falls at 10:00 PM, but it did not get to Redding until 2:21 in the morning. It was going to be a long day for Rod, but he was up for an adventure and had never ridden on a train before. When he went with his parents they had always driven or if it was a long distance, they had flown.

Alicia knew that her parents, BJ and Ralph, were tight financially, they always seemed to be, but with the economy the way it was she was sure that they didn't have much money to spare. Since they had plenty of money and her parents were going to be watching Rod for the summer, she gave Rod an envelope with five one hundred dollar bills in it and she booked them a room in Klamath Falls for four nights and put it on her credit card. She knew that the train would not get into Klamath Falls until late and she didn't want them trying to drive home after picking up Rod or in staying in some cheap, flea-bitten, out-of-the-way motel which is where they usually stayed when they had to spend the night away from home on their dime. Plus, she also knew how much her mom really wanted to see Crater Lake, so this would give her time to do that and it would be good for Rod to see it too. He had seen Crater Lake before when he was seven, but thought he might appreciate it more now that he was older. Besides, he could be the "tour guide" for his grandparents and keep them out of trouble. She had just heard about the couple that had stopped at the viewpoint overlooking the lake and had forgotten to set their emergency brake. The car started rolling down the hill towards the lake with their dog in the car. Fortunately, they had an open sunroof and the dog was smart enough to jump out it before it hit the bottom and into the lake. The authorities had to use a helicopter to retrieve the mangled car as it is so far down to the lake, it is so steep and there are no access roads to the lake. Alicia really didn't believe her parents would do that, but it would be nice to have someone with them that was a little younger than them and had done quite a lot of traveling, especially for someone as young as Rod was.

"Ralph, did you get it all squared away with Jack to take care of the animals while we are gone," asked BJ?

Jack was the next door neighbor (actually he lived a quarter of a mile away) boy that had just graduated from high school that spring. His family had a small farm like Ralph and BJ and had taken care of animals since he was old enough to walk.

"Yes, I told him where everything was and how much to feed everyone. I also told him when we usually milk Bertha. I told him how upset she gets when you don't milk her on time," said Ralph.

"Jack is a good kid. We can trust him," replied BJ.

Ralph said, "BJ, you'll have to be the navigator."

"You know I don't do well reading maps. Just don't have a fit when I miss the road that we are supposed to be on," replied BJ.

"We just need to take Highway 199 leaving Crescent City then we don't have to worry until we get to Grants Pass," said Ralph.

The drive was uneventful, with Ralph stopping in Medford to stretch and to relieve themselves. While they were stopped they ate a snack before heading off again. They almost missed the off ramp to get off of I-5 and onto Highway 66 since Ralph was unaccustomed to driving on a freeway, but they did get off and they did make it to Klamath Falls.

Ralph asked, "What's the name of that hotel we are staying at and what is its address?"

BJ said, "It's called the Best Western Olympic Lodge and it's on South Sixth Street."

"Sounds like some fancy place that we don't belong in," said Ralph.

"Ralph! Turn! Turn! There's South Sixth Street," BJ said excitedly!

"There it is Ralph! There's the Best Western," said BJ.

"I won't know what to do in there," said Ralph.

After checking in and getting settled into their room, Ralph and BJ thought that they had died and gone to heaven. They had never seen such a beautiful place. It was still a few hours until the train arrived, so they decided to go out and see the town, get something to eat and make sure they knew where the train station was.

"Ralph, the train is coming! I see the headlight down the track," said BJ!

"BJ, don't get so excited! That won't hurry it along," replied Ralph.

"BJ, look over there! There's our Rod," said Ralph.

"Grandma, Grandpa," exclaimed Rod!

"My, look at how big you have gotten," said BJ.

"How was the train ride," asked Ralph?

"It was a lot of fun, but I'm glad it's over. That is a long way. I met another boy that was going to San Francisco with his parents and we explored the whole train together," said Rod.

"Are you hungry," asked BJ?

"I did have some food on the train, but that was hours ago. Yes, I am hungry," said Rod.

"I saw a burger joint not far from here on the way to the motel. We'll stop and get you a bite, before we turn in for the night. We have some things to see and do tomorrow," Ralph said.

The four nights went all too quickly for Ralph and BJ. They made it up to see Crater Lake (a couple of times since BJ enjoyed it so much) and to the Lava Beds close to Tule Lake. Rod liked the Lava Beds the best. They had lava tube caves that he could explore and roam around in.

This time they decided to go back on highway 140 since it went north along the West side of the lake and they had already traveled along the East side of the lake when they had visited Crater Lake. And this time Ralph didn't have any trouble getting off of I-5 onto highway 199 heading home to Crescent City.

"Grandpa, do you have animals at your house," asked Rod?

"Oh, yes, do we ever have animals. And you get to help me take care of them this summer," said Ralph.

It wasn't long until Rod nodded off and when he woke up, they were pulling into his grandparents' driveway.

# 6

"Did you have a nice weekend Stan?" Asked Frank Bostrum, colleague and fellow guard at the Pelican Bay State Prison (however, usually not in the SuperMax area of the prison).

"It was OK!" replied Stan, less than enthusiastically.

"That's your normal answer. Don't you ever have a *fantastic* weekend? Did you go camping at your cabin again? Or do I even need to ask that one?" said Frank.

"I do other things – occasionally! And yes, I did go camping!"

"When are you going to take me to that cabin of yours?"

"It's nothing special. What's been happening around here? Anything more on the layoffs or cutbacks in hours?"

"Nothing more on layoffs – or cutbacks. I think the union used a little persuasion to help them think straight. Oh, and there's a new guy in D-22. I believe his name is Mark. His wife/girlfriend or whatever was in to see him right away too! Cute little thing."

"Did you catch her name?"

"She's taken! What you going to do, go hitting on her?"

"No! No! These gals that hang around here aren't my type."

"What is your type Stan? I have never seen you with a lady. I was wondering if you liked the men instead."

Stan takes a swipe at Frank, but Frank has already moved out of range, so the strike just fans the air.

"Just joking Stan! Lighten up! And I almost forgot, the state board of prison inspection is the end of this week and not the next, so we have to hump to get everything ready to meet their approval. It seems like someone's been complaining about our little commune here! Don't they know that this town's survival depends on how we do here at Pelican? This town would become a ghost town in a few months if this prison closed up."

"Maybe it would be good for those complainers to spend a few months in one of the cellblocks! Get a new 'girlfriend'! Eat some gourmet meals! Have to watch their backs all the time! And have you constantly chewing on their backside, Frank."

"Come on, Stan! You know that you're the one that rides them hard."

"Whatever! Let's get on with our rounds! I'm sure that the men have missed us," said Stan sarcastically.

"Stan, you go on ahead. I have some paperwork that the office wanted me to catch up on. Besides, this is my '*Friday*' and I wouldn't want to strain myself and ruin the '*weekend*'. I am taking an extra long one this time since I have so much vacation time built up."

"An extra long weekend? What are you going to do, Frank?"

"I am taking the family to San Francisco. The kids just got out of school and it has been quite a while since we were there. We are going to Golden Gate park, Fisherman's Wharf and then out to that new 'green museum' by the art museum."

"That sounds like it should be fun. I haven't been to San Francisco in forever. It just seems so far away and to take so long to get there!"

"Stan, you could go there if you didn't go camping every spare minute."

"Maybe I will have a little more time now. I just split up with my girlfriend."

"I'm sorry Stan. How long have you two been an item?"

"Not that long, only about 4 months."

"Long enough to start to get to know someone...and, to get them pregnant," said Frank.

Frank wasn't sure where that last sentiment came from, but he wished that he could retract it, because as soon as he said it, Stan turned on his heel and went off down the corridor without saying another word.

Frank went to the office to complete the paperwork that the office wanted him to fill out, but his mind was elsewhere and he had to ask for another form and start over because he realized that he was filling it out wrong. He couldn't help wondering about the strange reaction that Stan had when he said 'get them pregnant.' Maybe that was why they broke up. Some men just aren't ready to be fathers. He would have to remember to apologize to Stan the next time that he saw him.

In making his rounds, Stan purposely swung by D22 to introduce himself and size up the new guy that Frank had mentioned earlier in their conversation.

"I'm Stan Wosniak. What's your name number 533621?"

"I'm Mark Noyes."

"What are you in for? And how long?"

"I...I..."

"I'll find out sooner or later Mark Noyes," said Stan.

"I'm in for armed robbery and accessory homicide-seems as though the convenience store that I was supposed to have robbed, didn't go so good and the little clerk was shot and killed. Someone framed me as the getaway driver and I ended up here. I have 20 years to sit here and rehabilitate."

"Noyes, every one of these men in here tell me that they are innocent, but a jury of their peers says otherwise. Now who do you think I'm going to believe?"

"No one believes me – except my wife!"

"Yeah, Frank told me you had some pretty little thing visiting you while I was gone."

"She's a good woman! You leave her alone!"

"What are you going to do Noyes? You have twenty years to look at the other side of those bars. So I don't think that you are in any kind of a position to be telling me what I can or cannot do. If your pretty little woman needs some company on a cold winter night, what are you going to do to stop me?"

"Just stay away from her Wosniak," screamed Mark!

"It's *Mr. Wosniak* to you Noyes! Oh, and what's her name, Mark?"

At lunch time Frank caught up with Stan in the cafeteria. "Stan, I want to apologize for what I said about getting your girlfriend being pregnant. I don't know why I said it. I just blurted it out without thinking. It is none of my business and I'm sorry."

"Apology accepted. I guess I was a bit touchy on the subject and reacted very badly. And no, she is not pregnant; at least, not that I know about. Hey, I went by and met the new guy you said checked into D22. A little touchy about his woman if you ask me! Told me to stay away from her! I haven't even seen her yet! He must have a little bit of jealousy going on there."

"Well Stan, you do tend to rile up the men talking about their women!"

"All in good fun, Frank. All in good fun."

That afternoon, Frank and Stan were assigned to the visitation room when Tricia Noyes came in to visit her husband, Mark.

Stan noticed her first and said to Frank, "She is a looker isn't she? How did a loser like him wind up with a good looking woman like her?"

"Yeah, I would be jealous too, if my wife looked like that and some guy was making a pass at her," said Frank.

"Frank, I didn't make a pass at her."

"Just keep it on the up and up, Stan! We are professionals here. We have a job to do and we shouldn't let that interfere with our personal lives...or the personal lives of the inmates and their families."

"OK, warden! I get the message!"

"Time to wrap it up! Visitation hours are over!"

# 7

"Good Morning, Rod" said BJ the morning after their arrival back in Crescent City after she and Ralph had picked him up in Klamath Falls a few days ago.

"Mornin! I guess! Sure is early to be getting up" exclaimed Rod!

"Things start moving early on a farm. You'll get used to it shortly. How did you sleep?"

"Sure is quiet here. Sort of spooky."

"You'll get used to that too! So used to it that you will have a hard time when you go back home to that noisy Seattle life."

"Maybe"

"What would you like for breakfast, honey? I think I have just enough time to make you breakfast, unless you want some fancy gourmet dish."

"Grandma, do you have any Pop-Tarts?"

"No, dear!"

"What about those Jimmy Dean breakfast sausage sandwiches or those breakfast Hot Pockets?"

"We don't eat those store-bought prepared meals. We can't afford to eat like that. We make our own meals from scratch with good, fresh, wholesome ingredients."

"Really? You can do that?"

"Sure! And you hang around here long enough and I'll show you how to as well. I showed your mother, but I suppose she's forgotten how to do that or maybe she's just too busy to take the time to cook."

"So, would you like pancakes, or bacon and eggs, or biscuits, or oatmeal, or maybe French Toast?"

"Can we make pancakes? I love to get pancakes when we go to IHOP!"

"Sure we can! But, mine probably won't taste like IHOP's."

"Probably better!"

"What do you mean probably? They are definitely better!" said Ralph coming in the back door having finished up his chores outside for the morning and looking for some breakfast himself.

"Morning, grandpa! You heard? We get to have pancakes!"

"Good morning, Rod! And yes I did hear that we get pancakes."

"Don't I get a good morning?" asked BJ.

"I'm sorry dear! Good Morning!" said Ralph as he gave her a little kiss.

"Alright! You are forgiven this time. Go wash up and we should be about ready by the time you finish. And Rod, you can help me set the table with plates and utensils. Then you can put the butter, syrup, peanut butter, and jam on the table."

It's not long until the table is set, the griddle is heating up and the coffee is starting to brew.

"Come to the table!" said BJ.

BJ puts a stack of cakes on Rod's and Ralph's plates. Rod hurries and fixes his cakes with lots of butter and drenched with warm syrup. As he starts to take a bite of his food BJ says, "Young man, we say grace at this table before we eat! I taught your mom how to do that too. I guess she's forgotten everything I ever taught her."

After Ralph says grace, BJ says, "Alright, you may eat now."

"Thank you, grandma! Those were really good pancakes. Definitely better than IHOP's, but I won't tell them," said Rod.

"Thank you, honey! I am going to have to hurry up or I will be late for work. Can you two men clean up things here?"

"Sure we can," replied Ralph as BJ is scooting out the door heading to the Chart Room Restaurant for her shift.

BJ pulls into the parking lot at the restaurant with a couple of minutes to spare. She didn't like to cut things so close. It made her too "on edge" for half of her shift when that happened. Some of the other waitresses would consistently cut it down to the wire. Steve Marcus, the restaurant manager, didn't like it much either. He was a rather high-strung individual; always hopping around from one place to another. It made BJ nervous if she had to work too close to him for very long. But the owners, Pat and Jennifer, liked him as he was a very good manager. The restaurant was always clean and the décor/decorations always up to date. The customers liked him. The help liked him. And, He made money for the owners so naturally they liked him.

"Good morning, BJ" said Tricia as BJ hurried through the door as she was putting on her apron. "Running a little behind schedule this morning I see. You are very rarely this late. How was your vacation? Did you pick up your grandson? What's his name again?"

"What is this, the inquisition? So many questions as soon as I walk in the door," said BJ.

"I'm sorry," said Tricia, "I missed you! I haven't had anyone to talk to-really talk to."

"I missed you too! Maybe, we will have a moment later to talk some. Right now, it looks like we have several hungry customers that need us," said BJ.

The rest of the morning and on through the lunch hour was a blur. It was all that the two of them could do to keep up with all of the customers. There was no chance for either of them to catch a breath, let alone find some time to talk to each other. It was not until the middle of the afternoon before it slowed down enough and they had caught up with the things that needed to be done on a regular basis; filling the salt and pepper shakers, restocking the sugar packets and the little jam containers, filling the napkin holders, bringing out clean glasses and cups from the kitchen, sweeping, and the myriad of other little things that are necessary to do to keep a restaurant running smoothly and the customers happy. And that was the object, wasn't it. If you didn't keep the customers happy, it wouldn't be long until the doors would be locked for good and you wouldn't have a job. So, keep the customers happy; the number one rule. And usually, BJ did a very good job of that and from what she could see so far, BJ thought that Tricia was going to be one of those that went out of their way to 'keep the customers happy.' Not that you could keep everyone happy all of the time, but it was a goal to strive for. Some people you simply would never be able to please or to make happy. BJ didn't like to wait on those kinds of people. Nothing was ever good enough for them no matter how much you tried to please them or how much you did for them it just wasn't going to happen.

"I think we might have a little bit of a breather now," said Tricia!

"Yes, it looks like it. I'm sorry about this morning-of what I said about all those questions," said BJ. "Let's sit down and take a break and do a little catching up."

"Sure, my feet are killing me," said Tricia.

"I don't know if I can remember all of those questions that you asked me earlier. But yes, we did have a wonderful vacation and yes, we did pick up our grandson, Rod in Klamath Falls," said BJ.

"What all did you do there? Did you get to see Crater Lake," asked Tricia?

"We saw it two times! It is more beautiful than any picture could ever show. I would like to live there-except for the winter. They get lots of snow there. Did you know that there are several months that they get over a hundred inches of snow? That's over eight feet of snow. Guess I won't have to worry about ever living there. We also went to see the lava tubes and the caves that they make. Rod really liked those. He liked to explore in them. What an imagination that boy has. He was fantasizing all kinds of adventures in those caves."

"Where did you stay? Was it nice?"

"My daughter, Rod's mom, booked us at the Best Western Olympic Lodge. The name even sounds too rich for my blood. We thought we had died and gone to heaven in that place. They have a pool, a room that you can get on those fancy exercise machines, complimentary breakfast, huge rooms with a refrigerator and a microwave in it. They even had real paintings on the walls," said BJ. "I don't know how much the room was, but I know that we could never afford to stay in a place like that."

"Sounds wonderful! Maybe someday we'll be able to take a trip like that. This is the only time and the farthest away from Los Angeles that we have ever been," said Tricia.

"Well, Ralph and I had never been to Klamath Falls before this. San Francisco is all the farther from here that I have ever been before," said BJ

"Say Tricia, how about you and your kids come over for dinner tomorrow night? That way you can meet Rod. And your kids can start getting to know Rod a little bit and he them. I know that your son, Timmy, is watching your daughter Candy while you are at work, but if you want, maybe you can drop them off at my house and they can play together with Rod. Ralph is there most of the time so he can keep an eye on them."

"That would be wonderful. Timmy is a pretty mature 11 year old, but I still worry about him and his sister alone all day. You know that "Home Alone" syndrome and all that. Is there something that I can bring to dinner," asked Tricia?

"No, just yourselves. I have everything under control. And by the way, do you mind if I invite Pastor Grime (pronounced gre-MAY) to eat with us? His wife is out of town for a conference and to visit her sister. I thought he might like a home cooked meal. I'm not trying to play matchmaker so just put that out of your mind. You are both married," said BJ.

"That's fine. I have wanted to get to know him a little bit better anyway. We just say hi at church on Sundays and I haven't really had much time to talk to him."

"That was the ulterior motive of mine," said BJ.

"What time is dinner?"

"What time are you off tomorrow," asked B?

"I don't work tomorrow. So anytime will work for me," said Tricia.

"I am off early so I should be able to have everything ready by 5:30," said BJ.

"Then 5:30 it will be. Guess our break is probably about over."

"I think so. I'm surprised that Steve hasn't been pacing back and forth here waiting for us to get back to work."

BJ and Tricia finished off their shifts without having much more time to discuss anything else in detail besides work. Tricia left earlier than BJ since she had started earlier, saying, goodbye to BJ and promising to see her tomorrow evening as she walked out the door.

# 8

❦

"Good morning, Stan! Warden wants to see you in his office right away!"

"Thanks Jack! I will head right there!"

On his way to the warden's office Stan begins to play all kinds of scenarios through his mind as to why the warden wanted to see him and it sounded so urgent as well. It feel like he was a schoolboy again getting called to the principal's office for some misdeed that he had done-and there were plenty of those instances. But his mother always came to his rescue and bailed him out of whatever trouble he found himself in. He had no recollection of a dad so he couldn't have bailed him out of anything, even if he had wanted to. His dad had run off with some young thing shortly after Stan had been born. His mother thought that he really couldn't get his mind around the idea of being a father. So Stan grew up hating someone he didn't even know or hadn't ever met. He dreamed about what he would say or do to him if he ever had the opportunity to meet him. His mother had become very protective of her little boy and fought every one of his battles for him-at least the ones that she knew about. And now he was marching off to the "principal's office" again, except this time there was no mother. Who would fight this battle for him? Who would plead his case? His mother had died fourteen years ago. Now he would have to go it alone. Had they discovered his secret life? Did they know about his cabin? Had they somehow found Julie? The closer he got to the warden's office the more apprehensive he became.

Opening the door to the warden's office and poking his head in Stan said, "Good morning, sir! Jack said that you wanted to see me!"

"Yes, Yes! Come in Stan! Glad you came right away. I think you knew that we are having an inspection here at Pelican Bay today and we will be hosting some distinguished guests. But before they come here they are going to meet with the mayor and the city council at the Rotary luncheon and they would like some of the representatives from the prison there as well. I have chosen you as one of those representatives as well as Fred Noonan and Jose Rodriquez. Fred and Jose will meet us there. I told them about this yesterday while they were here on their shifts. You can ride with me. We will be leaving in about an hour," said the warden.

"That sounds fine to me, sir," said Stan.

"Very well, meet me back here in an hour and we'll take off. You might tell the other guards on duty that you'll be out for two or three hours. If they have problems with that, tell them to come see me."

"Thank you, sir!"

As soon as he stepped out of the warden's office, a flood of relief swept over Stan like a tsunami rushing up on a beach unexpectedly. And just as suddenly, Stan had to relieve himself and hurried off to find the nearest men's room. With those pressures off, Stan noticed that he was wet and clammy from perspiring under the stress of the situation that he had just found himself in. He splashed cold water onto his face to help cool him off and to calm his nerves. That's when he saw that his hands were trembling.

"Come on, Stan! Get a grip! It's over! It was nothing! They know nothing," Stan said to himself out loud as no one else was in the restroom at the time. Not that Stan felt any guilt over his past; he just didn't relish the idea of being found out.

Stan told the other guards that he was going to be gone for a couple of hours and they seemed to be OK with that. Not much was going on anyway. The inmates were on lockdown anyway so they wouldn't be going to the dining hall. That was usually the roughest;

and then it was good to have as many guards posted around to keep order as the system would allow. Stan managed to look busy and fill up the hour before he was to meet the warden at his office.

Opening the door once again to the warden's office, but without the trepidation that he had earlier Stan said, "I am here, sir. I'm ready to go whenever you are."

"Wait outside, will you Stan? I will be right with you," said the warden.

The ride to the luncheon was quiet and uneventful. It was almost too quiet for Stan. He was glad that the place that they were having it was close so that he didn't have to endure the quiet for too long. Once there, they were ushered to their table and their seats. They even had placards with their names on them to indicate where they were to sit. Fred and Jose were already there. Jose was sitting next to Stan on Stan's right and the warden was on Stan's left. This was not the sort of event that Stan was comfortable with. He hoped that it didn't last too long or he might have to get up in the middle of things to find a bathroom and forget to come back for a long, long time.

It wasn't long before the meeting was called to order and a few pleasantries were said and they started serving the food. They were served a plate that had a piece of cooked chicken breast (chicken was always served at these things Stan thought), a sourdough bun, a slice of tomato, and some lettuce on it. All sorts of condiments were already on the table like little sentinels waiting to go into battle. It was one of those make your sandwich affairs, because we are too busy to make it. And besides we don't know what you want on your sandwich. Each place setting also had a chocolate brownie there beckoning any who dared look at it.

When everyone was about finished and the servers had gathered up the empty or in some cases half empty plates, the MC of the luncheon got up and said, "Ladies and gentlemen, it is my great pleasure to introduce our illustrious governor of the great state of California, Governor Arnold Schwarzenegger. Will you give him a warm round of applause as he makes his way to the podium?"

As the applause begins to die down, Governor Schwarzenegger steps to the microphone and begins his speech in that distinctive accent of his that has become his trademark in the movies and as governor. "I want to thank all of you for taking time out of your busy schedules to meet with me here today. I also want to thank the mayor, the city council and the citizens of Crescent City for inviting me here today. It was most gracious of you. And I must thank the Rotarians of Crescent City for sacrificing their time to allow me to speak at their luncheon.

Let me begin by saying that I am aware of the struggles that the people of Crescent City and of Del Norte County have gone through in the last fifty years. I know about the economic toll that the loss of the timber industry and the commercial fishing industry has had on this area. And I know about the physical toll on individuals and families that the tsunami has taken on the people that lived through that destruction. But I also know and see how strong and resilient you people are. You have looked adversity in the face and said, 'I'll be back!' I like that kind of tenacity.

I want to commend you for seizing on an opportunity when it was presented to you. When the California Department of Corrections presented the residents of this city and county with the option of building a modern, state-of-the-art incarceration facility, you people had the foresight and courage to proceed with the construction of the Pelican Bay Prison Project. Now, Pelican Bay has fueled resurgence in new businesses; which translates into new jobs, a lowering of the unemployment rate and a better standard of living for the community.

Other communities, where a similar facility had been proposed, were opposed to having the facility located in their environs. But the good people of Crescent City and Del Norte County were far-sighted enough to see the benefits of having the facility built here. As your governor and as an interested party, I have looked at the crime statistics for your area. Those statistics would say that you were wise in allowing the California Department of Corrections to locate the prison here. The track record for over 20 years shows that crime in this city and county has not increased over that time frame, but economic growth and prosperity has.

So again, I want to thank you for allowing the State of California to site Pelican Bay in your fine city. You are helping to make this state and your streets and every other city's streets in this state to be a safer place for you and your families. We want to continue to have a good working relationship between the State of California, Pelican Bay Prison, the local authorities and the citizens of this city and county. If there are any issues that are a concern to you about Pelican Bay we would like to know about them as soon as possible and we will try to mitigate them as quickly as possible.

And now, one of my most favorite parts of an event such as this; it is my honor and privilege to present the Medal of Valor award to one of your own. As many of you know, the Medal of Valor award is a special award that is given to a California State employee who selflessly put service and sacrifice above all else, and I am proud to present this Medal of Valor to such an extraordinary individual. This honor recognizes that not only has this individual devoted their professional lives to serve California and it citizens, but have at one time risked their own safety to protect the safety of another. The selfless act of this employee clearly shows that when faced with adversity, they can stand tall to the challenges life presents. If I could please have Stan Wosniak come to the podium so that I may present this award to him."

Stan slowly, reluctantly rises from where he has been sitting, observing all that has taken place so far, at the enthusiastic insistence of the warden and his two colleagues, Fred Noonan and Jose Rodriquez. The audience began applauding and Stan could feel his face flush. He was definitely out of his element here; like that proverbial fish out of water. He just hoped that he didn't make fool out of himself as he made his way to the front. Those next to him as he passed by were patting him on the arm, shaking his hand and in general congratulating him.

Upon reaching the front, Governor Schwarzenegger continued, "Stan, I want to congratulate you and to thank you for your service to California and to its citizens. In particular you helped protect the lives of two of your fellow guards, Fred Noonan and Jose Rodriquez, when a few of the inmates decided to take matters into their own hands over a year ago. You risked your own safety for their sake to rescue them when the inmates had them on the ground and were beating them mercilessly. Are Fred and Jose here today? Would you please stand?"

As Fred and Jose stand, the governor says, "I want to thank the both of you for your dedicated service to the Department of Corrections and I am glad that you were not injured any more than you were. I am also grateful that we have employees like Stan who can come to the assistance of their coworkers like he did for Fred and Jose. Thank-you gentlemen, you may be seated."

"Stan, as your governor and boss, I am proud to present this Medal of Valor to you today. And again I want to thank you for your service and your heroics. Keep up the good work. You have joined a select few individuals that have received the Medal of Valor Award. If you are ever in Sacramento at the State Capitol building you will find the Medal of Valor Award Kiosk at the east entrance. Your name has already been added to that kiosk along with the other extraordinary individuals that have distinguished themselves by winning this award. Thank you and good luck."

After making a few closing remarks, the MC adjourned the meeting and the audience hurried over to shake Stan's hand and congratulate him on his achievement. All of the attention was making Stan nervous and he was relieved when the warden announced that they needed to get back to work and were leaving.

The return ride to Pelican Bay was quiet between Stan and the warden; which Stan was grateful for as it gave him some time for some introspection. He wished that his mother could have been there-she surely would have been proud of this accomplishment. It never did seem like anything else that he ever did made her proud of him. She was always telling his older brother how proud she was of him and what he did, but not Stan. Nothing that Stan ever did was good enough for her. Then his mind drifted off to think about all of the townspeople congratulating him and whether they would change their minds if they knew what Stan Wozniak was really like. What would they say about Julie? What would they say about the others; he couldn't even remember their names he had pushed them out of his memory that far? Well he would bask in the glow while it lasted. He knew that people were so fickle and that one minute you would be their hero and the next the devil himself.

"You can wake up now Stan, we're back," said the warden. "And thanks for making this such a great team here. I really appreciate the work you've been doing here at Pelican Bay."

"Oh, you're welcome. I guess I was just still caught up in the reverie. I suppose I have to come back to earth."

# 9

Tricia and her two children, Timmy and Candy, showed up about 15 minutes early for their dinner engagement at BJ's house. They knocked on the door just as BJ was putting the last of the dinner into the oven to cook. Opening the door, BJ said, "Come in. Come in. Make yourself at home. Ralph and Rod are outside finishing up with the chores and should be in, in a minute. How are you Timmy? And look at you Candy. I think you have grown 2 inches since I saw you last."

"I'm fine, thank you," said Timmy

And Candy piped in with, "No I haven't. But I wish I would have."

"BJ it smells divine in here. I hope you haven't spent all day cooking," said Tricia.

"Just good old fashioned meat and potato cooking. Ralph doesn't go for all that fancy foo foo gourmet stuff. Besides, I wouldn't know how to cook that kind of a meal anyway. No, I just put a pot roast in the oven along with some potatoes to bake. I just stuck some biscuits in the oven so they should be done shortly and I have to heat up some vegetables and we will be ready to eat," said BJ.

"I thought Pastor Grime was coming to dinner as well," said Tricia.

"He is supposed to be here any time now. And if he doesn't hurry up we will eat without him. I better go call Ralph and Rod to come in and get cleaned up," said BJ.

"Is there anything that I can help you with," asked Tricia?

"If you like, you can put those plates and silverware around the table. I got them to the table, but that's all the further I got," said BJ as she opened the back door to call Ralph and Rod.

Tricia and Candy began distributing the plates, napkins and silverware around the table. Ralph and Rod came right in as BJ called them; like they were waiting beside the back door.

"I would like you to meet my grandson, Rod. Rod, this is Tricia and that is Candy and this is Timmy," said BJ.

"Hi Rod," Tricia, Candy and Timmy said in an echo of one another.

"Ralph, you and Rod hurry up and get washed up. Dinner is almost ready to serve," said BJ.

Ralph replied, "I thought the pastor was coming!"

"He is. And he better hurry up or he will be eating cold food by himself. I'm going to start putting it on the table right now. What does anyone want to drink? We have milk, apple juice, lemonade or water," said BJ.

Everyone shouted something different, but the waitress in BJ caught all their requests and started pouring glasses of what everyone wanted. As she was putting the food on the table, there was a knock at the door.

"Timmy, would you get the door please? It is probably pastor," said BJ.

"All right," Timmy said as he bounded for the door, glad to be of some assistance in this cacophony of activity. Opening the door, Timmy said, "Come in, Pastor gre-maaaay!"

"Why thank you, Timmy. It smells so wonderful in here I don't think I can resist," said Pastor Grime.

"Resist? Why would you resist? Aren't you hungry," asked Timmy?

"Of course I'm hungry! And these smells are making me even hungrier," said pastor.

"Hello Pastor! Welcome! I think you know everyone here. When Rod comes out from washing up, I'll introduce you to him. How's the bachelor doing," asked BJ?

"I didn't realize that I hadn't been eating very much or very well until I came into your house and my olfactory senses were hijacked," said pastor.

"How did you get away if you were hijacked," asked Candy?

"Honey, he wasn't really hijacked. He just means that the wonderful smells of dinner captured him to make him really hungry, just like they did to you," said Tricia.

"Now that everyone is here, pastor, I would like you to meet my grandson, Rod. Rod, this is Pastor Gre-may," said BJ.

"How do you do, Rod? It is a pleasure to meet you. You have a wonderful grandmother and grandfather," said pastor.

"Thank you. It is nice to meet you too," said Rod.

"Everyone can find their seats. I have little name tags by their plates. I think I got everyone's drink order right. Oh, pastor, what would you like to drink? We have milk, apple juice, lemonade or water," said BJ.

"I believe that I will have some lemonade, thank you," said pastor.

"Here you go pastor. Would you say grace please," asked BJ?

After grace was said and the food platters were passed around the table, the contented sounds of quiet chatter mingled with the clink of silverware against plate and the 'Um, good' filled the room like a sweet perfume on a still, summer evening. Finally, everyone had overstuffed themselves until they were miserable and couldn't take any more from BJ when she offered it just to be polite; even though it tasted so good, it wasn't a matter of just being polite, they truly did want more, but when the saturation point comes, any added load would be courting a disaster with potentially embarrassing results. The children were becoming restless as well, so Rod invited Timmy and Candy (although reluctantly since she was a girl and a younger one at that, but he did have some manners) to go outside to show them something. That freed up the adults for more grown-up talk. Even though they were not going to discuss anything that was of a particularly adult theme or about the children, it's just that some issues and ideas are easier to discuss without them present.

"Tricia how is your husband, Mark, doing," asked pastor?

"He is getting really discouraged. And he worries about me and the children," said Tricia.

"How is he being treated in the prison," asked pastor?

"He won't talk about it to me. I have asked him, but he just keeps saying that it would be better for me not to know what went on inside of those walls," said Tricia.

"Tell pastor what you told me about that one guard in there," said BJ.

"Mark said that it was probably nothing. One of the guards was taunting him when he first arrived that he was going start seeing his wife and take her away from him and things like that," said Tricia.

"Sounds like that guard was just trying to intimidate him so that he could have control of Mark," said pastor.

"That's basically what I told Mark, but it didn't seem to help calm him down. He was ready to take that guard out," said Tricia.

"Tricia, I believe that you said one other time when we were talking that Mark had an appeal in the works and that they had some new evidence or something. What is happening with that," asked pastor?

"I haven't talked to the lawyer for a few days, but the last that I heard was that he had filed an appeal and was waiting for the court to give him a hearing date. It seems like it moves so slowly. Doesn't the court know that people's lives are affected by their inaction? It just gets so frustrating sometimes; and I know Mark is really frustrated," said Tricia.

"Tricia, do you think he would see me," asked pastor?

"I don't know pastor. I have been telling Mark about you, but he says that he is mad at God and anything that has to do with God. He blames God for putting or at least allowing him to be in prison," said Tricia.

"That is a very common reaction, Tricia. But God is big enough to take any and all criticisms. In fact, you should be encouraged," said pastor.

"Encouraged? How so, pastor," queried Tricia?

"It says that God has been dealing with Mark, and Mark is trying to resist. Blaming God is Mark's excuse to be able to push God away. God's love will open that door to change Mark's attitude," said pastor.

"I keep telling him that God loves him and that He has a plan for him. I also tell him that I'm praying for him and he tells me to stop," said Tricia.

"That is exactly what Mark needs. Continue to show him love; continue to pray for him. Trust God that He will work it out," said pastor.

"I know. God keeps telling me to 'Trust Him'," said Tricia.

"Didn't you tell me that is what God said to you the other day when that couple left you two – one hundred dollar bills for a tip and they were just passing through the area," asked BJ?

"Yes, and that was right after I had told God that I didn't know how I was going to make it. What with my meager salary, rent, utilities, food, the kids, school, and on and on. And then God gives me a little down payment to insure that I do trust Him," said Tricia.

"Incredible! Our God truly is incredible. Do you mind if I ask you to share that story Sunday during worship time. There are some other folks in the congregation that need a faith booster too, and I think your story just might help them as well," said pastor.

"I don't speak well to a group of people," said Tricia.

"Those people are just like the people around this table. They care about you. They are anxious to hear what you have to share. You don't have to come up front if you don't want to, just share the story like you told it to us tonight," pastor said.

"I'll try," said Tricia.

"Good! And when Mark is ready for me to come visit him, I would be more than willing to go and talk to him," said pastor.

"I'll see what he says," said Tricia.

"This has been a wonderful evening. But I really must be going. I told widow Armando that I would come over after dinner. She said she had something important to talk to me about," said pastor.

"Isn't it rather late to be making house calls," asked BJ?

"Normally yes, but widow Armando said that she stays up until 2 or 3 in the morning anyway. Says she has trouble getting to sleep if she goes to bed too early," pastor said.

"When is your wife supposed to be home, pastor," asked BJ?

"The day after tomorrow. And I will be so glad to see her! Well, good night all. And thanks again for the delicious dinner and the stimulating company," said Pastor Grime as he went out the front door.

"Come on, BJ. I'll help you clean up this mess and wash the dishes," said Tricia.

BJ objected strongly, "No! You are company! I can finish this up after you leave. We can sit and visit awhile over a cup of decaf."

"I insist," said Tricia, "with two of us it will be done in no time and then we can have our coffee chat."

"Ralph, why don't you go out and look in on those kids of ours. Just make sure they haven't wandered off too far and are behaving themselves," said BJ.

BJ and Tricia tackled the dishes and left over dinner and just like Tricia had predicted, they had everything put away and the kitchen was once again spotless. Just like BJ liked to keep it. She became anxious and felt out of control and sloppy when the house, especially the kitchen, looked like a tornado had just passed through. And since Rod had come to stay with them, it seemed that it always was in that state. BJ loved her grandson and enjoyed her time with him, but right now she was not sure if she could make it the two and a half months until the end of summer and he got back on the train and went home.

As BJ visited with Tricia, BJ began to fill in her picture of Tricia. She had known that Tricia was struggling financially, but she hadn't realized how insecure and almost terrified of the position that she now found herself and her family in. But she could also tell that she was learning to lean on God and to trust Him in all things. What a hard, hard lesson that is to learn. She thought of the difficult times that she and Ralph and the kids had persevered through in learning that valuable lesson. Not that she felt like she had fully learned that particular lesson, because each season and each age seemed to bring its unique challenges and opportunities to relearn and to put into practice that valuable lesson once again. But one thing that she could say with certainty, God was trustworthy. He always keeps His promises; is always faithful; and He always makes a way even though it may be rough and not the way she would have chosen.

Tricia too gained some insight into BJ through their conversation that night. She learned that BJ's faith was strong; that her relationship with her Lord was vibrant and real; that she was strong and a fighter; and that Tricia garnered strength from BJ just by being in her presence. And on her way home that night, she felt like all of her problems were like nothing more than pesky gnats and that she could be a winner in this game called life. She couldn't wait to tell Mark all about the evening and her new found friend, BJ.

"BJ, I'm going to round up the kids and take them home to bed. I have early shift tomorrow at the restaurant and need to get some rest before then. Thank you so much for having us over. The dinner was marvelous and the company was a real treat," said Tricia.

BJ replied, "You are most welcome. It was a pleasure to get to know you and your children better. We will need to do this more often. And if you and your children would like, you can bring your kids over here during the day to hang out with Rod. Ralph is usually here all day if I am working so he can keep an eye on them and out of trouble."

"That sounds wonderful to me. I have been concerned about leaving them home alone all day while I'm at work. When school was in session it wasn't quite so bad, as it was just a few hours that they were home alone. Not like during the summer when it is all day. And I can't afford to pay someone to watch them," said Tricia.

"No need to do that. They will have a great time here. And it will keep Rod from getting too bored by himself," said BJ. "And by the way, if you and the kids don't have anything to do next Wednesday, you are welcome to come with us to a little beach we know about south of town a few miles. It used to be the town garbage dump and you can find a lot of really cool beach glass."

"I believe that I am scheduled to work that day, but the kids would love to go I'm sure. They just love the beach and I haven't been able to get them there very much even though we've lived so close to it," said Tricia. "I really do need to go. Come on kids, let's go home."

And friendships were struck; BJ and Tricia; Rod and Timmy and Candy. Friendships that would grow and stretch and hold firm as true friendships do over time.

# 10

Tricia awoke early. It was her usual waking time when she was on duty at the restaurant, but she didn't have to go in today. And today was Sunday. She didn't have very many Sunday's off. She had one out of every fourth Sunday off. She wished that she would have more Sunday's free. She enjoyed being able to go to Sunday morning worship at church. Although she did get to go to a small group meeting in the evenings after she got off of work, it just wasn't the same. She missed the camaraderie of the others that came to worship. She missed the music, but most of all she missed the sermons that Pastor Grime gave. They seemed so alive and strengthening. Right now Tricia needed all of the strengthening that she could get. She had her own personal devotion time, but sometimes God seemed a million miles away from where she was living. But Pastor Grime made the scriptures come alive. It was like God was right there; talking to her; telling her things she needed to hear; giving her comfort; bringing peace to the turmoil bubbling in her inner self; assuring her of the future and giving her hope; hope to live.

But today...today, she can go back to morning worship. Be renewed, charged up to handle what she is facing right now. Tricia just lay there thinking about her life, her situation and the service that she was anticipating. She felt like a wanderer lost in the desert some times. So parched and dry. She wondered if the others that came were like her. Could they see how hungry, almost desperate, she was. She didn't care; not really. She needed what she received there and no one was going to take it away from her. Her goal was to get to the place where she could have every Sunday morning off so that she didn't have to miss any Sunday mornings.

And as Tricia lay there she also thought about BJ and what a good friend she had turned out to be. Even though BJ could have been her mother, she had taken Tricia under her wings and had become the mother, the friend, the confidant that Tricia had never had. Tricia didn't know how she would ever repay her for all her kindness. And just the other night at dinner at BJ's house, BJ had offered to have her kids over while she was working. That would relieve some of the anxiety that Tricia was feeling. Knowing that her kids were safe and not home alone all the time that she was working. Tricia had plenty of other issues to fret over so it was so good to be relieved of one of them.

As she was laying there, the sun suddenly came streaming through a small crack in the well worn curtain covering her bedroom window. The sunbeam played an interesting pattern on the blanket next to her. It was an inviting little dance; almost a beckoning call to get up and come away with me. The sun had been hidden in the gray, gloomy, fog-shrouded days for a very long time. So long, that Tricia had often wondered if the sun had given up on the place. But now, it was inviting; inviting her to get up; inviting her to lift her spirits and feel the warmth of the sun deep down where it really mattered. It was going to be a good day. God was already preparing her for it. She knew, just knew deep down inside of her, that it was going to be a special day; a special time; a time of healing and renewing; a time to drink in the rain and the sun and all else good that was going to come that day.

Tricia smiled to herself as she threw the covers off and leaped out of bed. That is, if you could call what a thirty something that was out of shape and not at all athletic did when they got out of bed exuberantly, expectantly as "leaping", then that is what Tricia did that Sunday morning. Making her way to the bathroom to get her shower and get ready to go, she poked her head into Timmy's room first and then Candy's room to begin the process of getting them up and ready to go. It was so difficult to get them into bed at night when it was bedtime, but it was also equally difficult – and maybe even more difficult – to get them out of that same bed in the mornings.

By the time Tricia had showered and all of the other myriad of things that needed to be done to get oneself presentable in the morning and out of the bathroom, the kids had barely stirred from where they were when she had called them before going into the bathroom. Now she would have to get serious about getting them up or they would be late for service. Obviously they were not as excited about going as she was this morning. There were times when it would be so much easier to leave them there sleeping and go on without them, but she knew that was not the solution. They needed to be at church as much as she needed to be there. They simply had not realized it yet. Tricia wondered when that would happen. How many disappointments, how many failures, how many wrong turns, how long in trying to control their lives would it take before they came to that realization that they needed to be there too. She only knew what it had taken to bring her to that place. And now, it was just the opposite. Tricia could only go so long without that connection before she knew she had to get recharged or like a battery she would have no power to do anything.

Tricia was not sure how they did it, but they did make it to church with even a few minutes to spare and were able to greet a few people before the service started. Timmy and Candy wanted to sit with Rod and his grandparents, but Tricia decided to sit next to Claudia. Claudia was a young mom like Tricia whose husband was incarcerated at Pelican Bay. Tricia had met her the last time she was at church; four no five Sundays ago. Claudia seemed to be having trouble adjusting to her new situation and in making friends here in Crescent City so Tricia felt like she should reach out to her.

"Hi Claudia," said Tricia! "How are things going for you?"

"Oh! Hi Tricia! I didn't see you come in. I'm fine. It has been difficult finding a job that will give me enough hours to live on though," said Claudia.

"May I sit here with you," asked Tricia? "I know how you feel. I too struggle to be able to support myself and my kids. But you know what? Every time things start to get tight, God always reminds me to 'Trust Him.' And somehow or another He always comes through."

Claudia replied, "Sometimes I wonder why I bother. I can't see God working. I can't hear Him. I feel like I'm sinking deeper into a pit and I doubt if there is even a God or if there is, if He knows who I am or cares about me."

"Oh, Claudia! Of course He knows who you are and God loves you. He loves you more than you can imagine. And it is not just my words. Those are His words. He has a plan for your life and He wants to give you hope and a future," said Tricia.

"I want to believe that, but the doubts seem to shout at me to the contrary," said Claudia as a couple of tears began to form in the corners of her eyes.

"Claudia, I am going to write down a few of the scripture verses that have helped me when I start to feel that way and give them to you. Will you read them," asked Tricia?

"Yes! I know I haven't been very faithful in reading my Bible, but if you say it has helped you, then I'll give it a try," said Claudia.

About that time, the music for the service started, but Tricia was having a hard time focusing on what was being sung as she couldn't help but think about Claudia and the struggles that she was in. And under her breath, she breathed a prayer for Claudia that God would make Himself real to her and show her how much He really did love her. When Pastor Grime finally got up to speak, Tricia finally could focus on what he was saying and not on her friend Claudia.

He was talking about how when he was younger the other kids would always make fun of his name and pronounce it like the dirt grime instead of the correct French pronunciation of gre-MAY. But it didn't matter how they pronounced his name, he knew that he was a gre-MAY and that no matter what they said or what they did they could not change it. Then Pastor Grime said, "There is a new contemporary song out called 'Come Home'[1] by Luminate that has a line in it that says, 'Mercy doesn't care what you have done.' God's mercy doesn't have strings connected to it. It is available to all. It does not have a limit. It cannot be earned or bought. It has already been paid for at a cost far greater than any one of us could ever repay. That song 'Come Home' also says that we have been looking in a place where we don't belong and that we have been running for too long and searching for something and that we need to come home. God was there waiting for us with enough mercy to cover anything that we have ever done. It didn't matter what anyone else said about us. No one has done anything or messed up their lives so badly that God's mercy can't cover it and for Him to forgive us. Mercy doesn't care what you have done. God loves you! Come Home! Stop running! Stop searching for the thing that will not satisfy! Come Home!"

Tricia glanced over at Claudia and noticed that the tears were flowing freely now. She had stopped trying to keep them in check. The message that Pastor Grime was delivering had found its mark. Tricia slid her arm around Claudia's shoulder and began to cry along with her friend.

Pastor Grime then said, "In conclusion, if there is someone that needs to come home, this morning. That needs to experience that mercy that doesn't care what you have done, Jesus is more than willing to give it to you; he is more than willing to welcome you home. Just ask him to forgive you. Then after we close the service, come down and see me."

After the service had ended and the congregation had started to file out, Claudia said, "Tricia, thank you! I feel so much better than when I came here today. The doubts just seem to have evaporated and I do feel like God loves me. Pastor hit on the very area that I have been struggling with. I didn't think that God, if He did exist, could ever love a person like me who has lived such a rotten life and been so self-centered. But I know that was a lie. He does love me and His mercy doesn't care what I have done. I feel so liberated and free."

"Claudia, I whispered a prayer for you while we were singing that God's love would be revealed to you in a very real way. I knew that He would answer," said Tricia. "I am glad that you came home."

Tricia and Claudia stood together, hugged and let the tears flow; tears of joy and happiness. Claudia had lost her way and now she too had "Come Home."

"Pastor, have you met my friend Claudia," asked Tricia?

"Yes, I have. Nice to see you here again Claudia. Did Jesus do something here for you today, Claudia," asked Pastor Grime?

"Like you said pastor, I was running and looking in all the wrong places. And I didn't think that God could love me after all that I have done in my life. But you made it so clear today with that phrase you quoted from the song about 'mercy doesn't care what you have done.' Today God's love touched me and I 'Came Home.' I really did 'Come Home!' I feel so at peace and so encouraged," said Claudia.

"I don't want to discourage you, but your problems have not gone away. The only difference now is that you have Jesus to help you with them and you have a whole new family here at Living Waters Fellowship to come along side you and give you a hand when you need one. And I might add that I will be the first to offer whatever services I can to assist you. I am a pretty good listener and I know my way around Pelican Bay if you have someone in there that you would like me to visit," said Pastor Grime.

"Thank you, pastor. I will keep that in mind. I don't know if my husband would talk to a pastor, but I will ask. He does get awfully lonely in there and might welcome anyone from the outside visiting him," said Claudia.

"Hi BJ, have you met my friend Claudia," asked Tricia as BJ came up the aisle close to where Tricia, Claudia and Pastor Grime were talking?

"Hi Tricia, I have not met her, but I have seen her from across the way a couple of times. Hello, Claudia! I am Billie Jean, but most people call me BJ — right Tricia," said BJ.

"Billie Jean takes too much time to say; it's much easier to say BJ. Besides it fits you better than Billie Jean," said Tricia.

"I will leave you ladies to your getting acquainted and Claudia I am so happy that you stopped running and 'Came Home' today. There is rejoicing in heaven because of your decision. And remember, we are all on the same journey and we try to help each other as much as we can along the way so don't feel ashamed if you have to ask for help," said pastor.

"Thank you, pastor," said Claudia

BJ and Tricia chimed in with a, "Goodbye pastor."

"Tricia, how would you and our new friend Claudia like to come to my house for some lunch. It won't be anything special. Your kids have already agreed to come over. How about it Claudia? That is if you don't already have other plans," said BJ.

"BJ, you already do so much for us. I feel like I am imposing," replied Tricia.

"Nonsense! I still cook for a big group even though the kids have been gone for years. And Ralph and I just don't eat as much as we used to. That will give us a little more time to get to know one another. So that settles it; the both of you are coming to my house. Claudia, do you have a car," asked BJ?

"My car is sitting in the driveway and doesn't run right now so I walked here this morning," said Claudia.

"Either Tricia or myself can give you a ride to my place and then take you home when we get tired of gabbing," said BJ.

"OK," replied Claudia.

"And I am going to talk to Ralph and see if some of the men can't stop by some time and have a look at that car of yours to see if they can fix it without costing a lot of money," said BJ.

At that Claudia's emotions completely overwhelmed her and she began to cry once more. But these were happy tears; tears of pent up anxiety and fear that had just been melted with that little bit of love and kindness that BJ had expressed without even thinking about it. It was just who she had become; an extension of the Master that she served and tried to emulate every day, in every circumstance. BJ moved into Claudia's space and gave her a big hug to let her know that it was alright and that it would be alright. She had "Come Home."

# 11

Since both Tricia and Claudia had husbands incarcerated at the Pelican Bay State Prison, they had agreed on Sunday during their dinner with BJ and Ralph, to go together on Wednesday during visiting hours to see their husbands. Both Tricia and Claudia were free then and it had been awhile since they had been there to see them. Tricia volunteered to drive them because Claudia still didn't trust her car to make it there and back even though Ralph and another fellow from church had stopped by on Monday and supposedly had fixed the thing. Claudia had no clue what was wrong, what they did or if the car would leave her stranded some place like it did the last time it quit. But they had assured her that it was all fixed and that she shouldn't have that trouble again. Although they couldn't guarantee that the rest of the car would hold up. The car was old and looked as if it had been through at least one war zone if not two. Claudia figured that the car was probably older than her – especially when you counted car years. She didn't know what one car year was equal to in human years and maybe from the abuse that this one had been put through it was even equal to more years than the normal automobile -as if that made any kind of sense at all or even mattered. Cars were meant to perform a function and if they didn't, they weren't good for much. All that aside, Claudia was short on funds to be able to put any gas in the tank. So running or not, without fuel it was still going to sit where she had parked it. Ralph and put a couple of gallons in the tank when they were working on the car to make sure that it would run, but two gallons, less what the men had used in getting it running, would not go very far since the car had been made before anyone really cared about mileage figures. But now Claudia did care – the only problem was, she couldn't do anything to change the situation. So, she kept pouring gasoline into the tank when she could afford it and kept going as far as she could on what little she did put in.

Tricia had worked Wednesday morning at the restaurant and then went by to pick up Claudia about two in the afternoon. Timmy and Candy were still at BJ's house playing with Rod. BJ didn't seem to mind. It kept Rod occupied and out of trouble and it gave Ralph something to do watching them and helping them make things and giving them ideas on what there was to do and explore. Ralph had really enjoyed that. It appeared to BJ that he had become bored and maybe even a little down with where he was at. Nothing had seemed to change. There was no challenge to life. He really did take pleasure in helping other people. And now that he had someone, or more specifically three some ones, to pour his energy and assistance into, it had invigorated him. It gave him purpose. It gave him a reason to look forward to tomorrow. So with the kids safely in BJ's and Ralph's hands, Tricia could turn her undivided attention and worries to other matters – namely a husband languishing in prison.

Claudia was anxiously awaiting Tricia's arrival. She had changed her top three times. She was not happy with any of them, but finally decided on the one that she was now wearing. Not because it necessarily pleased her and made her feel confidant but simply because she was running out of time before Tricia would pull up out front and want to go. She didn't want to be in the middle of changing it a fourth time when she came and then have to wait on her. So Claudia resorted to pacing around the room, even though it was so small that just a few steps was all that she could take in any one direction, straightening and dusting things that she had just straightened and just dusted. She felt like she was going to be a nervous wreck unless Tricia came real soon. Why was she so nervous? She couldn't quite figure that one out. Was it because she was going to see her husband? She had visited him other times at the prison and had not felt this way. Was it because she was going with

Tricia? Even though she had just met Tricia last Sunday, they had hit it off like they had known each other for years. Was it that she was getting help from someone else? Claudia was self-reliant and did not like to have to depend on anyone else for anything. Or was she misinterpreting her feelings? Maybe she wasn't anxious and nervous at all. Maybe the feeling that she was experiencing was more a feeling of excitement and anticipation of what was going to happen that threw Claudia into her emotional turmoil. Whatever the case, Claudia was ready to be on her way.

At last, Tricia's blue car pulled in front of Claudia's house and Claudia went bounding out the door and down the walk towards the car. "Hi Tricia! How was work this morning," asked Claudia?

"Hi" responded Tricia! "It was pretty slow at the restaurant this morning. In fact, Steve, the manager was threatening again to cut our hours if business doesn't pick up soon. I think he just likes getting everyone worried and worked up by saying that. Not that I'm not concerned. I can't afford to have my hours cut. I'm barely making it on what I make as it is, without making less money. But hey, we're not here to have a pity party or start a worry fest. We are going to see our husbands and they don't need any more to worry about. Besides, God keeps telling me to trust Him and I am trying to learn that lesson. And it is definitely a hard one to learn!"

"Trust Him for what? How does one 'trust' God? Why would God do anything for me," fired off Claudia with rapid fire questions?

"Like I said, I am just trying to learn that lesson. Pastor Grime would be a better one to ask. Or maybe even BJ. But I think that the first step in trusting God is to come to the realization that He loves you. I know I'm still trying to understand how or even why God would love me. I'm used to having people want something from me and not to love me for whom I am. To have someone love me like God loves me is foreign to me. And because God loves me unconditionally and without strings, He wants the best for me. Even when I don't understand what is going on in my life. There is nothing that can separate or change God's love for me. When I get anxious and start worrying about things, I have to remind myself of God's love for me. Some times that is all that I can do – and do – and do. If I stop reminding myself, my mind starts to wander into all sorts of troubling scenarios that drag me down," said Tricia.

"You seem so strong, Tricia. I don't think I can ever be as strong as you," said Claudia.

"I don't feel very strong some times," said Tricia. "You will learn that it is one day at a time, one step at a time, one lesson at a time. As God comes through for you one time, your faith and trust in Him slowly grows. You may not even notice it for awhile, but it will happen if you can just let go of your fears and rely on Him."

"You make it sound so easy," said Claudia.

"In one way it is easy. But another way it is hard. We want to control everything about our lives. We think we know best. We think we have the resources to take care of everything. We think that if we plug our lives into such and such a formula, that a certain result will pop out," said Tricia.

"We should probably get going, but maybe you can pray for me and encourage me in this area," said Claudia.

"I would be glad to Claudia. Another thing that has helped me in this area of trusting God is to read the stories of how God was faithful to men and women in the Bible and in modern times," said Tricia as she pulled away from the curb and out into traffic.

The two rode silently the rest of the way to Pelican Bay each lost in her own thoughts of what they had just been discussing - a rather heavy topic and one that neither of the women was taking lightly. And before either of them had fully contemplated the topic, they arrived at Pelican Bay and Tricia was turning into the parking lot. It snapped them out of their reverie and back to the task at hand.

"Here we are," said Tricia.

"I really appreciate the lift. The last few times I came out here I walked and it seemed like I would never get here," said Claudia.

"There is no reason to do that unless you really want the exercise," said Tricia.

"I am sure that I need the exercise, but I would rather do it without being forced into it," said Claudia.

"If I am not working, I can give you a ride to wherever you need to go. Don't be afraid to call and ask," said Tricia as they were walking up to the entrance.

Stan happened to be coming on to his shift as he was working swing that day and just happened to be approaching the entrance from the opposite direction just as Tricia and Claudia were arriving. "Hello, ladies. You look lovely today," said Stan as he met them.

"Hello," said Tricia and Claudia in unison without commenting on his remark about 'looking lovely.' But a chill ran down both of their backs, but they could not understand why and they did not share that bit of information with each other. They only knew that this guy was not someone that they wanted to spend much time getting to know or be around even if he was a guard.

As the ladies entered in front of him, Stan slowed up so that he could be behind them and watch them. His thoughts drifted to desire; no, that was not quite accurate was it? It was probably closer to lust than desire. But what was so wrong with good old fashioned lust. He had heard that lust was one of the seven deadly sins, but who decided that anyway? They had never asked him. It was probably some of those religious killjoys that never wanted anyone to have a little fun and enjoy life. What was so deadly about lust? He could turn it on and off when he wanted to. He could control it. It would never control Stan. Stan was the master of his own destiny. And he saw a couple of fine looking ladies that he wouldn't mind getting to know a little bit better. He had never had two "girlfriends" at one time. And his mind began to wander in that direction of what it would be like to have two women in his little tree house bungalow. It certainly would be cozy. And the two of them seemed to get along quite nicely. He had always wondered how the ladies kept from fighting when a man had more than one wife/girlfriend living in the same house at the same time. Maybe the Muslims and the Mormons had something going for them after all.

The more Stan contemplated that thought of having two ladies at the same time the more that it intrigued him. And the more that he watched Tricia and Claudia walk down the hall in front of him the more he wanted those two. He would need to begin his planning, his study of them — he didn't particularly like the word 'stalk', although that was essentially what he would be doing. Stalking sounded so unromantic, so unchivalrous; which Stan wasn't even sure was a word, but it said how he felt anyway. Stan thought of himself as a ladies' man; a man that knew what a lady wanted and he knew he could supply it. But, when it came to the ladies, Stan's ego was so much bigger than what he could actually deliver. Nevertheless, Stan was blind to that fact and continued operating under an inflated opinion of himself. So it was not stalking – it was studying; getting to know them; getting to know their habits; know their routines; know their likes and dislikes; know them better than they knew themselves. This was going to be a real challenge; getting to know two ladies at one time and keep them separate. The more Stan thought about it, the more he liked the idea, the challenge, and the game. Yes, the game. And it would begin now!

Both Tricia and Claudia were glad to have put some distance between themselves and that "guard," whoever he was, as they were led into the visitation room waiting for their husbands to be brought in for that – oh, so short – visit. Mark came in first and sat down with Tricia. But, Ricardo, Claudia's husband, was slow in coming in and she began to get anxious thinking that something was wrong and that he wasn't going to visit with her today. Finally, he came in as well and sat down with Claudia.

Tricia was busy catching Mark up on all the latest that had happened to their family since she had last visited him. She thought it important that, even though Mark was incarcerated, that he knew what was going on with the family and be able to make a connection with them in some small way through her stories of their life and struggles. At one point she began telling Mark about Pastor Grime's sermon last Sunday. "Mark," said Tricia, "you would like Pastor Grime. He really cares about people and his messages are right where I live. Last Sunday he was talking about 'Coming Home' and how we have all run in the wrong direction and have looked in the wrong places for something to satisfy. And that was me. He was talking about me. He also quoted a line from a popular song that goes, 'Mercy doesn't care what you have done,' Mark I needed to hear that. I have felt for so long that God surely couldn't love me, or that He couldn't/wouldn't forgive me for my past or that He would never be able to use me because of how I had lived and what I had done. But, Mark, mercy doesn't care! Mercy is given no matter what – no matter how rotten, how evil, how unlovely we have been. No one deserves mercy, but God gives it anyway. All we have to do is repent and ask for forgiveness."

Tricia could see moisture forming in the corners of Mark's eyes and thought that there might be some hope for her husband. Maybe he would accept the forgiveness that Christ offered; that he had died for. But as she was thinking this, Mark said, "maybe that's for you or someone else, but not me. God could never forgive me. I am too bad; too far gone; God could never find me here."

"That is where you're wrong Mark. God does know where you are and He still loves you. He still extends His mercy and His forgiveness to you. If you want, Pastor Grime offered to come see you here and talk to you, to be your friend," said Tricia.

Mark replied, "I don't want to talk to a pastor. Do you know how I would be treated when word got out that I was talking to a pastor? It would not be pretty! NO pastor!"

"OK Mark, if that's what you want. He just offered to talk or just listen to you if you want to talk to him," said Tricia.

About that time the "end of visitation" sound began its incessant racket to inform the inmates and visitors that it was time for this visitation period to be over. Both the prisoners and the visitors alike would undergo the mandatory pat down to make sure that no contraband had passed between either the prisoner or the visitor during their exchange. When that was finished, Tricia and Claudia watched until the last possible second as their husbands filed out the door and were led away back to their cell blocks and to their cells. They slowly turned and walked quietly together in the opposite direction from where they had just watched their husbands go. Tricia and Claudia's hearts were heavy; almost to the point of breaking. How could they continue to live like this? Their emotions were being ripped apart at their core. Humans were not designed to go through situations like this. Something had to give.

# 12

✠

"**M**r. Monroe, will you please help us build a birdhouse like the one that you made over there for those pretty little birds," asked Timmy?

"First of all Timmy, what have I told you about calling me Mr. Monroe? That sounds so stuffy; like I should be in some big tall building with lots of glass and me ordering people around to do this or to get that. That's not me. I do not belong there," said Ralph.

"But sir, I've been taught to respect my elders and I just can't call you 'Ralph'," said Timmy.

"Fair enough. I appreciate that you have been brought up with some manners. Most of the youngsters that I see these days don't respect anyone, especially someone in authority or someone older than them. So what if we work on a compromise here? How about you and Candy call me 'grandpa' just like Rod does," asked Ralph?

"Really? Could we really call you 'grandpa'," asked Timmy? "We have never known either one of our grandparents. It would be awesome to have a grandpa. Especially a grandpa like you. You are the best grandpa anyone could ever have!"

"I would be glad to share him with you, since you don't have any grandparents and I have four of them," said Rod.

"That is really generous of you Rod," said Ralph. "So it is agreed, you call me grandpa?"

"Agreed," said Timmy.

"That would be so cool," said Candy jumping up and down while clapping her hands together.

"Second, Timmy, those 'pretty little birds' are called purple martins. They are of the swallow family. And they eat lots of bugs so I like to give them a place to live so that they'll hang around here and help keep the insect population down. I don't like to spray pesticides all over the place to control the bugs so I try to do it naturally – with purple martins, swallows, praying mantises, lady bugs, and the like. And to answer your question, yes, I would love to help you make a bird house for the purple martins. But I must warn you, you probably won't get anyone to move in this year. It is already well into the season and most of them already have their nesting homes picked out already. But, then you might get lucky and get some straggler that forgot to check his calendar. When I go into town later this afternoon I will stop by the lumber store and pick up enough materials so that you each can build your own 'martin' house."

"Neat! Way cool! Wow," the children all kept saying over and over. It was starting to annoy Ralph so he made some excuse to take his leave from them, leaving them to carry on like someone that had just won a radio contest.

After Ralph had gone, Rod said, "Hey, let's go down to the creek and check on the tadpoles to see if they have changed yet or not."

Candy was a little bit reluctant. She was afraid of the creek and what lived in and around it, but she was not going to let the boys know this and she certainly was not going to be left out of anything that might happen. Timmy on the other hand, got so excited at the mere mention of going down to the creek to explore and play that he said, "Last one to the creek is a rotten egg." And at that challenge all three of them took off running towards the creek. No one wanted to be that last one – that rotten egg.

The three of them spent the rest of the afternoon at the creek. They spent their time watching the tadpoles, that hadn't changed appreciably since yesterday. They floated sticks down the creek in make believe boat races. They dangled their feet in the water while sitting on a tree that had fallen down across the creek in one of the last strong windstorms that they had had in Crescent City. However, they had been warned not to get in the creek, but they had decided that they were not really in the creek and in the spirit of the law the water was merely splashing up onto their feet. They were careful not to tell or let their parents know what they were actually doing as they might forbid them from coming to the creek at all and that would not do; the creek was their most favorite place to play and fantasize. They would swing out over the creek on a rope that they had tied to a limb up in a tree; although only Timmy and Rod would do that while Candy watched and feared for their lives. Even though it looked awfully fun, she couldn't be persuaded, goaded or shamed into giving it a try.

When Tricia was finished with her shift at the restaurant, she stopped by BJ's place to pick up the kids. No one came to the door so she went around to the back and found BJ working in her garden. "Hi BJ! How are things going," asked Tricia?

"Oh, Hi Tricia! Everything is going good," replied BJ. "I think that the kids are down by the creek playing."

"They sure love to play down there," said Tricia.

"Say Tricia, I have been going to ask you how your visit with Mark went the other day and I haven't had a chance to ask until now," said BJ.

"We had a good visit. I told Mark about Pastor Grime's sermon on 'Coming Home' and then I told him that Pastor Grime offered to come see him if he wanted him to. I could see that what I was telling him was affecting him. He had a little bit of moisture in the corner of his eyes and I've never seen him cry before. But he didn't want pastor to come visit with him. He was afraid of what the others would say or do to him," said Tricia.

"You know that is a good sign. God is speaking to Mark and he is resisting. Just keep praying for him. If it is alright, I will share that with the prayer group at church," said BJ.

"That would be great. Mark really needs all the help that he can get," said Tricia.

"I want to invite you and the kids to go with us to that one beach that I was telling you about; the one that used to be the city landfill many, many years ago. You can find lots of beach glass there. We can make a picnic lunch and make a day of it," said BJ.

"Ohhhhh," moaned Tricia.

"What is it? Aren't you off tomorrow?"

"No! I volunteered to take Tammy's shift tomorrow as she had an appointment that she had to be at and I really need the money," said Tricia. "But you can take the kids if you want to."

"I hate to go without you. You need a break from all this too. But if we don't go tomorrow, it will be quite awhile before we will be able to go and Rod has been hounding me for days to go down there again. He really enjoys that beach and finding that beach glass. He won't be able to pick up his suitcase by the end of the summer from the weight of all that beach glass he will have put in it," said BJ.

"There will be another time when I can go. That beach is not going anywhere," said Tricia. "I wonder where those kids are! Timmy! Candy! It's time to go home!"

The afternoon had slipped by so quickly and they had lost track of time so easily that it was not until they heard Timmy and Candy's mom calling their names did they realize that it was getting late. They should have probably been heading back towards the house long before this. That decision was now out of their hands. Tricia's voice was getting that edge on it that said, although not in so many words, *'you kids had better get up here right NOW or else heads will roll.'* It was that tone that both Timmy and Candy knew too well, and respected equally well so they dropped whatever had been so important a moment ago and took off at a run for the house. It had happened so quickly that Rod was left by himself wondering what had happened.

Timmy and Candy came running up to where BJ and Tricia were standing talking and Timmy said, "Guess what mom! Mr. Monroe told us to call him grandpa!"

"That's pretty special. Are you sure that he wants you to call him grandpa," asked Tricia?

"Yes, mom! He doesn't like us to call him 'Mr. Monroe.' He wants us to call him grandpa. We've never had a grandpa, mom! Isn't that cool," said Timmy.

"That is very cool, Timmy! Make sure you obey and respect him then. He has given you a great honor and you both need to treat it like the valuable gift that it is," said Tricia.

"That husband of mine does come up with some pretty good ideas once in a while. If he wants you two to call him grandpa, then you should call me grandma," said BJ.

"Oh, Wow! We get a grandpa and a grandma all in one day! This is the best day of my life," exclaimed Timmy.

"BJ, I think that you and Ralph have given Timmy and Candy the best gift they could have ever been given. They have never had grandparents that they knew. All four of them were gone by the time they were born. Several of their friends that they used to play with would always talk about going to their grandparents' house and doing this or that with them. Timmy and Candy would come home in tears because they had no one like that in their lives. Sometimes I would find them holding the pictures of their grand-parents and staring longingly at them like that would somehow bring them back. You'll never know how great a gift you have given them today," said Tricia.

"Well, we better get you guys home, fed and into bed. Sounds like you are going to have a busy day at the beach tomorrow," said Tricia.

"The Beach!" exclaimed Timmy and Candy in unison.

"That's right! BJ and Ralph, I mean grandma and grandpa, are taking you to the beach tomorrow," said Tricia.

"Tricia, don't you worry about the picnic. I will have plenty of food for everyone. Those two eat like birds anyway," said BJ.

"BJ, I am going to be in your debt for the rest of my life for all that you have done for us," said Tricia.

"Don't even go there girl," said BJ. "The only thing that you owe me is love."

"That's easy! Who couldn't love you, BJ for all the things that you do for people," said Tricia.

"Just trying to be like Jesus, that's all," said BJ meekly.

"You certainly do a very good job of it if you ask me," said Tricia. "Well, let's go kids. It's not getting any earlier and I have to go in to work early tomorrow."

"Goodnight grandma," said Timmy.

"Night grandma," said Candy.

"Goodnight, Timmy. Goodnight, Candy. And Goodnight, Tricia," said BJ

"Night," said Tricia.

# 13

❧

"Hello, Frank! How are the animals today? Oh, did I say animals. I'm sorry, did I really say animal? That was a slip. I meant to say *'reformants,'*" said Stan. "Have you been here all night or just starting?"

"And hello to you too Stan. I've been here all night. I'm about ready to check out. Just trading places with you. Stan, I don't think 'reformant' is a word. And you better not let the warden hear you calling them 'animals.' He thinks they are his own personal projects and takes great offense when someone maligns them," said Frank.

"Well, you and I both know these guys in here will never change. Never be reformed. They may get out for awhile, but they will be right back in here or someplace like it all too soon."

"Stan, you're pretty cynical this morning! Are you needing a girl-friend or is something else getting under your skin?"

"Oh, I don't know! It is so hard to meet a decent lady these days. They all seem to have so much baggage and demand so much from a guy. It's always about them. They never seem to think about my needs or pleasing me. Frank, how did you get so lucky with the woman you have? How long have you been married now? It seems like a long time – you have been married to her since I have known you. That's been what, ten plus years now?"

"We have been married quite a few years now Stan; twenty three years next month to be exact. Stan, maybe you are looking in the wrong places for your women. It seems to me that you are always finding your women at the bars. I am not the brightest guy Stan, but I don't think that the women that hang out in bars are the homemaker type of women. Delores and I met at the same church that we were going to at the time. And it is not that we haven't had our difficulties. Those first few years were rough. But, we were committed to each other and to making our marriage work. And I can't neglect to give credit to one other help that we had…"

"What help was that Frank? Your parents? A friend? What?"

"Stan, before Delores and I ever got married we decided to make Christ the center of our home. We wanted him to be leading us; to be shaping us into the couple that he wanted us to become. So we stepped out in faith, trusting that he would do just that. And he has not failed us yet. We've let him down many times, but he never gives up on us. He gently picks us up, dusts us off and helps us clean up the mess that we have made and move on with our lives."

"Sounds so simple Frank. You Christians with your faith and trust! God has never been there for me my entire life! Nothing has ever worked out! My mom made my brother and me go to church every Sunday when we were growing up and she lived like the devil and treated us like it too. I have no use for God, Christ or his church. They are all a bunch of hypocrites."

"Stan, I am so sorry that you had such a bad experience with the church when you were younger. It doesn't sound like those people were living a Christ-like life. You shouldn't judge every Christian by them. There are some Christians who have a genuine relationship with Jesus and live out a Christ-like life, but ultimately everyone is responsible for following Jesus, not another person. No one is perfect. Jesus was the only perfect human that has ever lived since Adam and Eve fell."

"Don't tell me that you believe that Adam and Eve story too. That is just a myth to help those ignorant people of old explain the origins of the earth and man. We of the scientific age are too enlightened to believe old wives tales."

"I'm not going to argue with you Stan, but I do believe the Bible is God's inerrant Word and that all of it is truth – including the story of Adam and Eve."

"I thought you were smarter than that Frank. I have to go. It's time for me to check in."

As Stan walked away, Frank breathed a short prayer under his breath for Stan that God would open his eyes to the truth and that he would understand God's plan of redemption for mankind. But Frank couldn't help but have a heavy heart for Stan. He was so close and yet he was still so far away. How sad that his childhood experiences with the church and Christianity had soured him. Frank knew that with God all things were possible and that He loved Stan as much as He loved anyone in the world, but would Stan respond to that love? That was the million dollar question wasn't it. Frank believed in freewill and right now Stan's choice was keeping God at arm's length. He would be praying that Stan would tear down those walls and allow God to come close and heal him.

Frank had put Stan in an even fouler mood than when he had walked in the door that morning, and so he resolved to start putting his plan into motion as soon as possible. He needed to "convince" those two ladies to his little "love retreat" in the woods; his sphere nest in the trees where he made beautiful music like a songbird with his mate. Later today Stan would access the prisoners' personal files when there was a lull in the place and no one would notice what he was doing in order to get the information that he needed on those two lovely prisoners' wives. He was convinced that they needed him as much as he needed them. He was sure that they were lonely and could use some male companionship and that he, Stan Wosniak, was just the man to do it.

Stan's decision to begin the next chapter of his life helped his mood immensely. His spirits were lifted just at the thought of having two women under his control at the same time. Just think how much better he would feel and be once he had them 'safe and sound' in his love nest.

The rest of Stan's day was hectic. It seemed like everyone had demands on his time. Why today? Most days Stan was bored out his mind; but not today. Not on the day when he had decided to move forward on his plan. Why was this happening? He was getting more and more frustrated as the day wore on; and more and more irritable as well. He had even snapped at the warden when he had asked Stan to do something for him. He had to get himself under control. He definitely was not himself.

Finally, during the last hour of his shift Stan had everything under control in the cellblock, no one else had a demand on his time and he could slip unnoticed into a room with a computer. Stan had used his charm on the clerk who was in charge of the prisoners' personal files and sweet talked her into giving him permission to access the files. He had used some lame excuse about needing their information so that he could take 'Care' packages to the prisoners' families on the outside from the Guards' Association at Pelican Bay. Being a woman and with his way with women, she had relented despite her many objections. Stan had to promise that he would only use the information for honorable purposes and that he would limit the number of times that he accessed the files so that it would be less likely that anyone would notice.

"Let's see, Ricardo...what's Ricardo's last name?" Stan said to himself as he opened the program that accessed the database containing the prisoners' personal information files. "It is Sanchez, isn't it? So many Sanchez's! Here we are Ricardo Sanchez. Says his wife's name is Claudia. Here's her address, her phone number, her parent's information, his parent's information, no kids – that's good." Stan quickly copied down the information he wanted in cryptic form so if someone found the paper they couldn't easily tell what it was. They would just think that it was some random notes that he had jotted down.

Finished getting Claudia's information, he quickly typed in Noyes. Fortunately there was only one Noyes – Mark. Stan copied Tricia's information in the same manner that he had copied Claudia's, except that he did notice that she had two kids. When he saw that he groaned. That could present a problem. Kids would need tending to and would notify someone of Tricia's absence sooner than he would have liked. He liked to have a few days pass by before his girlfriends were missed. The longer it went before someone noticed, the colder the trail would become and the easier Stan would breathe.

Stan had just put the paper with the information that he had just gleaned into his pocket, closed out of that program and restored an innocent enough screen that had been minimized in the tray when the door handle turned making that all too familiar Shhhhh-clunk sound as the door opened and in walked the warden.

"Hello Stan. Catching up on reports or surfing the web for a new fishing pole?"

"Oh, hello warden! I was just trying to locate an article for one of the inmates, sir."

"That's what I like to see in my guards, Stan. A little bit of initiative to try to get these men educated and started out down a different road than the one they have been on."

"Yes, sir! Thank you, sir. I didn't find what I was looking for and I really need to finish up with my shift so I can check out. So if you will excuse me sir..."

"Oh, of course Stan, keep up the good work. Like I said I appreciate a man who takes some initiative around here. You have a good rest of your day."

"Thank you, sir! You too," said Stan as he exited the room as quickly as he dared without looking too obvious that he was trying to hide something. As Stan made a swift retreat down the hall he muttered to his self, *'that was close, too close.'* But his excitement was building as he could sense the hunt was near. Could he really bag two at once, that was the question? No, that was the challenge.

# 14

Tricia got up having a pity party for herself. BJ had offered to take Timmy and Candy with them to the beach today. Actually she offered to take all three of them, but Tricia had already committed to pick up Tammy's shift at the Chart Room Restaurant and she really needed the money. It seemed as if each week she would slip a little further behind financially. She just couldn't ever seem to get caught up. And when she started to make a little progress some crisis would happen – one of the kids would get sick, the car would break down, it would be extra cold and would have a huge heating bill, or some totally unexpected thing would come up that demanded money; money that she didn't have.

She was grateful that BJ offered and that she cared enough to go out of her way to provide what she did feel like she could provide. That was another straw on the proverbial camel's back. She couldn't provide for her kids like she would have wanted to – someone else was doing that. It was not like she didn't want to do things with and for her kids; she really did want to, but the resources simply were not there – the resources of time and money of which she lacked on both counts.

It had taken an enormous effort to drag herself out of bed this morning and an equal effort to go through the motions of getting ready to go to work and then getting the kids up and ready for a day at the beach. Tricia couldn't get her heart into the motion. She was on mechanical. She did shoot up the one sentence prayer,

"God, where are you in all of this?" over and over as she shuffled around. And it did not help that when the kids did get up they were so excited about going to the beach that they were bouncing off of the walls and she had to keep reminding them to calm down and take care of the business at hand, which was to get ready to go.

She was not quite sure how it had gotten accomplished, but they did get out the door, in the car and headed in the direction of BJ's.

"Timmy! Candy! Did you remember to put sunscreen on? And remember to bring the tube of it to put some on later as well?"

"Yes, mom," said Timmy.

There was a long silence as Tricia waited for a response from Candy. Finally Tricia said, "How about you young lady? Did you put sunscreen on?"

"Do I have to? I don't like that stuff," said Candy.

"Yes, you have to! I don't want you getting all burned today. Timmy, help your sister put sunscreen on," said Tricia.

"Yes, you have to. Now hurry up before we get to BJ's. And make sure you put It on evenly. I don't want her all striped either."

After riding along in silence as Timmy liberally coated Candy's exposed skin with white sunscreen lotion, not bothering to work it in very well in spots, which gave the impression that Candy had leprosy or some other skin disease. Tricia cringed on the inside as she watched in the rearview mirror at the progress that Timmy was making and made a mental note to herself that she needed to rub some of that in once they had arrived at BJ's place.

Approaching the driveway that led up to BJ's, Tricia said, "I want the both of you to be on your best behavior today. Don't cause any problems for BJ or Ralph. Mind what they tell you. Alright?"

"Yes, mom," both Timmy and Candy said simultaneously.

"Good! And I want you to have fun today so you can tell me all about it tonight," said Tricia.

"We will," said Timmy.

"We will," said Candy a half beat behind her brother.

BJ came out to meet them as they were getting out of the car; them and all of their beach toys. Tricia could hide it from her kids, but not from BJ. As soon as she saw Tricia, she knew exactly where she was at and what she was struggling with so she came around to the driver's side of the car where Tricia was standing; went over to Tricia and gave her a big hug. BJ whispered in Tricia's ear, "It won't always be like this. This too shall pass. God still loves you. He still sees what you are going through. And He will always be there for you."

That was the touch that Tricia needed. She began to sob uncontrollably and BJ pulled her closer to her to console her in a mother-daughter embrace. Timmy and Candy, stood there with mouths agape, wondering what was wrong with mom, but afraid to say anything for fear that it would be the wrong thing to say. It finally dawned on Tricia where she was at and what she was doing out in BJ's front yard and felt embarrassed. She began sniveling and wiping at the tears that had by this time covered the majority of her face.

BJ said, "Honey, would you like to come in and freshen up a bit?"

Tricia replied, "No, I need to get to work. I'll work on it as I drive to work. I have some tissue in the car."

"Remember, Jesus loves you! And we all love you," said BJ.

"I know! And thank you! Bye Timmy! Bye Candy!"

"Bye mom," they both said together.

As Tricia drove off down the street, Timmy asked, "What's wrong with mom?"

BJ replied, "Nothing, honey. She just needs a lot of love right now. Are you kids ready to go to the beach and have some fun?"

Tricia got herself pulled together quite nicely on her drive from BJ's to the restaurant, but her eyes were still slightly puffy and red from having a good cry, so she tried to avoid direct eye contact with anyone for as long as she could so that her eyes would return to normal and she could avoid having to answer any questions about why she was crying.

Not many customers were in the restaurant right then, so Tricia busied herself, busing a couple of tables, filling the salt and pepper shakers and napkin holders. By then, a couple of different groups had come in, which she promptly seated. She supplied them all with menus and set silverware and water glasses at each place. After giving them a chance to look over the menu offerings, she began to take their orders. It was not long until she was in the groove of being the top-notch waitress that she always was. Her customers were enjoying themselves and she was feeling better about her life and situation. The other plus of all of this was that her tips were as generous as usual and some of them even more so.

Although the day had started out rather slowly, it had picked up steadily throughout the day so that Tricia didn't have much time to think about anything but serving her customers. By the end of the day, she could tell that she had been on her feet all day running between the tables and the kitchen. When she had about 15 minutes before her shift was supposed to be over, Steve, the restaurant manager stopped her and asked her to come see him in the office when she had a chance.

Tricia made one last round of the tables, put a few things away and then headed down the hall towards the office. Knocking on the office door Tricia heard a, "Come, In. It's open."

Opening the door and walking in Tricia said, "You wanted to see me, Steve?"

"Yes! Take a seat. I just wanted to chat with you a little bit."

Tricia was always frightened in situations like this. She always imagined the worse and even had plans revolving around in her head of what she would do next. But now she just knew that this was going to be her last day and she could think of no scenario beyond working here at the restaurant. Jobs in Crescent City still were not that plentiful, especially for someone without many skills or education. She was off in her own little fear driven fantasy and didn't really catch what Steve was saying at first.

"Tricia, are you alright? Did you hear what I said? I said that we, the owners and myself, are so pleased with your work that we have decided to give you a twenty five cent an hour raise. I know that may not seem like a lot, and I wish we could offer you more, but the way the economy has been we just didn't think that we could give you more at this time. But, as soon as things pick up again, we want to give you another raise. I just ask that you not spread this around. There are a couple of the waitresses that have been here longer than you and you will be making more than they are, but you are a harder worker than they are so I think you deserve it. I just don't need any hard feelings between any of you. Are you good with that?"

"Thank you! Thank you! I don't know what else to say. You will never know how much this means to me and how much this will help us out. Can I share this with BJ?"

"You can share it with her as long as she promises not to tell the others that work here. And I trust her to do that. There is one other thing that I need to discuss with you. You have asked several times if you could have Sundays off. Would you still like them off? I know that they have traditionally been one of the better days for tips and if you want to work that day I will leave you there on the schedule, but Tammy has asked if she could trade one of her days for your Sunday. Like I said, if you want Sunday you can keep it, but if you want it off I will work out the trade. But I do need to caution you, there may be a few Sundays when I will need you to help out in here."

"Really? That is an answer to prayer. I have been praying that I could get Sundays off more often so that I could go to church Sunday mornings. The answer is YES! I believe that God will more than make up what I don't make in tips on Sunday in the tips I get the rest of the week."

"Great! It's settled then. You will be happy and Tammy will be happy. Everyone gets what they want. Tricia, thank you so much for all your hard work and for being a team player. It makes it so much easier to manage a restaurant when I have an employee like you. I just wish that I could clone you. Between you and BJ, you pull 80% of the load around here. Thank you again. Is there anything else that I can do to make your life here more enjoyable?"

"I don't think so, Steve. You have done more than enough already. You are the best manager I have ever worked for in my life and I have worked for quite a few of them."

"Thank you! You probably want to get on your way to pick up your kids, don't you? I won't keep you any longer. I believe that you are off tomorrow, so have a good day and I will see you in a couple of days."

"Thanks again, Steve. Bye!"

Tricia could hardly contain herself as she scurried out to her car. She sat there in a daze trying to assimilate all that had just transpired in there. She had gone from fretting that she was losing her job to the exhilaration of getting a raise and having her Sundays off. God was so good to her. He truly did love her. Just when she had been at a particularly low point in her life, God knew what would pick her up and give her the lift that she needed to continue on. How could she not trust Him after this? He always came through. And it was always right on time. Trust! Trust! Trust! God had been pounding that into her head for how long now? And yet she still needed to be reminded to trust Him when life seemed so unbearable.

Tricia finally started the car and pointed it in the direction of BJ's. Once there, she couldn't remember exactly how she had gotten there; whether she had stopped at the lights and the stop signs; or if she had passed any cars; or which route that she had taken to get there. She had been reveling in the blessings that God had just poured out on her and thanking Him for them all the way there.

BJ, Ralph and the kids were back from the beach already and the kids were off playing somewhere when Tricia pulled in and stopped. BJ saw her pull in and went out to meet her. Tricia had been on BJ's mind all the time they were at the beach. She had wondered how she could help her friend ever since she had hugged her earlier in the day and Tricia had broken down sobbing. As BJ approached Tricia, she could see the drastic change that had taken place in her countenance from before so BJ said, "What happened to you?"

"Nothing! God just knows how to bless me," said Tricia.

"He truly does! How did he bless you this time," asked BJ?

"Steve wanted me to keep this quiet, but he didn't mind if I told you so please don't share it with anyone else," said Tricia.

"You know me, my lips are sealed."

"Steve gave me a quarter an hour raise in my pay. And that's not all. He is going to give me Sunday's off so I can come to church. Isn't that wonderful?"

"Tricia, honey! That is the most wonderful news you could share. God does look out for you."

"Yes, I know that He does. But there are times when you are in the middle of life and He just doesn't seem to be there with you.

That's when the doubts begin to grow and multiply and my faith and trust shrivels up and begins to die."

"That's one of the reasons that God does come through for us. He wants us to build up our faith and our trust. Just like the body builder that keeps lifting heavier and heavier weights; pushing his body to grow and develop stronger muscles to meet the challenge of the heavier weights," said BJ.

"That makes sense. I guess I had never thought of it in those terms. I must be the 95 lb weakling on the block then," said Tricia.

"You underestimate yourself. You are stronger than you think you are. And with God on your side all things are possible."

"Thanks BJ! You always seem to know the right things to say. I better find my two kids and get them home. You are probably about fed up with them."

"No, No! They were no trouble at all. We had a great time today. I'm glad that we could bring a little bit of joy into their lives. I think that they really enjoyed themselves. They should sleep well tonight."

"Timmy! Candy! Time to go home."

"Coming mom!"

"Thanks again BJ! I am off tomorrow, so I will spend a little time with the kids. But if you don't mind I will bring them over the next day."

"They are more than welcome anytime."

"Goodnight," said Tricia.

"Night all," said BJ.

"Goodnight grandma," said Timmy.

"G'night grandma," said Candy.

# 15

❧

Stan was so excited that he had gotten Tricia's and Claudia's information that he almost forgot that he had an appointment after work that he had made two weeks ago. He wanted to get home and onto his computer to look up what he could about them before he started his observation phase. Some people may have referred to his activity that he called observation as stalking, but observation suited Stan much better. Observation sounded so sci-entific; so up-to-date; so good; so right. Stalking sounded so base; so perverted; so evil; so wrong. In Stan's mind he was helping these women; without him they would have nothing; they would continue to scratch and claw for everything that they got. He would provide for them. He would protect them. Their husbands had failed them, but not Stan. He would come through for them; he was going to be their superhero.

It was not until Stan had driven past the Union hall on his way home that it dawned on him that he was supposed to be in that building in fifteen minutes. He wasn't late. He hated to be late for anything, but if he had gone on home he would have been late, if he didn't miss the meeting altogether.

Stan was on the administrative advisory board for the guard's union and they had some important issues to discuss before they took them to the members to vote on, so it was not like an ordinary union meeting where no one would miss you if you weren't there. There were only six members on the advisory board, of which Stan was one. He was so proud that he had been elected to the post. He received no extra perks for being a board member, but the status and what it did for his ego was enormous. Stan had to pull in a few favors and twist a few arms in order to get elected three years ago, but when he was up for reelection a year ago the members had realized his worth on the board and he had been reelected without much opposition.

So, at the next intersection Stan turned around and went back to where the union hall was located. And although Stan was physically there at the meeting, his heart and mind were not. His thoughts kept drifting off to his "game"; to his "hunt." His contributions to the decision making process were minimal, but they made it through all the items on the agenda with no major setbacks and Stan was relieved to finally be finished.

Once home, Stan grabbed a quick snack that he could eat while working on the computer and sat down to find out what he could about Tricia and Claudia. He first checked Facebook, but came up empty there. He had figured as much, but he still had to check. Both of them were probably too poor to have a computer or an internet connection or both. He then tried the California state site for court records and found that Tricia had been to court on a domestic issue nine years prior and Claudia had a DUI conviction five years prior. There was one other site that he was subscribed to that gives information on people, but they only gave him the same information that he already had; most of the time he wondered why he bothered to pay those people. There were a couple of times however, when they had provided some very useful information to his observations of different women that he had been interested in, but they had failed him this time. He would just need to do it the old-fashioned way; he needed to hone his detective skills anyway.

He had often wondered if the authorities would be able to track back to his computer and him that he had been making inquiries on the women that disappeared. No one had ever done that yet, but there was no assurance that it couldn't happen. Computer technology kept advancing so quickly that something wasn't possible one month would be the next. So Stan was always cognizant of that possibility every time he did a search on a specific person.

Next he pulled up Google Earth and typed in Tricia's address. He looked at the overhead, satellite view and became so familiar with all of the connecting streets around her neighborhood that it was like he was in his own neighborhood. Then he zoomed into the Street Level view and studied her house and her neighbors' houses. When he was comfortable with Tricia's neighborhood, he put in Claudia's address and went through the same process with her neighborhood.

The next morning Stan was up bright and early even though he did not have to work, he was eager to be about his observations. He ran through the same process with Google Earth that he had done the night before on each of the women's neighborhoods only he didn't need to spend as much time studying them as he had done previously.

With that accomplished, Stan washed down a cranberry bran muffin with a glass of orange juice. He always tried to eat healthy whenever that was possible. And for those times that it wasn't possible, he always felt guilty for a week afterwards and he was extra fastidious about what he ate until the guilt subsided.

Stan changed into his jogging shorts and shoes, slipped on an old ratty T-shirt that he had picked up at the thrift store that said "I Love NY" on the front with the love being a big red heart, and put on a NY Yankees baseball cap with the bill pulled down in front as far as he could without obstructing his vision. He pasted on a fake mustache and put on a pair of thick, dark rimmed glasses with plain glass in the lenses. He wished that it were sunny out so that he could wear sunglasses, but it was raining instead. It rained a lot in Crescent City, one of the things that he despised about the place. He liked sunshine and hated the rain. But this is where the work was so he put up with it. That was one of the reasons for the fake mustache, the glasses and the cap pulled down in front. He didn't mind being seen, but he didn't want to be recognizable.

Stan drove to within a half mile of Claudia's house and parked on a secluded side street. He had mapped out a route that he could jog that would take him past Claudia's house and then on to run past Tricia's house and back to his car. Stan estimated that it would only be about a four mile run which would only be a warm-up run on his normal jogging regimen of ten miles a day.

Jogging or riding his bicycle on his observation runs was Stan's preferred mode of operation. He figured that a car driving slowly past a house or parked on the street where one could watch a house would be more suspicious than a jogger or a cyclist. With jogging or cycling you could go slowly past the house and no one would think anything except that you were a little tired and needed to rest. Besides that, cars were too easily recognized and identified. It was harder to disguise a car than a person; you couldn't put a fake mustache on a car, or pull the bill of a baseball cap down over its windshield, or put dark rimmed glasses on its headlights.

Today, he had decided to jog instead of cycle, because he wanted to poke around a little bit and it was harder to do when you had a bicycle tagging along. Turning down Claudia's street, Stan knew from his Google reconnaissance that her house was in the middle of the block. He decided quickly as he turned the corner that he needed to be on the opposite side of the street from where he was, which also happened to be the side of the street that Claudia's house was on, to get a better view of her house and the pertinent other items of interest that he needed a view of. Jogging slowly past her house Stan noted that the house was a bit shabbier than the Google Earth photos had pictured the house and yard to be. Resisting the urge to sneak over and peek in the windows, Stan forced himself to move on past her house. There didn't appear to be any sign of life in the house even though there was an older car in the driveway. Stan made a mental note of all the information about her place that he thought was important and some things that probably didn't matter for anything, but you never knew what piece of information would be that one vital link to success.

Stan ran to the end of the block, turned the corner and headed towards Tricia's house. Tricia's house sat on a corner lot which afforded Stan a good look at two sides of her place. Just as Stan was approaching Tricia's house, Tricia and her two kids came out the front door and got into the car. Stan had to come to a stop and jog in place as the car backed out of the driveway into the street.

This was a fortunate turn of events for Stan. He couldn't believe his luck. He took it to mean that his venture was 'blessed' and that it was going to be successful. He was ecstatic. He had only hoped to observe her house and the neighbors' houses, but besides that, he was fortunate enough to see Tricia and her two children. All the way back to his car Stan was euphoric. He barely even noticed that he was running. It was like he was floating on air. It had truly been a successful day. The only thing that could have made it better would have been if Claudia would have been coming out of her house as well. But that would have been asking too much.

Stan began thinking about what he should do next. He thought about coming back over after it got dark and trying to peer in the windows, but Tricia's house was too exposed. There weren't enough hiding places and the backyard was all fenced off, which might mean that they had a dog. He usually didn't have much trouble with most dogs, but there was always that one that hated everyone and everything. And even if you could win their confidence most dogs usually barked a few times anyway until you could gain their confidence, so better not tempt fate, at least not until or unless it became necessary. He hoped that it didn't come down to that, but you never knew how these things would play out.

He figured that he probably could get away with peering into Claudia's windows as there were several bushes on each side of the house to hide in and the backyard was open. But in the end he talked himself out of it, at least for today. It had been a good productive day and now was not the time to do something stupid that he would regret later on.

The route that he had mapped out for his little jog was a good route and would serve his purposes well so he decided that he would continue running the route when he could so that he could become more familiar with each neighborhood and each house.

He needed to find out if either woman worked. Surely they must work somewhere. How could they live without working? That would be his next quest; find out where they worked and when. Maybe he could use that in his plans. He did know one thing after today though. He did know that whatever method of 'persuading'

Tricia to come with him that he decided on, he would have to be able to get her separated from her kids.

Nothing was ever easy. There always had to be some little glitch or obstacle to work around when you were trying to help someone; and Tricia's kids were going to be her obstacle.

# 16

✚

Tricia finished off the week without much incident. Timmy and Candy couldn't stop talking about their time at the beach and playing with the beach glass that they had collected. They had taken over one end of the dining table to lay out their treasures; rearranging them into a myriad of different shapes, colors and sizes. They had discovered that during a few hours in the afternoon the sun would come streaming into the window, strike the beach glass and throw off a kaleidoscope of colors. They were having so much fun playing with the glass that it had become an even greater chore to get them to bed at a half way decent hour. And now it was Sunday and it was time to get them up and ready to go to church, but they were not having any of it. Sleeping was their main priority at the moment.

When all other methods to get them out of bed had failed, Tricia threatened to swipe all of their precious glass baubles off the table and into the trash. It only took one threat to get them to jump out of bed and come screaming "MOM" at the tops of their lungs to protect their booty.

Once up and calmed down, Tricia directed them to the table to eat some cereal and begin to get ready for church. It was Sunday after all and their new habit was to be in church every Sunday now that Tricia had Sundays off from work. It was going to take Timmy and Candy some time to get used to the new schedule, but Tricia knew that in the end it would pay off and she breathed a silent "Thank You" to God, again, for blessing her with Sundays off.

Going out the door when they were finally ready to leave, Tricia noticed a man straddling a bicycle just standing there looking at her house. She thought that he looked vaguely familiar, but couldn't quite pin it down as to where or who or how he looked so familiar. But having his riding gear – helmet, shorts, gloves, dark glasses – on, distorted her recognition capability and she dismissed the notion as a figment of her imagination.

When he noticed that she saw him looking at her house he quickly started fiddling in one of the bags attached to his bicycle as if he were looking for something. That same chill ran up her back that she had noted earlier as Claudia and she were going into Pelican Bay to see their husbands. But Tricia put the thought quickly out of her mind as she hurried the kids into the car since it was getting late and church would be starting soon.

Stan had to be extra careful now that Tricia had spotted him watching her house and would be suspicious if he were to follow too closely. He didn't want to lose them, but he didn't want her to suspect that he was following her either. It would be a cat and mouse game to wherever she was going. He had an idea, but he was not certain.

Tricia swung by Claudia's house to pick her up and stopped out in front to wait for her. Following Tricia on his bicycle, Stan hadn't thought about her stopping at Claudia's house, although he did realize that they were in her neighborhood, until he came around the corner to her street and was coming up on the back of her stopped vehicle too quickly. Hoping that Tricia was too busy watching Claudia's door to notice him, Stan made a quick U-turn and rode back onto the street that he had just turned off of.

Stan found a fence and a shrub that he could pull in behind and still have a view of Tricia's car and Claudia's house without being seen by them very easily. Stan took a long drink from his water bottle while continuing to keep an eye on the quarry. Claudia still hadn't come out of her house so Stan pretended to make some adjustments to his bike while he watched so that the neighbors wouldn't become too suspicious of some stranger lurking in their bushes.

Stan's patience finally paid off as Claudia came out of her house and hurriedly got into Tricia's car and they sped off. It almost caught Stan off guard and he had to quickly get back on the street, on his bike, and pedaling after them. He figured that they must be late for something. And since it was Sunday morning, it was probably church that they were headed to. But which church? Stan wanted the answer to that major question; plus, Stan had other objectives in mind and he needed them to be away from their houses for a period of time that he could count.

Fortunately for Stan, the route that Tricia drove, took her through a couple of the cities few stop lights and slowed her down enough to allow Stan to catch up to within visual distance of her. Stan slowed and ducked in behind a couple of other cars so that it would be hard for her to see him. It wasn't too much further until Tricia turned into a parking lot of a small, well-kept church. It was not fancy and ostentatious, just simple and down-to-earth.

The sign over the door said, "LIVING WATERS FELLOWSHIP" in large, bold letters. Underneath of that was printed in smaller letters, "All Are Welcome." A flood of negative memories coursed through Stan's mind. This was just the kind of place that he had spent a lot of his youth in – and all of it forced on him by his mother, and most of the teaching he had rejected long ago. Stan didn't understand how his brother had embraced such a repressive, backwards belief system and had even become a pastor of a similar kind of church. Stan knew what he would hear if he ever would happen to go in there, but it might come down to that in order to get close to Tricia and Claudia. Stan sensed that these two women were not the sort of women that he could find in or invite to a bar.

Stan waited outside, out of sight until it looked like most of the late-comers – nothing had changed, there always were those that came well after the service started – had straggled in before making his move. He left his bicycle hidden and slipped into the parking lot, keeping the majority of the cars between him and the church building. Things were going well for Stan today; Tricia had not parked up close, but towards the back of the lot in the shadows of a large tree. Stan placed a small, GPS tracking transmitter up in the right, rear wheel well that was held in place magnetically. This would allow him to follow Tricia's movements when she was in her car.

Having accomplished that feat, Stan figured that he had less than an hour to do the rest of what he wanted – needed – to do. He had to be in and out of both of their houses before they got out of church and returned home and he wasn't sure if they would come straight home afterwards or go somewhere else, but he had to assume that they would go directly home which meant that he needed to hustle. Logically he figured that he should go to Claudia's house first since she would come home first if Tricia was dropping her off on her way home; so he headed back to Claudia's house.

Claudia's neighborhood was still quiet when Stan arrived back there. He ditched his bike in the same place where he had hidden earlier when he was following Tricia's car when she was on her way to church. He went the remainder of the distance to Claudia's place on foot. Stan had found that if you went to wherever you were going assertively even if you didn't belong there, it aroused less suspicion than if you were sneaking around; so that is how he approached Claudia's house – assertively. He went to the back door which was unlocked and went in quickly. Stan could tell right away that Claudia was not a housekeeper. It was probably a good thing that the place was small; otherwise it would have been a major disaster. Stan made a mental note to himself that he would have to help Claudia in that department. It would be his 'gift' to her. Stan needed to have things in order – everything. If Claudia was going to be his woman, then she would need to learn how to keep things tidy.

Since there was only one bedroom in the house, Stan located it with ease and the bathroom was right next to it. There was so much clutter in both rooms; it was easy finding an inconspicuous place to put his wireless camera transmitters. He wished that he would've had more time to make sure that they were working properly and that he had a good view of both rooms, but he knew that the clock was ticking and he still had to get to Tricia's house and set up the cameras there as well.

Before he left Claudia's though, Stan poked through her drawers to get a better idea of what she was like. He had always thought it strange that you could tell what a person was like by the kind of things they collected. He also found a blouse of Claudia's that he placed in his backpack before heading out the door. He knew that in all this clutter she would just think that it was buried in there somewhere and that it would turn up sooner or later. Gathering a personal item from the women that he was watching had become Stan's own personal fetish. He thought that it helped him get closer to his women. When he couldn't watch them he could fondle their clothing; he could smell it and get their scent; and at times he would even taste it.

Stan left Claudia's house as quickly and assertively as he had entered it and walked briskly back to where his bicycle was stashed. Putting his helmet back on and mounting his bicycle, he rode quickly to Tricia's place where he again hid his bike in some bushes close by, but not too close in case he had to flee her house quickly. It was easier to leave and remain hidden on foot than it was on a bicycle; even though you could get away faster on the bicycle. And once again, Stan approached her place assertively and headed straight to the back door. However, this one wasn't going to be as easy as Claudia's; the door was locked and it was a good stout deadbolt – good for Tricia; bad for Stan. He tried the windows in the back, but they were locked as well. Stan didn't want to break anything so he would have to work on that deadbolt lock and see if his lock picking skills had gotten too rusty to be of any use to him. The deadbolt was an older model that he was familiar with so it should be fairly easy to do. He took the lock picking tool out of his backpack, selected the blank that fit that lock and proceeded to unlock it. It took him a little longer than he had wanted to take, but he did get it open and was able to gain entry to Tricia's as well.

Stan could tell that Tricia was definitely not like Claudia in the housekeeping department. Her house was how Stan liked it; tidy, clean, organized, everything in its own place, the sink not over-flowing with dirty dishes. She was his kind of woman; a woman after his own heart.

Tricia's place was a little larger than Claudia's although it too was small. It did have three bedrooms, but they weren't much bigger than closets, except for one was a little bit larger than the other two. And from the things in that room Stan surmised that it was Tricia's room. The one bathroom was down the hall from her bedroom. All of them would use the one bathroom and the thought that he would have to view her children at times in looking for Tricia turned his stomach somewhat. He thought pedophiles were the worst animals alive, but he would do what needed to be done in order to carry on his reconnaissance. He would just try to limit the time that he spent looking at the children.

Since Tricia's place was tidier than Claudia's it was a little more difficult to find a suitable hiding place for the camera transmitters. He did manage to place one in her bedroom and in the bathroom in places that were not too noticeable and hopefully she would not be doing a meticulous cleaning job between now and the time he made her his. As he was mounting the last camera he heard a car door outside. Startled, Stan ran to the nearest window and peeked outside – it was just a neighbor coming home. But it did remind him that he needed to finish up quickly and get out of there before she did come home.

Stan started looking thru Tricia's drawers, careful not to disturb anything so that it would draw any attention to being out of place. At Claudia's it didn't matter – everything was out of place already, but here he was sure that every little thing was cataloged to a certain place. It would be hard to take an article of clothing from her without her noticing that it was missing, but he needed to take that risk. He finally found it – a pull-on sweater. Putting it in his backpack, he surveyed the room one last time to make sure it was all just like it was when he had arrived.

Leaving through the back door, Stan didn't bother to try to relock the deadbolt. He figured that they would assume that they had forgotten to lock it before they left and not think twice about it. Again Stan walked briskly and assertively back to his bicycle and rode home. He would come back later to check on the four cameras to make sure that they were working. The transmitters didn't have a very long range so he needed to at least be within a one block radius of them in order to pick up a signal. He wished he could afford more powerful ones, but they were too expensive for being throw-away items.

Riding home Stan was pleased with his progress that day. It was a good day, a very good day. He had made significant progress and it would not be long until his little hideaway was once again bustling with activity.

# 17

Tricia, Claudia, Timmy and Candy slipped into church just as the rest of the congregation was standing to begin the service with a few rousing, contemporary worship songs. Not many noticed that they were actually late. Tricia couldn't help but think how good God was to work it out so that she didn't have to work and could be in church on Sunday morning. She knew that some would attribute it to luck or coincidence, but not Tricia - and she truly was grateful.

The rest of the service went by in a blur for Tricia, that is, until it was time for the sermon. It was not because she did not like to sing or to be attentive and a participant in the other aspects of the service, but she could not help but marvel in God's goodness and faithfulness to her. But when Pastor Grime got up to give his sermon, she was snapped back into a total awareness of what was being said right then, instead of the autopilot mode that she had been in.

What brought her to attention was the mention of the book of the Bible that Pastor Grime would be preaching from. It was going to be the Book of Daniel, one of Tricia's favorites. She loved the stories in that book. She liked to read how Daniel and his friends had trusted God in the situations that they found themselves in and God always came through for them. It was an encouragement for Tricia. She knew that it was not quite the same, but she had imagined in the past that facing some of her really difficult times was like being thrown into a den of lions or into a blazing hot furnace and having God deliver you.

Now Pastor Grime was going to be preaching from Daniel and he was going to be using the story of when Daniel was thrown into a den of lions because he had refused to stop praying to his God. Before he even said which chapter of Daniel the story was found in, Tricia knew that it was found in the sixth chapter. She knew that because she had read and reread that story. She had almost memorized it because she had read it so much. It had sustained her when she was barren. It had given her hope when she was despairing of life itself. It had given her a role model for trusting God when there was no good reason to trust Him.

Pastor Grime didn't want to spend the time reading the story from that sixth chapter, but he did suggest to the congregation that they read it for themselves some time later that day. Tricia made a mental note to herself to do just that. Pastor Grime recounted the high points of the story to help remind everyone of the story that they may have forgotten parts of it or may have never even heard of Daniel's plight.

He said that because of the jealousy of some of the other administrators in the kingdom where Daniel was over them, they devised a plan to get rid of Daniel. Because the king liked Daniel a lot, their plan involved having the king sign into law a decree forbidding anyone to worship any god or man other than the king for thirty days. Not realizing that this law would entrap Daniel, the king signed the law which became irrevocable. Being a God fearing man, Daniel continued to pray to the one true God three times a day just like he always had done.

The jealous administrators knew that this was Daniel's routine, so after the decree was signed into law, all they had to do was wait and watch for Daniel to break it; and break it Daniel did. The jealous administrators ran straight to the king demanding that Daniel be thrown into the lions' den because he had broken the king's edict about worshipping only him. This disturbed the king a great deal because Daniel was his favorite and he knew that he could not save him. He had to carry out the sentence.

So, Daniel was ordered to be thrown into the lions' den, a stone was placed over the entrance and a seal placed on it so no one could enter and Daniel could not escape. After a fitful night, the king hurried to the den to find out Daniel's fate. Arriving at the den, the king called out to Daniel to inquire of his well being. Daniel's reply was that God had sent His angel to shut the mouths of the lions. The king was overjoyed and gave the orders to have Daniel taken out of the den.

Then Pastor Grime called everyone's attention to the second half of verse twenty three of the sixth chapter which reads like this, "...when Daniel was lifted from the den, no wound was found on him, because he had trusted in his God." For emphasis Pastor Grime repeated, "TAKEN OUT... UNINJURED...FOR HE TRUSTED IN HIS GOD." Pastor Grime let the silence hang in the air as he let the people chew on those words, '*Taken out... uninjured... for he trusted in his God.*'

Once again Pastor Grime repeated those words, "TAKEN OUT... UNINJURED...FOR HE TRUSTED IN HIS GOD...FOR HE TRUSTED IN HIS GOD...TRUSTED IN HIS GOD. Daniel trusted in his God and He delivered Daniel. And in case you were wondering about the rest of the story, the jealous administrators were bound along with their wives and children and thrown into the same lions' den that God had delivered Daniel from and before they reached the bottom of the den, the lions had overpowered them and had crushed all of their bones. And the king honored Daniel and gave glory to God."

Tricia was pumped after that sermon. She felt like she could be thrown into a den of lions and come out victorious because she had trusted in God and He had delivered her. But, she knew that it was not that easy. Daniel was a super believer... and she...she was nobody. She would probably faint the first time one of those lions let out one solitary roar, let alone stand up to them and believe that God would keep her from being harmed by them.

After the service BJ suggested that they take Claudia out to KFC for lunch since it was her birthday. Well, technically yesterday was her birthday, but it was close enough that they could still celebrate it anyway. Rarely did any of them go out to eat. Budgets were tight in all three of their households and eating out was a luxury. But they decided to splurge anyway. KFC was not a fancy place by any means, but everyone could find something that they liked to eat without it costing a fortune.

Lunch was a success all the way around. They made Claudia tell them some stories about her childhood and growing up. Although at first she was a little embarrassed by it, she warmed to the occasion quickly and had everyone's ear as she told story after story about herself and her family. It also helped them get to know Claudia better and make a connection with her that might have taken a long, long time otherwise.

It was later in the afternoon when they finally decided that they should probably head for home. Claudia couldn't think of any more stories that she wanted to share and they all had laughed and cried until it felt as if they had gone on a twenty mile hike. They did get their share of quizzical looks from some of the workers and other customers that were in the restaurant at the time. But they were oblivious to it all. They were having a good time and they were enjoying the company of each other.

Tricia dropped Claudia off before heading to her own home. The minute Tricia stepped inside her house; her inner 'radar' went off that something was not quite right. Not quite the way she had left it this morning when she went out the door to go to church. She did not have any specifics that she could put her finger on. She didn't see anything out of place; or notice that anything was missing at first glance, but something inside her was nagging at her that something had happened here while she was away. Tricia tried to ignore it; to push it deep down inside of her and override that sense, that feeling that she had. But it kept popping back up. She couldn't quite smother it. She didn't verbalize it to her children as she didn't want to unnecessarily worry them and besides she really didn't have any concrete evidence that something was amiss.

Failing to use the restroom at the restaurant, Tricia had laid claim to first use of the bathroom while they were still in the car on the way home after dropping off Claudia. Dropping her purse and Bible on the nearest and handiest piece of furniture that she could find, she made a beeline for the bathroom. Tricia froze in her tracks in the bathroom doorway staring at some strange looking, black thing lying on the bathroom floor. She crept closer to it and poked it with the toe of her shoe. It did not appear to be alive, but she couldn't quite figure out what the thing was. In all of the rush of adrenaline,

Tricia forgot why she had needed to come in here in the first place. She picked the object up off of the floor and began examining it in detail closer up. She noted that a piece of paint and plaster from her bathroom wall was stuck to it, so she began scanning the walls to see if she could spot where it had been stuck. It took very careful scrutiny in order to find where it had been sticking, but she did find the place. A portion of plaster about the size of a dime was missing its paint.

*But what was it? How long had it been up there? Who put it there? And why?* All of these questions kept running around in Tricia's head as she turned the object over and over studying it from every possible angle trying to figure the thing out. As a last resort, she called her son Timmy in there.

"Timmy, come take a look at this thing that I found on the bathroom floor," said Tricia. "What do you think it is?"

Taking the object out of Tricia's hand Timmy takes one look at it and says, "That's easy mom. It's a camera!"

Dumbfounded, Tricia says, "A camera? Why would a camera be stuck to the wall of our bathroom?"

"I don't know, mom. Probably somebody wanted to watch someone go to the bathroom," said Timmy.

That foreboding feeling leapt up in Tricia's throat and put a chokehold on her that forced her to involuntarily cough to try to shake it off. Again the questions began swirling around in her mind. *What have they seen? Did they watch me? Did they watch the children? Should she call the police or tell someone else about this?*

Timmy said, "It was probably left there by one of the renters that lived here before we came. It's nothing to worry about mom. Just forget about it. Can I have that thing?"

"No, Timmy, you can't have it. I am going to put it up in case we need to show it to the police or someone. But thank you for helping me figure out what it is. Now, if you will step out of the bathroom I need to use it real bad."

Timmy stepped out and Tricia pushed the door closed. As soon as the door was closed she put the camera underneath a heavy towel and pointed it toward the wall away from the commode just in case the thing was active and someone was watching her right now. It gave her the creeps just to think that someone may have been watching her and her children doing their business in the bathroom ever since they moved in to the house. She wondered if this was the handiwork of the landlord. She never was too comfortable around him. He always seemed unusually friendly in her opinion. She had to remind herself not to go passing judgment on him without having any evidence to link him to this. But she had to do this constantly as his name and face kept coming up in her mental gymnastics connecting him with the deed.

As soon as she was finished in the bathroom, Tricia took the camera and placed it in a drawer in her dresser in her bedroom where she kept her treasures and other important items that she wanted to save. She made sure that it was covered up good so that there would be no possibility of anyone seeing anything on that camera again.

Having put the camera away, Tricia began a sweep of the house to see if she could spot any other cameras. Since she was in her bedroom when she decided to examine the rest of the house, she started her scan in there. She stared at each square inch (at least she thought she did) of wall and ceiling to see if she could spot another camera. When she had finally convinced herself that there were no other cameras in there she moved out into the hallway and repeated the scanning process. She checked the living room, the kitchen/dining area, the children's bedrooms and finally moved to the back porch area having decided there were no cameras in those other rooms.

While on the porch she noticed that the deadbolt on the back door was unlocked. She had been certain that she had locked that door before leaving for church this morning because she had scolded the children for leaving it unlocked overnight.

"Timmy! Candy! Did either one of you go out the back door since we got home?"

"Not me," said Timmy.

"I didn't either," said Candy.

"Oh, dear," muttered Tricia under her breath. Again she didn't want to alarm the children to the possibility that someone may have broken into their house while they were gone. And again her suspicions of her landlord came rushing to the forefront. Of course, he would have a key. And he would know when they would be gone. He probably slipped in and put that camera up in the bathroom and went back out, forgetting to lock the deadbolt when he left. Then the question came to her, *Should she confront him about it?* That would be tantamount to an accusation, wouldn't it? Could she go that far? She still didn't have any hard evidence that it was him.

Tricia stepped out the back door away from the children and began to sob silently. What was she going to do? She decided that she would talk to BJ about this the next chance that she had. But the fear and the dread began bubbling up inside of her putting a stranglehold on her.

Suddenly, that still small voice that she had learned as God speaking to her, spoke and said, "Don't be afraid! Trust Me! Trust Me; the lions' mouths will be held shut." And with that voice, a calm peace swept over Tricia and instead of sobbing in fear she began crying for joy.

# 18

✤

The three children, Rod, Timmy and Candy, were so excited. They had anticipated this day ever since Ralph had suggested it over two weeks ago. He had gone out and purchased the materials that they were going to need for their project the same day that he had mentioned it to the children and they were so excited to begin that they had wanted to start building right then. And every day since then there had always been something to interfere with the start of their project, but that hadn't kept them from pestering Ralph (grandpa) if they could start today and every day since then it was always the same. It would have been reasonable to have assumed that their enthusiasm would have been tempered over time, but not so. In fact, their excitement had been building ever since it was first suggested to them and every day that they were told, "not today" their disappointment and their expectancy grew at the same time.

But today it was going to happen. They were positive of that. Ralph was finally going to help them build the birdhouses for the purple martins. Ralph had been telling the children all about the purple martin; sometimes he told them the same facts over and over, but the children didn't seem to mind. They were so excited and interested in the purple martins and in having a bird house of their own that they listened eagerly even if it was a repeat of what they had already learned.

They knew that they probably wouldn't have any guests living in their birdhouses this year since all of the martins had already nested for this breeding season and it would not be too long until they migrated south for the winter months. It did give them hope for next year though. They thought that maybe if they got their birdhouses up before they migrated that some of them would check it out and see what a great new place it would be for next year. Ralph did tell them that the purple martins that migrated to the eastern part of North America almost exclusively nested in bird boxes, but that their Western cousins preferred to nest in natural cavities. They were not quite sure what a natural cavity was, but they thought that maybe they could dress up their birdhouses to give it a natural look; maybe attach a few twigs and leaves to it, that sort of thing. Also, Ralph had several families of martins that came back to his birdhouses every year so maybe the purple martins that came to Crescent City were originally from the East and liked to live in birdhouses and not 'natural cavities.'

The children had been fascinated by the birds' feeding and drinking habits and could sit and watch them for hours. They were so acrobatic and agile. They knew that they ate winged insects and caught them in midflight. And if that wasn't interesting enough to watch, their drinking method was even more astounding to watch. They learned that the purple martins drink in midflight as well. They skim the surface of a body of water and scoop up water in their lower bill like a forest service airplane that scooped up water out of a lake to dump on a forest fire. Ralph had told them about how they drank, but when they saw it for themselves down by the creek on one of their forays there, they were astounded. They couldn't stop talking about it for weeks.

Ralph also told them that the purple martin is the largest of the North American swallows measuring about seven and a half inches long. And he told them – several times – that they could tell the male birds from the female birds by their coloration. The male birds were entirely black with a glossy steel blue sheen. And the female birds were similar to the males except that they did not have the steel blue sheen and had lighter colored feathers underneath on their bellies.

The children were all in the shop waiting for Ralph to come out of the house after going in to the house to eat his breakfast when he had finished his chores. They were fidgety and trying to dissipate some of their nervous energy and excitement by playing with some of the tools and gadgets in Ralph's shop and poking at each other as kids often do. When he had finished his breakfast and finally did come out to his shop, the children started jumping up and down and clapping their hands.

"Calm down! Calm down," said Ralph, "you need to be calm when you are working with tools, especially power tools. Now I am going to cut out all of the pieces that we will need to build your birdhouses and then I will help you assemble them. Here are some safety glasses that I bought especially for you. I want you to put them on. You can watch me cut the pieces out, but I want you to stand over there behind that bench. If you don't stay behind the bench, I will make you leave the workshop and you won't get to build a birdhouse. This saw is a very dangerous piece of machinery and I don't want you to get tangled up in it and lose a finger or hand or something else. So this is for your protection. Everyone understand?"

"Yes, grandpa," they all echoed in unison.

"Great! Let's get started building those birdhouses. The purple martins need a new home to move into."

"Alright!"

Ralph, carefully cut out each piece from the pattern that he had previously marked on the wood pieces. Since he had made several birdhouses just like the ones that the children would be making today, it went very quickly. And even though they were excited and really wanted to get closer to the cutting process, they also knew that Ralph was serious about being banished from the workshop and not being allowed to build a birdhouse. And they certainly did not want those consequences so they stayed put behind the bench where Ralph had told them to stay.

When all of the pieces were finally cut out and the saw turned off, Ralph motioned for the children to come near. He sorted the pieces into four neat little piles of wood pieces and gave each of the children one of the piles. There was one pile left over which he took for himself. Ralph had decided to build a birdhouse along with the children so that he could demonstrate the next step in the building process.

Ralph then had them line themselves up along his workbench so that everyone had plenty of space to work in. Ralph situated himself at one end of the workbench so that all of the children could observe him as he built his birdhouse and he could monitor their progress as well. Each of them was issued a file and three pieces of sandpaper of varying grits – from a coarse grit to a fine grit. Ralph showed them how to use the file and then the sandpaper to first take off the bigger pieces and round off some of the sharper corners that the saw either couldn't reach or had left a rough edge on. Ralph explained that the martins were an 'elegant' bird and liked the finer things in life and so they needed to make a finely crafted house for them. The children were not quite sure if he was pulling their legs or not, but they didn't want to cross him and run the risk of not being able to finish their birdhouse. So they worked diligently filing and sanding away until Ralph finally approved of each of their efforts and said that they could now proceed to the next step, but the first one finished didn't get to go on until all were finished. In the meantime, the first one finished which just so happened to be Rod, started to get a little antsy. He went off to the bathroom and to get a drink of water before turning his attention to pestering the other two children still filing and sanding away. And even though Ralph had made some suggestions to Rod about some of the places that could be finished a little better, he was having none of it. He had no more patience for filing and sanding and he was more than ready to move on to the next step. Ralph could see that Rod had grown weary of the tedium of filing and sanding so he stopped making suggestions of how Rod could improve his pieces of wood.

The next step was to glue and screw the pieces together into something that resembled a birdhouse and their finished product. Ralph drilled all of the holes for the screws and then showed them how to put the glue on and put the screws into the holes. Rod and Timmy managed quite well getting the screws turned into each hole, but Candy could only get the screws in a few turns before she didn't have enough strength to screw them in snug so Ralph had to help her put the screws in the rest of the way. Once all of the screws were in Ralph checked Rod and Timmy's screws to make sure that they were tight. Then he had them run the sandpaper over it a few times to smooth out any imperfections that may have appeared in the assembly process.

They had been working so intently all morning that they had failed to realize that it was lunchtime until BJ called them from the house to come get a sandwich. It then dawned on them that they were famished. They had worked up an appetite working on those birdhouses. And now they even looked like birdhouses. Not just a pile of wood pieces. When BJ called, they dropped what they were doing and took off on a run to the house. And as usual, Candy came in last. But she wasn't the very last. Ralph had stopped to straighten out the things that the children had just dropped in their haste to reach the house first and besides, he moved a little slower than the children did.

Refueled and reenergized, the children were raring to get back out to the workshop and their birdhouses. Ralph on the other hand would have been content to have relaxed and let the sandwich and chips digest for a while before plunging back into work. Maybe even slip in a short cat nap for a few minutes. But it was not to be. The children wanted to finish the birdhouses so Ralph would oblige them.

They had a few more pieces to attach to the birdhouses before they could begin to paint them. Most of the pieces were more of an appearance matter instead of being a structural component or having a function that would make it easier and more attractive for the purple martins to move in and live there. One of those items that needed to be added were short pieces of ¼" doweling right below the entrance to that the bird could land on it before entering the opening to the nest area. Again Ralph drilled the holes for all of them and showed them how to glue them in place.

Once all of the pieces had been attached, they began cleaning and prepping them for paint. They would need to put a coat of paint on them and then wait until tomorrow to put the final coats on. Ralph said that they should put two coats on since they would be outside and needed lots of protection from the sun and rain. The children however, wanted to go put them up right then. They didn't want to wait for paint to dry – especially not three coats of paint. Ralph found each of them a paintbrush and poured some primer paint into paper cups so that each one would have his own paint bucket and there would be no fighting over the paint can. Ralph had to show each one of them how best to hold their paintbrush, get a little bit of paint on the brush wiping off the excess on the side of the cup and then how to stroke the paint on making sure that the paint went on evenly, smoothly and that all of the exposed wood was covered with paint. Once that was completed, Ralph showed them how to put the remainder of their paint that was in each individual cup back into the paint can, close the can tightly with the lid and how to clean out their brushes. When all of that was finished, the four of them stood back to admire their handiwork and daydream about the purple martin families that would be moving in any day now.

It was not long until they were snapped out of their reverie by Tricia, calling for Timmy and Candy. The children all started groaning in chorus. They knew that they had to wait until tomorrow to put the finish coats on, but yet they didn't know that. And so, they groaned. But Tricia can be very persistent in situations such as this. So the children decided that groaning was going to get them nowhere and that they better do as their mother had bid them do.

Tricia had had a very busy day at the restaurant and was in no mood to listen incessantly to the children drone on and on about their day building birdhouses. All of the way home they chattered about the purple martin birdhouses and each and every step that they went through to get to where they were then. Then they told the same thing over and over reliving their day of birdhouse building for the purple martins. Tricia was never so glad to see her driveway as she was that night. Her question that kept running through her mind was, *"how am I ever going to get them settled down for bed tonight?"*

# 19

❧

S tan set tonight when he would activate the cameras in at least one of the women's – his women – house. He had decided that they belonged to him, they were his wives, it didn't matter if they didn't agree or if no official ceremony ever took place or any legal certificate ever was issued. They were his. He had claimed them. That was all that mattered. It didn't even matter if they were legally and morally committed to another. They were his – end of story.

As a guard, he loathed the perverts; especially the ones that preyed on the unsuspecting and the weaker. And he thought that the voyeurs were the lowest of the low. He put them right down there with the ones that exploited children. But, because these women were his, he was justified in observing them. After all how could he know how to provide for them adequately if he did not know what they needed?

Stan had decided that he would observe Tricia first since he had discovered and selected her first as his next "wife" and if he had time he would go observe Claudia. And if time didn't permit it he would observe her tomorrow night. He had also reasoned that Tricia would probably go to bed earlier than Claudia since she had young children. He had ordered some new equipment which would allow him to sit in the comfort of his home and watch what his cameras were seeing, but it would probably not be here for another two weeks or so and he couldn't wait that long to get started especially since the cameras were already in place. And that was another thing; he also wished that he would have had the new cameras that he had just ordered in time to install them in their houses. Next time – if there was a next time. He didn't feel like risking entering their houses again to swap out the cameras. But the new cameras would have been nice. They were supposed to be able to "see" in really low light situations like the night vision goggles that the military wore when they went on night exercises. Oh well, there was always some new gadget coming out that made his job easier, but usually too late to help him when he needed it.

The spot near Tricia's house that Stan had used before was perfect. He was off of the main thoroughfare, he was partially hidden, he could visually see her house and it was within range of the cameras. He couldn't have asked for a better place. On the other hand, Claudia's place left him more exposed, more vulnerable so he would have to limit his exposure there. That was probably another reason, at least subconsciously, that he had chosen Tricia's place to start with. It had been quite a while since he had been in this phase and he felt a little rusty. He needed a nice safe place to get his groove back and then he could be a little more daring, a little bolder.

Stan had driven by Tricia's house a few times and had decided that 9:30 to 10:00 PM was usually bedtime at her house; at least he surmised that from the pattern of when the lights went out; which would be perfect. It would be fairly dark by then and still give him some observation time; after all he had to be up for work the next day too. Fortunately for him he was not on the early morning shift rotation right now, otherwise he would have been forced to take a nap when he got home from work and then get up and go do his observing.

About 9:00 PM Stan headed over to Tricia's house and his hiding spot. Once there, he set up his laptop and picked up the signal from the cameras; or should I say he tried to pick up the camera signals. The only signal that he could get to come in was the camera in the bedroom. The bathroom camera was dark; pitch-black dark. Nothing. Not a peep of light, not even an indication that it was on or that it had ever existed.

Stan filled the air with obscenities. He was livid. "How could this happen? Why isn't the camera working? How did he get so lucky? Was the battery dead? Did someone find it?" And with that thought voiced, Stan started getting panicky. Was he about to be discovered, he wondered? He was so preoccupied with his anxiety that he failed to notice that the lights in the living room had been turned off and it was dark in the front of the house. "When did that happen," asked Stan to himself? Lights were still on in the back of the house and working in Stan's favor, Tricia's bedroom faced where Stan was parked and there was a window on that side of the house so he could see that her bedroom light was still on.

Tricia had been in the habit of dressing and undressing in the bathroom and this night was no different. So, when she came back into her bedroom she was dressed for bed with a robe on. Stan groaned when he saw that. He was so hoping to see much more. He watched as Tricia crawled into bed and proceeded to take a book off of the nightstand and read. His camera wasn't good enough to pick up the title of the book, but he sat there watching for 15 or 20 minutes as she read. He was recording all of this so that he could pour over it later at home just like he fondled the clothing every day that he had taken from the two women's bedrooms a few days ago when he had planted the cameras in their houses.

When the book started bobbing and weaving around Tricia decided that she was too sleepy to read any more and sat the book back on the nightstand where she had retrieved it from, got up and went over to turn off the light. For some unknown reason, being fully clothed excited Stan more than if she had nothing on. The light went off and the camera went dark for an instant as it read-justed itself to the available light level. In that split second, Tricia had managed to slip off her robe and was back under the covers. As the camera "sight" came back Stan could make out some of the major features in the room and he could only make out a lump lying on the bed, no features would appear no matter how much he squinted or what adjustments he tried to make with the picture. The "glow" in the room from the windows and the digital clock was just not bright enough to let the camera see very well. It was a good thing that he had spent the extra money for drones with the night vision capability on them. He could see now that he was going to need it. Then the next thing would be to learn how to use them.

Stan saved the file that he had been recording and since it was still relatively early, decided to move over to Claudia's house and at least check out the cameras there and see if both of them were working or if he had been compromised there as well. Because he was going to be using everything right away, Stan didn't bother to shut it all down only to have to start it back up again.

Arriving at Claudia's place, he noticed that it wasn't completely dark, but there wasn't much light on either. Stan pulled to a stop in the conspicuous place that he had used before and not wanting to draw much attention to himself he had decided that he wouldn't stay very long at any one time. He connected easily with both of the cameras. Claudia was in the bathroom taking a shower, but Stan couldn't see very much because the shower curtain was opaque with some sort of ugly design on it.

While he was intently watching, a rap came on his driver side window. Stan just about jumped out of his skin it startled him so much. When he regained his composure, he closed the screen to the laptop so that it wasn't viewable and rolled down his window.

Standing outside his car was an older gentleman obviously out walking his dog and he said, "Are you lost? Can I help you?"

Stammering a bit, Stan replied, "Oh, aww, I was just making some notes for a presentation that I thought about while I was driving and I didn't want the possibility of forgetting my thoughts until I got home. I am fine, thank you for checking."

"OK! We have had some strange things going on around here lately and I like to keep an eye on what's happening. So, if you are up to no good you will have me to contend with."

"Don't you think that it is best to leave that sort of thing up to the law enforcement; after all that is their job?"

"Young man, they can't be everywhere at the same time. People need to watch out for their neighbors and their neighborhood. I am not saying anything against our police force because as far as I can see they are doing an excellent job, but like I said part of the responsibility for a safe neighborhood falls on the neighbors' shoulders for watching out for each other."

"Well sir, I just don't want you to get involved in a situation that would endanger yourself. There are a lot of unsavory characters out there that wouldn't think twice about hurting you."

"You never mind me. I am always packing, especially when I go out at night. I have a concealed weapons permit. I know how to use a handgun and I am not afraid to use it. I was in Vietnam and I put more men down than care to remember, so don't worry about me, I can take care of myself. And if I can't, I know where I am going when I check out of this place."

"Suit yourself sir. I was just finishing up. I will be on my way now. You have a good night now. And take care of yourself."

"Good night to you."

As Stan drove away, the older gentleman made a mental note to himself to write down the car make and license plate number when he returned home. He didn't like the feeling that he got from that guy. He might have been perfectly legit, but he still felt like he was up to no good.

# 20

Tricia had not seen Timmy and Candy's birdhouses yet. They had wanted to have them finished before she could see them so they had kept her out of Ralph's workshop yesterday when she came to pick them up after work. The birdhouses were all put together and had a coat of primer on them. Today the children would put the final two coats of paint on them along with some garnishing touches of some little bric-a-brac that they had found while rummaging around in Ralph's cupboard of miscellaneous parts and pieces of different screws, knobs, trim and doo dads of varying usefulness.

Tricia had promised them that she would take them with her when she went to Pelican Bay this afternoon after work to see their dad. They were excited about that. They had not seen him in over a month. Tricia didn't like to take them too often. She didn't think that the prison visiting room was a very healthy environment to take children to even though they wanted to see their father more often than that.

And of course they were excited about finishing their birdhouses. She couldn't tell which one excited them the most – finishing the birdhouses or visiting their father. Tricia had the early shift which meant that they had to get up and go to BJ's early as well. BJ didn't seem to mind. Her and Ralph were always up; whether she had to work or not. Rod on the other hand would not be up for a while yet. He liked his sleep. So, Timmy and Candy usually curled up in a chair or on the sofa to get some extra sleep of their own while Rod was still sleeping. BJ was always so happy to see them and to help Tricia out in any way that she could; that was one of her endearing qualities that had attracted Tricia to her so quickly. Ralph on the other hand was more reserved than BJ and even though he would go out of his way to help you, he was not as forthcoming as BJ in his access and consequently not as approachable. Be that as it may, both of them were fine friends. She couldn't have asked for better, more caring friends than BJ and Ralph. And she owed them a debt of gratitude for their help with the children this summer.

Timmy and Candy got almost another three hours of sleep before Rod finally decided that it was time to get up. BJ fixed them all some breakfast while Ralph sat there finishing his third cup of coffee for the morning and reading the paper. When they all had finished it was Candy who finally asked, "Can we go finish our birdhouses now?"

"Yeah, let's go," said Rod.

"I'm ready," said Timmy.

And Ralph said, "I have been waiting on you three!"

This time it was Candy that made it out to the workshop before any of them could even think about it. She made it out there and grabbed the can of paint that she wanted to paint her birdhouse in. It was a deep, metallic purple that Ralph had used to paint a toy truck that he had restored and brought back to usefulness from a life of neglect and disuse. He had found the truck in a basement that he had helped clean out almost twelve years ago. When he found the truck he had asked the owners of the place how much they wanted for it, but they just gave it to him as it looked like the rest of the junk that they were throwing away; but not to Ralph. Ralph saw the potential that lie dormant under all of the rust, dents and abuse that little boys subject such a toy to. Ralph worked his magic on that toy. He scraped and sanded and hammered and filled and painted until it looked better than when it was purchased and taken out of the store to make some little boy happier than he had ever been.

Candy had picked out her color yesterday and was not about to change her mind now. Timmy wanted to paint his camouflage color, but the others didn't think that was a very good idea. If it was camo how in the world would the purple martins ever find it when they were looking for a new place to live? Wasn't that the whole idea of camo — to blend in to the surroundings so that you became invisible? And if your point was to try to attract the birds there, why would you want to paint it so that it would become invisible. But Timmy was not to be dissuaded and Ralph had decided to stay out of it a long time before this so that the birdhouses would be their own creation and no one else's. Rod had not decided for sure, but he was leaning towards a plain white one like his grandfather Ralph made. He would take a look at the colors that were available one more time to see if anything other than white jumped out at him and said, "Use me! Use me!"

Ralph helped Candy get started painting her birdhouse since she was more than ready and the others were still fiddling around. Once he had her started, he suggested to Timmy that he use a pencil to mark out splotches where he would paint the various colors to complete the camo look. Ralph had four different colors of paint that had the "natural" look that was most often used in camouflage coloration schemes. Timmy picked one of the colors to be the base or background color that would go between all of the other color swatches and began painting that in between the shapes that he had drawn on his birdhouse. Once that was completed, Ralph showed him how to clean out his brush and start painting a few of the splotch shapes in with that color. In the meantime, Rod finally decided on the white that he had originally selected and began to paint his birdhouse. And once Ralph had all of the children busily painting their birdhouse, he shared Rod's can of paint and started painting his own birdhouse. So soon there would be two new white birdhouses, a new camo birdhouse and a deep, metallic purple birdhouse in the neighborhood.

Candy, Rod and Ralph were all finished with their first coats well before Timmy finished putting his first coat of camo paint scheme on. But it didn't matter. It was taking shape. It was looking like something. And it was something that he had put together with his own hands. He had never done anything like that before and he was taking pride in it. It made him feel good. He had a real feeling of self worth and a strong image boost from this simple little exercise.

Ralph said that they had to wait a couple of hours for the paint to dry before they could put the second and final coat on so he sent them off to play and he went back into the house to his favorite recliner to sneak in a cat nap while he could. Not that he really needed a nap, but he had gotten into the habit of dozing off for a few minutes when he came back in from doing the chores; that is when time permitted and there was nothing else pressing that needed to be done at the moment.

When he woke up, Ralph went back out to the workshop to check on the paint and discovered that it was not quite dry; especially Timmy's birdhouse since he had been the last one to finish painting. So, Ralph started puttering around the shop straightening and cleaning what he could. Not that it needed straightening or cleaning, because Ralph couldn't stand to work in a messy place. Everything was in its proper place unless it was being used and then when you were finished with it, back into its place it was supposed to go. But he did find a couple of things not quite to his liking and proceeded to put them in order. As he did, he wondered to himself who had left it like that. Certainly not him - could it have been?

Completing that little project, Ralph was heading out the door of the workshop to call the children and tell them that the paint was dry and that they could come and put the second coat on when he saw them running back towards the house from having been down at the creek. Ralph watched them running for a few seconds, half envious of their carefree, exuberance they exhibited in their run back to the house.

The second coat went on much quicker – even Timmy's montage – than the first coat. And when they had finished painting them, they all stood a few feet away and admired their handiwork. Ralph broke the quiet with, "Those will be the best looking purple martin birdhouses this side of the Mississippi."

"What do you mean by that, grandpa," asked Candy?

"It's just a figure of speech, honey. It just means that those are some mighty fine looking birdhouses and I would be proud to live in any one of those if I were a bird."

All of the children started giggling at the thought of Ralph – grandpa – living in one of those purple martin birdhouses. It was more than even they could imagine. But they did think that they were great looking birdhouses and could hardly wait to get them put up somewhere and to have a family of purple martins move in.

Then the children started picking out and arranging the decorative pieces that they wanted on their birdhouse and where, being careful not to touch the drying paint in the process. Once that was done, it was time to get cleaned up for lunch. BJ had promised them soup and toasted cheese sandwiches for lunch – all of their favorites. And she had said that if they did a really good job on their birdhouses she would make them some cookies. They hadn't quite figured out how she would know if they did a good job or not and still have time to bake the cookies, but they didn't fret over that conundrum too long. BJ always came through with her promises. And if she said that they would have cookies if they did a good job, then they would do a good job and they would get their cookies.

The children were hoping that the paint would dry soon enough that they could add the decorative pieces after lunch and before Tricia came to pick them up. They so wanted to show her what they had been so diligently working on. And they wanted to be able to tell their father this afternoon when they saw him at the prison that they had made a birdhouse, that it was all finished and that it was beautiful.

Lunch was quiet as all of the children were intent on eating so that they could get back out to their birdhouses. Rod and Timmy devoured all of their food and had a smaller second portion of soup. Both of them had worked up an appetite. Candy didn't do as well as the two boys. She had a few spoonfuls left of her soup and a couple of bites of her sandwich left when she announced that she was full, but BJ noticed that when she brought the plate of cookies out that Candy ate her share of them.

As they were working on the cookies, Ralph slipped out to check on the paint because he knew what would happen once the children were finished eating. He met the children coming out of the house and heading for the workshop only to disappoint them with the news that the paint was not quite dry yet. Another half hour he said. This time they found something close by to play with instead of going off to the creek to play. They wanted to be close by when Ralph said that it was OK to add their decorations. It was going to be close. Secretly they hoped that their mom had to work a little overtime, like she did some days, so that they would have time to finish their birdhouses, but not too much over or she would not want to go out to the prison afterwards. They hadn't quite figured out the visiting hour time period at the prison yet, but they could relate to when their mom said that she was too tired to do something that she had promised them earlier that they would do after she got off of work and then didn't do it.

But it all worked out. They didn't have to worry about a thing. The paint dried in time. Tricia didn't have to work overtime and she came just as they were attaching the last of their decorations to the birdhouses. They made her wait outside while they cleaned up and set the birdhouses in a nice neat row – like a condominium development. When all of that was completed they made her close her eyes and led her into the workshop and faced her towards the "Purple Martin Condominium Park" and told her to open her eyes.

When Tricia opened her eyes she exclaimed, "Oh my, they are BEAUTIFUL! You have done such a wonderful job. I am so proud of all of you."

"Me too," joked Ralph?

"Yes, you too Ralph! Especially you, for all your help and patience."

"Can we take them home," asked Timmy?

"I thought you wanted to put them up here. And besides, I think that they should sit here for a day or two and make sure everything is good and dry before you handle it too much," said Ralph.

"I forgot," said Timmy.

"You can take them home if you want to, but I would still wait before you do that," said Ralph.

"We have time to decide that later. We better get going if we are going to make it out to see your father this afternoon," said Tricia.

"I almost forgot that too," said Timmy. "Let's get going then."

"Thanks for everything, BJ. Thank you, Ralph," said Tricia as a tear sneaked down her cheek not unnoticed by BJ and Ralph.

"Bye grandma! Bye grandpa," said Timmy and Candy in unison.

"Goodbye, children," said BJ as they headed down the walk.

BJ and Ralph stood there watching and waving as they pulled out of the driveway and off down the road towards town and the prison.

"A couple of great kids. Thanks for spending time with them dear. Hopefully it will make a difference as they grow older," said BJ.

"It's a lot of fun. Tiring, but fun," said Ralph as they walked arm in arm back to the house.

# 21

❧

All the way to Pelican Bay the children sat in the back seat and chattered non-stop from BJ's house. They were excited about their birdhouses and the purple martins that were going to move in there, they were excited about going to the prison and they were excited about seeing their father. They wondered if he missed them or even if he remembered them. They couldn't wait to tell him about their birdhouses, and about BJ, Ralph and Rod, about the creek that they had been playing in with Rod and about all that they had been learning about in the youth group at church.

Tricia on the other hand had grown pensive. She was apprehensive about taking the children in to the prison. She knew that Mark would ask her how his appeal was going and she didn't have any answers for him. She didn't want to burden him with their financial struggles and she didn't want to lie to him either, but she knew that he would ask – he always did. And she felt like she should share her faith with him, but he had made it clear from previous visits that he had no use for God, if in fact he did exist. And he certainly didn't want a minister visiting him there in prison. Tricia used to look forward to going to see Mark, but the last few times it had become strained and unnatural. What was happening to their relationship? She could sense it drying up and dying, but she didn't know what to do about it.

She breathed a silent prayer as she turned into the parking lot, asking God to work a miracle in their lives – in her and Mark's relationship. She knew that it was possible and she also knew that she really needed one. And just as quickly as she breathed that prayer she heard those reassuring words, "Trust Me! Tricia, Trust Me!" The tears flooded into her eyes so that she couldn't see and had to stop driving. Fortunately she was in the visitors' parking lot of the prison and there wasn't much traffic moving about.

Timmy said, "What's wrong mom? Why are you crying?"

"Nothing honey. God was just reminding me to 'Trust him,' that's all"

"What does he mean mommy, when he says, 'Trust Me,'" asked Candy?

"It means that God has everything under control and that we don't have to worry or fear what will happen next. Like when those evil men had Daniel thrown into the lions' den. Daniel trusted God for the outcome."

"I remember Pastor Grime preaching about Daniel and the lions' den a few Sundays' ago," said Candy.

"That's right honey. He did preach about that. And God has to keep reminding me about that too. I forget too easily. I don't have a good memory like you do."

Wiping away most of the tears, Tricia could see well enough to pull into an empty space and park the car. "Let's go see your father before it's too late."

"Too late? Why would it be too late? What are they going to do to daddy," asked Candy?

"They are not going to do anything to daddy, dear. But if we don't hurry the prison visiting hours will be over and they won't let us in today," said Tricia.

"Race you to the door," said Timmy and off he took like a rocket.

"Not fair," shouted Candy as she took off after her brother.

"Kids! Slow down!"

By the time they got through security, into the visiting room and had Mark brought up from his cell, they only had twenty minutes left to visit with him. And while they were waiting, Tricia reminded the children that they couldn't touch their father. No hugging, no touching, no kissing. And when he came into the room, Tricia had to grab Candy to keep her from running to her father and throwing her arms around his legs.

They settled in around an empty table and after a few awkward moments of silence, the children finally broke the ice and began their chattering. They blurted out all the things that they had talked about in the car on the way there that they were going to share with their dad. The parts of the story were coming at such a rapid fire pace and so intertwined that Mark was having a hard time following all that the children were trying to tell him.

When they finally came up for air Mark said, "Let me see if I get this straight. This Ralph guy helped you two and this Rod build birdhouses for these purple marions and you just finished them today..."

"No dad. Purple martins. The birds are purple martins. Ralph told us all about them. They are really cool birds. They eat lots of insects so we need to help them have houses to live in," said Timmy.

"OK! Purple martins. And you have been playing down by the creek with this friend of yours Rod. What exactly do you do there? You aren't in the creek are you?"

"We don't get in the creek. We play with the frogs and the tadpoles. We have a fort built in the bushes and the cattails. We make boats and float them down the stream. We just play. Didn't you ever get to play by a creek when you were a kid, dad?"

"No, creeks don't run through the asphalt jungles where I grew up. It sounds like fun. More fun than sitting in here all day being bored out my mind."

"Daddy, Pastor Grime told us the story about Daniel in the lions' den. Do you want to hear it? He said that it teaches us to put our trust in God. And on our way here, mommy said that God had to remind her to 'Trust him," said Candy.

"No. I don't need to hear the story of Daniel and the lions' den. I believe your mother has already told me that story," said Mark.

"You could hear it again. Maybe God needs to remind you too," said Candy.

Feeling a little uncomfortable with the direction that the conversation was going, Mark said, "You kids sure have grown since I saw you last. You are growing like weeds."

"We're not weeds daddy," said Candy.

"You're right honey. You're not weeds. You're my big girl and my big young man. And I am proud of you both," said Mark.

"Tricia, have you heard anything about my appeal," asked Mark?

"No, Mark I haven't," said Tricia.

"I think that lawyer guy is just getting rich off of us. I don't think he has lifted one little finger to advance my case," said Mark.

"Mark, you know these things take time. They will work out in due season," said Tricia.

"I don't have much time. This place is starting to get to me. I don't think I will be able to take it much longer. The food is bad. You can't trust anyone – not even the guards. I don't get a decent night's sleep. I have to keep watching my back. There is always someone that wants you to be their girlfriend."

"Mark please. Not in front of the children," said Tricia.

"I'm sorry, I forgot," said Mark. "So what else have you two been doing this summer?"

"We went with BJ, Ralph and Rod to the beach and collected a lot of really cool beach glass. They are little pieces of glass that have been polished nice and smooth by the water and sand rubbing on them," said Timmy.

"I would like to see them some time," said Mark.

"Mommy said we couldn't bring them in here. I wanted to, but she said you might try to cut your way out with them," said Candy.

"No dear. I did not say that daddy would try to cut his way out," said Tricia.

"That's OK. You can show them to me when I get out," said Mark. "And maybe, you can even take me to that beach and help me collect my own pieces of glass."

"Yeah, can we go right now," asked Candy?

"No dear. Daddy can't leave here yet," replied Tricia.

"Tricia, how are you doing with the finances," asked Mark?

"Mark, don't be worrying about us. God has been providing for us. We don't have a lot of extra, but God sends what we need when we need it. He is teaching me to trust him – just like Daniel as he faced the lions' in their den," said Tricia.

"What is with you two? Are you ganging up on me with this lions' den story? And how can you say that God provided for you? Aren't you working and making money? Aren't you the one doing the providing," asked Mark?

"Mark, I am working, but God provides opportunity for overtime or an extra generous tip from a customer when I need a little extra money for a bill or something. Or, BJ and Ralph, send a big box of food home with us. Or someone at church slips me a twenty as we are leaving the church just because God told them to. Or some of the men came over and fixed our car when it was not working and didn't charge me anything. Mark, those things are not just coincidences. God is providing for us. He is looking out for us," said Tricia.

"Maybe you should marry this God guy instead of me. I can't seem to do a very good job of taking care of my family," said Mark.

"Stop it Mark! I am married to you. I love you. And one day you will take care of us again. And hopefully we will be able to help someone else that is struggling like we are now, but until that time God has told me to 'Trust Him,'" said Tricia.

"I am not convinced, but you do put up a pretty good argument," said Mark.

"I am not arguing with you Mark. I am merely stating the facts. Believe them if you want to, but those are the facts. God is taking care of us," said Tricia.

"Daddy, guess what we found in the bathroom the other day," said Timmy.

"Quiet honey. Daddy doesn't need to be bothered about that," said Tricia.

"What did you find in the bathroom," asked Mark?

"It was nothing. Nothing at all," said Tricia.

"It was not nothing mom. It was a camera. A peeping, spy camera," said Timmy.

"A camera! What's a camera doing in my families' bathroom? What kind of pervert has been watching them? I'll kill them. Let me out of here! I am going to rip their heads off," said Mark.

"Mr. Noyes, you are going to have to settle down there or your visiting privileges will be over and you will not be able to have visitors for a month. So just sit back down and lower your voice. Don't do anything stupid. I don't want to have to report this, but if you keep it up I am going to have to," said one of the guards on duty in the visitation room.

Mark sat back down, but he was furious on the inside. Someone had threatened the security of his family and he wasn't going to have any of it.

"Mark, we figured that it was probably left there from one of the previous renters. It didn't even have any wires connected to it. It probably didn't even work. Don't get yourself all worked up about it. I don't want you to lose your visitation privileges. I would miss seeing you too much. Promise me that you will let this go. Forget that Timmy ever brought it up. OK?"

"How is a man supposed to protect his family when he is stuck in this place," asked Mark?

About that time the horn sounded to signal the end of visitation.

"Mark, promise me you won't do anything stupid," said Tricia.

"I promise," said Mark reluctantly.

"Goodbye Mark. I love you," said Tricia.

"I love you too. Love you Timmy. Love you Candy. Take care of mommy for me," said Mark.

"Bye daddy. Love you," said Candy.

"Bye daddy. I will take care of mommy," said Timmy in as brave a voice as possible.

Then the guards came and took Mark and the other prisoners out into a vestibule where they searched them all over individually before opening the door and leading them back into the prison, and their cellblocks and their cells.

Then it was the visitors turn to be searched before being escorted to the outside, to the parking lot and to their cars.

The mood was tense and silent in the Noyes' car all the way from the prison to their house. No one spoke until they got home and then Timmy said, "I'm sorry mom. I thought that dad should know about the camera."

"No, Timmy. There are some things that are better that he didn't know right now, especially. It just upsets him and he can't do anything about it," said Tricia.

Tricia fixed them some supper. They cleaned up after supper, but no one was in the mood for doing much of anything so they all went to bed – or at least to their bedrooms- early. What had started out as a day of excitement, at least for the children, turned into an unsettled, downer of a day for all of them.

# 22

❦

Stan sat in the lunch room at the prison staring at the blank wall in front of him with his half eaten lunch there before him. He was pondering his dilemma. He wanted to get recordings from the cameras that he had placed in Claudia's house, but now he had a nosey neighbor butting into his business. If he showed up there again he would probably arouse the old guy's suspicions and he might do something rash; like notify the police or worse yet pull his gun on him. No, he would just have to cool it for a while there; at least until his new equipment came that would allow him to monitor and record the video feed from his house. He certainly couldn't afford to be drawing any undue attention to himself.

Then of course there was Tricia's house. He was only receiving video from the camera in her bedroom. Something had happened to the camera in her bathroom; and that troubled him. For one, he didn't know if the camera had aroused any suspicions and if they did, what did she do about them? Secondly, it seemed as if Tricia was in the habit of dressing in the bathroom so he wasn't seeing what he had hoped to see. So he was in a quandary as to what he should do there as well. At times, he felt like he should leave well enough alone and at other times he was ready to sneak back in there and put up another camera. But that was risky, very risky. It was risky enough to sneak in there without getting caught, but also she would now be looking to see if another camera appeared in there.

What to do? It was in the middle of this mental struggle that the door flew open and Frank, Stan's buddy that was also a guard, came barging into the room. "Hey Stan, what's wrong with you? You sick? You're just staring at the wall. You're not eating your lunch," said Frank.

Stan jumped at the sudden intrusion into his space and thoughts. He replied after a bit of hesitation and stammering, "I...I...was just thinking about the cabin. I haven't been there since Julie left me and I need to get over there and straighten it up, restock the cupboards, that sort of thing."

"You have a new girlfriend you're going to take there Stan," asked Frank?

"No, not yet. I'm working on some things, but I want to be prepared if and when I do pull something together. You never know about matters of love. It could happen at any time and anywhere," said Stan.

"Well Stan, I'm glad that you are getting back in the game. I was starting to worry about you. You never seem like the type to go very long as the single, bachelor type. At least not since I've known you. I think the longest that I can remember you without a girlfriend was maybe a month at the most. And how long has it been since Julie left – 3 months, 4 months," asked Frank?

"I know, I can't live with them and I can't live without them. But don't go jumping to conclusions now. I didn't say that I had anyone – just a possibility."

"A possibility is a start. It's a good sign. You haven't been quite yourself lately. I think a woman in your life would help bring some normalcy into your life."

"Normalcy? Are you saying that I am not normal Frank?"

"No! No! That's not what I meant. Maybe normalcy wasn't quite the right word to use in this situation. I just heard them using it on the radio this morning and thought it was a great word. You don't hear it used much, at least I don't. I just meant that you haven't been the same old fun-loving Stan since Julie left and I miss that Stan."

"So you don't like this Stan? Is that what you are saying Frank?"

"Stan, you're blowing this all out of proportion. I still like you as friend, Stan. It's just that the other Stan was more enjoyable and engaging to be around."

"Frank, you better quit while you're ahead. You're digging yourself in deeper every time you open your mouth, buddy."

"Fine! I have to get back to work anyway. I just popped in here to see if you were OK, but I can see now that you are not. Bye Stan, enjoy your lunch – what's left of it. Hope you get indigestion."

"See you around Frank!"

As the door clunked shut behind Frank as he exited the room, Stan muttered under his breath, "As if I don't have enough on my mind, I also have to worry about keeping the rattlesnakes in their den so they don't bite me."

Stan started picking at the rest of his lunch while thinking about the exchange that had just taken place between him and Frank. He decided that he didn't need a friend like that. In fact, he didn't need any friends period. He could survive just fine without friends. They were overrated anyway. He was so absorbed in that thought and at picking at his lunch that he almost forgot to watch the clock. When he realized it, he saw that he only had two minutes to clock back in and get back on his rounds. He scooped up what was left of his lunch and tossed it in the garbage can, ducked into the restroom and then down to the time clock just as the clock was dead on to the time he was supposed to be back to work. The prison didn't look too favorably on those that clocked in late. And if you were late too many times, they asked you to look for employment elsewhere. But on the other hand, they didn't want you clocking in early either unless they had asked you to come in early. If you came in early it meant that they had to pay you overtime and they hated that as much as if you came in late. So Stan always tried to be at work 15-20 minutes early, but not clock in until the time was dead on. It kept him on the good side of the administration at the prison.

The entire rest of his shift Stan tried to avoid Frank. If he saw Frank down one corridor, he went down another. One time he was taking some paperwork into the office and Frank was already in there, so he turned around and went back out. He decided he could turn the paperwork in later, hopefully when Frank wasn't there.

They had exercise yard duty together and normally they would stand together and talk while watching the inmates, but not today. Today, Stan moved to the opposite side of the yard from where Frank was standing, to watch the inmates.

The day didn't end any too soon for Stan. He just wanted to retreat to his home and get lost in handling Tricia's and Claudia's clothes and watching the little bit of video that he did manage to get of them – even as poor a quality as they were and without being able to see very much he still found pleasure in watching what he could view. But that would have to wait for a little while. He had decided that since he had the next two days off he would take a trip out to the cabin and see if everything was in order. And since he wanted to leave early in the morning, he needed to stop by the grocery store on his way home and stock up on some things that he knew that he needed to replenish at his little hideaway in the treetops.

Morning came way too early for Stan after spending a restless night without much sleep, but even though he had no real time frame or schedule that he had to meet, he thought that wouldn't be as suspicious if he left early in the morning. It would appear to anyone that might be watching that he was just another fisherman going out to fish at the best time of the day for fishing.

Stan had a pretty sweet set-up; at least he thought so. His house sat on a cul-de-sac that was close to a secluded bay and his back-yard was adjacent to the bay. If he wanted to go out in his boat, all that he had to do was walk out of his back gate, down a short path that was about 100 yards long and onto a semi-private dock anchored in the bay. He kept his boat moored there as did a half dozen other residents of the cul-de-sac. No one seemed to bother anything there and he very rarely saw anyone else in his comings and goings to and from the dock, which was just fine for Stan. The less people knew about his business, the better Stan liked it.

It took Stan 18 minutes to load all of his supplies onto his boat, having to make several trips back and forth from his house to the dock and that was even using his little two wheeled garden cart. The trip to where he docked for his cabin usually took about 45 minutes depending on how rough the sea was, whether there was any wind and whether the tide was coming in or going out. Everything seemed perfect right now which meant he might be able to make it in a little over 30 minutes, but the ocean was fickle and could change within a few minutes. His boat was one of the larger ones moored at the dock there, but it still was pretty small out there on the ocean when it was stormy and the waves were much over 8 feet high.

Since there was not much else to do besides steer the boat, Stan had decided to do a little fishing on the way. He really didn't like to fish, but it helped to pass the time and it gave the added benefit of anyone watching that he was just another fisherman out for the day to catch some fish - nothing more.

Stan wasn't really in the mood to mess with cleaning fish, but he did catch a couple of nice looking sea bass on the way so he decided that would make a nice meal tonight. It would go well with his new red potatoes, asparagus spears and that Chardonnay that he had brought along. He could have the steak tomorrow. Tonight it would be sea bass. His mouth started to water just thinking about it.

The small bay that he docked at was well hidden and a little tricky to navigate into. He had put a nice little scratch down the one side of his boat that was still there from the first time he had tried to maneuver into it. But he had the trick down now and it had become almost automatic as to when he needed to cut power, when to steer left or right and when to put the engine into reverse thrust and how much. He pulled in perfectly, congratulating himself once again for a job well done.

He took his freshly caught sea bass and a handful of other items and headed up the trail to where the sphere was anchored up in the tree. He would take those few things there, open up the sphere and get the two wheeled cart that he kept there for just the purpose of transporting the goods from the boat up to the cabin. The cabin was almost a quarter of a mile away from the dock and gained a little bit of an elevation, but not too much – maybe 10 or 12 feet at the most.

It took Stan almost an hour to haul all of the stuff from the boat up to the cabin. Well not quite into the cabin. He brought it to the base of the tree and piled it there. He found it easier to do it that way and then haul it all up the cable lift from there. It was at times such as these that he wondered why in the world he would build a cabin in such a remote place and up in the tops of the trees. But then he would answer the question himself and he knew why he would do that.

Once he had it all up into the sphere, Stan took a short rest, got a bite to eat and then began putting stuff away, cleaning and preparing for his next wives. He could envision it now. His little sphere would be tight with the three of them living in there, but that wouldn't be all the time, just for a couple of days. And it would be a bit awkward at first, but the three of them would get used to it – maybe even enjoy it after that adjustment period.

The rest of the time there at the cabin, Stan could do nothing else except fantasize about the two women that would soon be living there with him – Tricia and Claudia; Claudia and Tricia.

# 23

Tricia's visit to the prison with her husband left her feeling down and all during her shift at the restaurant she felt like she needed to be able to talk to someone. About an hour before her shift was finished Tricia decided that she would ask BJ if they could get together sometime soon and have a heart to heart talk session.

The remainder of her shift dragged on and on and seemed like it would never come to an end. All the way over to BJ's house she kept playing over and over in her mind what and how she was going to say to BJ. The difficult part she decided was how to bring it up. How do you start a conversation like the one she felt liked she needed to have?

She was still mulling it over in her mind as she walked through the front door. Then it all came crashing down. She was in a safe place and she could not control it any longer. The sobs and the tears came uncontrollably. The emotions bottle had come uncorked and it was gushing out like a shaken up soda that was just opened. BJ met her coming in and hurried over to her and put her arms around her and held her for the longest time. That mother/daughter connection that cannot be replaced by any other connection or relationship began working its miracle and Tricia began to gain a semblance of control of those raging emotions.

When BJ saw that Tricia had released most of her pent up emotions she directed her towards the sofa, sat her down with her arm still around her shoulder and said, "I'm here for you. Do you want to talk about?"

"I do. I just don't know where to start," said Tricia.

"Take it slow. I have all night if need be. What are you feeling right now?"

"I am so confused... and overwhelmed... and depressed... and adrift without any support... and I feel like my marriage is falling apart... and..."

"Are you struggling with your finances again?"

"When aren't we struggling with finances? That has always been a challenge at our house and probably will be until the day I die. But no, we are not struggling any more than we usually do. It is just one more straw on the proverbial camel's back"

"Ralph and I don't have a lot of money, but we do all right and have a little bit of money and if we can help in any way you make sure that you let us know. And if we don't have enough, we will take the matter to our church family and give them an opportunity to minister to you."

"BJ, you and Ralph have been more than generous to me and my family. I don't know how I will ever repay you."

"Tricia, you and your kids are like family. And we take care of family. You don't have to repay us anything. But if you are ever in a position to help someone else and do it, that will be repayment enough."

"Thank you again for all that you do."

"So that is not what is eating you alive," asked BJ? "Did all of this start because of your visit to your husband?"

"Yes!"

"Did he say something that upset you?"

"All he seemed to care about was himself. The kids tried to tell him about their birdhouses that they made and he wasn't the least bit interested. All he wanted to talk about was how bad it was in there. How bad the food was. How badly the other inmates and the guards treated him. How bored he was and if he didn't get out of there soon he would go crazy and do something stupid. He didn't say what, but the way he said it didn't sound good at all. He was asking about his appeal again. He just asked about it last week.

Doesn't he think that I would tell him if something had changed? He didn't ask how we were doing."

"I don't want to excuse him, but I am sure that he is under a great deal of stress and is not thinking straight. How much time do you spend praying for him? I know that you are limited on the ways that you can do this, but do you go out of your way to let him know that you still love him. Be creative about it. He is probably feeling insecure about where he stands with his family right now."

"Oh BJ! I never thought of it in those terms. I guess I may have been a little selfish myself; having my own little pity party."

"Can I get you something? A drink? A tissue? Anything?"

"I am a little dry now that you mention it. Maybe a glass of water. And I can probably use a tissue if you have one handy."

As BJ got up to get the glass of water and the tissue she said, "I know that you are not finished, so don't let this interrupt you. You need to get it all out."

"BJ, Mark and I used to be so close, but lately we have grown so distant and he doesn't seem like the same man that I married. I don't know what to do about it."

As she hands Tricia the water and the tissue BJ says, "Tricia, it's understandable. You really don't have that much in common any more except the children. You need to find some way to reconnect. Do you like to read? Does Mark?"

"Mark likes to read more than I do. I'm not a very good reader... at least out loud in front of people."

"I am not talking about reading to a group. I might suggest that the both of you pick a book that Mark and you have access to; although you will probably have an easier time getting any title particular than he will. So pick a book and then decide to read a chapter or two before you visit him again. When you come back together you can discuss what you read. Maybe that will start to form a reconnection point and you can begin to develop something in common once again. And don't be afraid to talk about how it makes you feel and what thoughts went through your mind as you read those chapters."

"About the only thing that I read anymore is the Bible and I don't think that he would read that. I wouldn't even know what to suggest that we read."

"Why don't you leave it up to Mark to decide? That way he will know what books he has access to and he will feel like he still has some control and influence in his family."

"BJ, you are so smart! I would never have thought of that."

"Don't underestimate yourself girl. You are pretty smart yourself. Now, I know that there is more, so out with it."

"I don't know if I should say anything or not. I have been arguing with myself about whether I should say anything to you or anyone else."

"You tell me and I will decide!"

"I was not going to tell Mark about this, but Timmy brought it up and then I had to tell him all about it. When Mark found out about it he went ballistic. The guards threatened to have him put into solitary confinement for a month if he didn't calm down."

"Then it probably isn't just smoke. It must have some sort of substance to it," said BJ.

"A couple of weeks ago we found this little tiny camera in our bathroom. It had been attached up in one of the corners of the room and because it was hooked to some loose paint it fell down. I didn't know what it was at first, but when Timmy saw it he recognized it immediately. I figured that it had belonged to one of the previous renters. I don't want to cause any trouble with the landlord. It is so hard to find a decent house to rent in this town so I don't want to have to move. I can't prove anything. And like I said when Timmy told Mark about it he flew into a rage. He wanted out and was ready to kill the guy that put the thing up in our bathroom."

"I can see what you mean. That is a difficult one to decide what should be done. But you know that we serve a God who is all wise and he knows exactly how to handle this situation. I think we need to be praying about this. Pray that God would give you discernment and wisdom on what steps that you need to take, if any, and that he will give you peace in knowing that he has it all in his control."

After a moment of silence BJ looked into Tricia's eyes and could see that she was still troubled about something so BJ asked, "What is it now honey? Still troubled about that camera or is there something else bothering you?"

"God continues to speak to me about 'Trusting Him.' Sometimes that is the most difficult thing to do. I want to trust everything else but him and turn to him only as a last resort. You would think that after several rounds of this same lesson that I would finally learn it, but it hasn't happened."

"Honey, you don't have a corner on that market. I find myself having to learn and relearn the same lessons over and over. But God is also patient and longsuffering with us. He never gives up on us; never gets discouraged with us; and he never stops loving us, no matter what. And you can take that to the bank! God has always been faithful to his people. You can read story after story in the Old and New Testaments of men and women who put their trust in God and he didn't disappoint them. In my own life I can recount many times when God has been faithful to me. And I am sure that if you think about it for a little while you can think of some instances when God was faithful in your life. What helps me when I get in one of those tight spots is to think of how God was faithful to me in the past or how he was faithful to someone else in their past."

"BJ, you are a godsend. I am feeling better already. I am so glad that I talked to you. I have been really depressed since I visited Mark this last time."

"May I suggest that you visit Mark again tomorrow or as soon as you can and try some of those suggestions that I mentioned. Focus on him and on his needs. Let him know that you still care about him and that you still love him. Start on a book together and begin a connection point. But most importantly, pray for him."

"Speaking of prayer, would you mind saying a prayer for me right now BJ. I can sure use all that I can get."

"I would count it a privilege!"

After praying a short prayer for Tricia and wiping a few tears away, BJ said, "why don't you and the kids stay for dinner? It's nothing fancy, but we have plenty and it will do you some good to be in a different set of four walls."

"BJ, I impose on you too much already."

"Tricia, stop that. You are not imposing. You are family. You know that you can eat here at any time; even without an invite."

"OK, if you insist. I know the kids would love it. They get sick of the same old things that I fix. The days that I work I don't feel like doing a bunch of cooking when I get home."

"That is what has been a real blessing to me. The days that I work late Ralph almost always has something started for dinner when I get home. It may not be gourmet, but it is good wholesome food."

"Well then, what can I do to help you with dinner? Set the table?"

"Dear, you just sit yourself right back down there, kick your shoes off and relax for a few minutes. I can finish off the dinner and either have Ralph or the kids set the table. Who knows, you might even doze off for a minute or two and you probably need it."

# 24

After her talk with BJ and the nice meal, Tricia went home and slept soundly all night; something that she had not done in two or three weeks. In fact, she couldn't even remember when the last time was that she had slept so well. When she awoke she was rested and ready to go. Ready to meet the day's challenges head on. She felt so good that she was half humming and half singing as she fixed breakfast for her and the kids and got everyone ready so that she could make it to work on time.

Timmy asked, "Mom, are you ok?"

"Yes, why? Do I seem sick," asked Tricia?

"Oh no, I just haven't heard you singing around here in the morning for a long time and you are singing today."

"I just feel really good today that's all; better than I have felt in a long time."

"Have you been sick," asked Candy?

"I think my heart has been sick."

"Are you going to have a heart attack," asked Candy?

"No dear! It has just been really heavy. It's been weighed down with too much stuff; too much worry. God keeps telling me to 'trust him' but, I don't do a very good job of doing it. Yesterday I had a nice long talk with BJ and then she prayed for me... and it has helped to take some of that weight off of my heart so I feel like singing."

"That's pretty cool, mommy! We have been studying in our Sunday School about how Jesus heals the broken hearted and I guess he did that for you, didn't he?"

"Yes, honey, I certainly believe that he did that just for me. Now you better hurry up and get ready to go to BJ's, I need to be to work in about 30 minutes."

Tricia already knew that there would be no way that she could make it to the prison in time for visiting hours that day, but she had tomorrow off and had made a mental note that she would make it there then. She felt like BJ's suggestion would help her and Mark get back on track with their marriage. She was committed to keeping it intact and alive and wanted to do anything in her power to make that happen.

She was still humming/singing as she walked in the door at the Chart Room and Steve met her coming in the door. He heard her and asked, "Why so cheerful? You win the lottery or something?"

"No, nothing like that. Candy said that Jesus healed my broken heart and I think that she is right," said Tricia as she put her stuff away, put her apron on and checked the schedule to see who and when would be working that day.

"Tricia, you just get too wrapped up in this Jesus/church thing. It's a good thing that you are such a good worker. I don't know if I could handle it otherwise," replied Steve.

"Steve, Jesus loves you too," said Tricia.

And with that, Tricia was off to start her shift waiting on tables leaving Steve standing there wondering what she had meant by that. The day went very well for Tricia and she couldn't help humming under her breath as she went about doing her work. The tips were even quite generous. Unusual enough that Tricia paused in the middle of the day and breathed a silent prayer of thanksgiving and forgiveness for not trusting God completely when he had specifically told her to 'trust him.'

Tricia had about 20 minutes left in her shift when she came out of the kitchen carrying two armloads of plates piled high with steaming hot food, when she noticed a familiar looking person sitting in one of the booths. Looking closer, Tricia saw that it was Claudia. She took her load of food to its' owners and took care of all of their requests before stopping by the booth where Claudia was seated.

"Hi, Claudia. This is a pleasant surprise. Can I get you anything?"

"No, I came to see if you were working and when you got off and whether you would have a few minutes to talk to me," said Claudia.

"I have missed you the last couple of Sundays at church and have been going to call you to see if you were OK. I'm sorry, I just didn't get around to it. Let's see...actually I get off in about 15 minutes. I do have the kids to pick up..."

"Maybe we can get together another time," said Claudia.

"No, I was just about to say that they are at BJ's place and neither one will mind if I am late. So if you want to stick around for a little bit we can talk when I am finished," said Tricia.

"I can wait," said Claudia. "Maybe I should wait in my car so that I am not taking up a booth."

"You are fine. We are not that busy in her now anyway. Let me get you a soda or a cup of coffee... it will be on me."

"A soda sounds good. Thank you."

Tricia finished her shift and Claudia sat there in the booth sipping at her soda. When Tricia had checked out and had hung her apron back up on its hook, she came and sat down opposite Claudia.

"Do you want to talk here or go out and sit in my car and talk," asked Tricia.

"I think I would be more comfortable talking in your car than in here if you don't mind," said Claudia.

"No, I don't mind. Finish your soda and then we'll head out," said Tricia.

"I think I'm about finished. I wasn't very thirsty anyway."

"OK, let's go then. Here I will put your glass in the dirty dishes container."

"Thank you!"

Opening the passenger side door, Tricia scooped up some papers and one of the kids' toys and tossed them into the backseat. She held the door for Claudia to get in and then went around to the driver side and slid in behind the wheel. Neither one said anything for the longest time and the silence was starting to become uncomfortable.

Finally Tricia said, "Claudia, I am really sorry for not contacting you sooner."

"It is mostly my fault. I haven't felt like making the effort to be in church and then I started feeling guilty about not going... and then I started feeling like it didn't really matter anyway and that no one missed me..."

"That is not true Claudia. I have missed you a lot. And I am really sorry that I haven't contacted you."

"Claudia, you don't have to beat yourself up over missing church, but it is really important that you are there as much as you can be. You see, you started a relationship with Jesus and that relationship needs to be cared for. And the way that you care for it is to spend time with him. You need to spend time in his Word, the Bible. You need to spend time talking and listening to him. And you also need to be around others that are growing their relationships with Jesus just like you. They can help you grow your relationship and you can help them grow theirs. That's the way it works. We all need each other. It is pretty hard to make it on your own."

"I know, I am beginning to see that. I am going to make a commitment to be in fellowship as often as I possibly can."

"That's great Claudia. I know that you'll be rewarded for that commitment. I had to come to that place in my relationship with Jesus and when I finally made that commitment a huge weight lifted off of me and a great peace flooded over me. Our relationship with Jesus should be no different than with anyone else that we love. If we love them, we will want to spend time with them."

"That's the other thing that I need to talk to you about Tricia. Your husband is in prison just like mine. Do you ever get lonely? I know you have your kids, but I mean lonely for a male companion, a male friend to talk to, to do things with."

"Tricia, I would be lying if I said that I didn't have those feelings. I am human just like you. Sometimes I don't think that I can make it."

"Have you ever thought about getting a divorce or just about going out... I mean, just as a friend, nothing more?"

"Claudia, Mark and I are going through a really difficult time in our marriage right now but I made a commitment to him when I married him and I am going to stick with it no matter what. Have you been thinking about divorcing Ricardo?"

"It seems like it has been preoccupying at lot of my thoughts lately and there is this guy at work that wants to go do something together, but I keep telling him that I am married and that I don't want to go there. But the temptation is getting really strong and he is so persistent. Do you think it would be wrong to just be friends?"

"No, I don't think that it is wrong to 'just be friends.' But it is a dangerous road to go down; the more time that you spend with a friend of the opposite sex the more that you will want to spend time with him, especially if you get along well together, and then the physical attraction starts. And once you get there, it is very hard to control it."

"I know, Tricia, but I am going to be 40 years old when Ricardo gets out. How can I survive that long, I am already lonely and I am only 24?"

"Claudia that is why you need to grow and develop your relationship with Jesus. He can help fill that loneliness and give you a sense of purpose in your life. I won't say that it will be easy, because it's not going to be. But if you do it, you will be rewarded beyond anything that you can imagine. Did you ever think what it must be like for Ricardo? BJ helped me see that with Mark. They are struggling as much or more than we are. We have the privilege of helping and supporting them through a difficult time in their lives."

A tear slid out of the corner of each eye as that though struck home with her. She really did love Ricardo and she wanted it to work out for them.

"Claudia, there is one thing that you might want to think about. If you are pouring yourself out helping others, you will not have time to be lonely and the satisfaction of helping others will help ease the desire for companionship. I didn't say take it away, I said ease it. You will still have your moments and you will still have to struggle with temptation, but the struggle won't be as difficult. You know, the church has just started a food bank that you could volunteer at in your spare time or the day care that they have at the church always needs people to help in it. Find something like that to pour your heart and energy into and God will bless you."

"Thanks Tricia! I have known what I should do with the advances of that coworker, but you have just given me the courage to do it and to live up to my commitment to Ricardo. You are right; it would be a dangerous road to go down; a road I can't afford to take."

"Claudia, have you read or heard the story of Joseph in the Old Testament?"

"No, I don't think that I have."

"I would like to suggest that you read it when you have time. Joseph was sold into slavery in Egypt by his brothers and how even when he was treated badly by those around him Joseph always did the right thing. And at first it didn't seem to pay off for him, but in the end God used him and blessed him for doing the right thing in those difficult circumstances. I think you might identify with him a little bit, I know I do at times."

"Where do I find this story of Joseph?"

"Oh yeah, I almost forgot the most important part. It starts in chapter 37 of Genesis and then skips chapter 38 and picks up again in chapter 39 through the end of Genesis. It is a pretty interesting story. I don't think you will have trouble reading it."

"I'll read it tonight! And thank you again, Tricia. You are always so kind and understanding and you don't judge me for what I've done."

"You're welcome. I hope I've helped."

"You have been a big help. You are like a big sister to me. I really appreciate it. I better let you go. I will see you on Sunday."

"And if I don't see you at church, I will be knocking on your door."

"Promise?"

"Promise!"

The days until Sunday passed quickly without much excitement or fanfare. When Claudia showed up at church she made a point of looking up Tricia the first thing.

"Tricia, I went home after talking to you and read that entire story about Joseph. It is amazing. How could he do that? I figured that if he could live like that under the terrible circumstances that he lived in, then I should be able to live and do the right thing in my life."

"I thought you might identify with Joseph. I know I certainly did."

"And do you know what else? You will never guess how God answered my prayer about that situation with the coworker."

"I don't know, how," asked Tricia?

"He started in pestering me to go out with him that next time that I saw him and I said to him, 'I am committed to my husband and I love him and I do not want to do anything to jeopardize that relationship. I'm not interested in a relationship with you other than as a coworker. If you continue to pressure me to go out with you, you will force me to go to the manager and file a sexual harassment charge against you.' When I told him that he got all red in the face, called me some awful name under his breath that I can't repeat and then he went stomping off. About 2 hours later the manager called me into his office and asked me what had happened between the two of us. After I told him what had happened, he said that he had fired the guy because he had heard some of the other female employees complaining about him and his advances."

"It's too bad that he had to get fired, but maybe God will be able to use this time in his life to speak to him about what is important. I'm so proud of you for the way that you made the right stand. The more times that you do that the easier it will become," said Tricia.

"I felt really good about it afterwards. I was sorry that he lost his job, but it did feel good to take that stand in favor of Ricardo and our marriage."

About that time the music started, indicating that the worship time was about to begin and Tricia and Claudia made their way to where Timmy and Candy were already seated with BJ, Ralph and Rod.

# 25

Tricia was still feeling good the next day. She was planning on visiting Mark after lunch. She wanted to spend the morning with Timmy and Candy. She felt like she had been neglecting them in all of her busyness so she was going to devote the morning just to them. She did not want to take the children when she visited Mark this time, but promised them that she would start taking them more regularly. She thought that it would help their family connection and bond if Mark and the children could be together as much as she was. There was one phone call that she wanted to make before going to the prison, but she figured that she would have to wait until a little later in the morning to catch him in his office.

Until that time, Tricia made the children their favorite breakfast. It started cooking while they were still sleeping so that they would wake up to the aroma of it in the air. When it was almost finished and the table all set, she slipped into each room, kissed them gently on their cheeks and said, "Your favorite breakfast is almost ready for you!"

One whiff of the bacon sizzling and the pancakes cooking brought them up with a start. And it didn't take them long to get out of bed, hit the bathroom and seat themselves around the table. They ate a leisurely breakfast, laughing and talking and enjoying each other's company. It warmed Tricia's heart and almost sent a tear coursing down her cheek, but she held it in check as she didn't want the children to think that she was sad or not enjoying her time with them.

Timmy finally said, "Mom, you made me eat too much. I am so stuffed I don't think that I'll be able to move from this chair the rest of this day."

"Timmy, you are exaggerating. You will be hungry again in a couple of hours. I know you; you are a growing young man; and a fine one at that. I'm proud of you."

"And Candy, I'm proud of you too. I couldn't ask for better children. I love you both very much. God really blessed me when he gave me you two."

"Mom, do you think daddy misses us," asked Timmy?

"Of course he does Timmy. He misses us all a lot. But right now is a very difficult time in his life and he is having a hard time just surviving. We need to keep showing him love and let him know that we miss him. Plus, we need to keep him in our prayers. Daddy really could use a miracle right now and God is in the miracle making business."

"How about now, mommy? Can we pray for him now," asked Candy?

"Why not? God hears us anytime we pray. Do you want to say a prayer for daddy?"

"Can I," asked Candy?

"Yes, of course you can. Your prayers are as important and heard by God as much as mine or anyone else's prayers."

"OK! Dear God, my daddy is in jail and he needs to have a miracle. Would you please give him one of your miracles? I know that you have a lot of them and I think that you should have an extra one that you can give my daddy. We love our daddy. Please God, tell daddy that we love him and miss him. Amen," prayed Candy.

"Amen," said Tricia.

"Amen," echoed Timmy.

"That was great Candy. I am sure that God heard that prayer and he is getting that extra special miracle ready for daddy right now. I don't know what it is or what he is going to do for daddy, but I do know that it will be special," said Tricia.

All of them sat around the table looking at each other and fiddling with the dishes and silverware still on the table from breakfast for what seemed like a half hour, but in reality was only a couple of minutes. Getting a bright idea, Timmy said, "Come on Candy. Let's clean up the breakfast dishes. Mom, you sit there finishing your coffee while we clean up."

He didn't have to suggest it twice to Candy. She was up taking dishes and left-over food to the kitchen almost before Timmy had finished suggesting it. And although, they didn't quite put things away and take care of things the way Tricia might have, the thought and initiative of it thrilled Tricia and she couldn't help smiling to herself as she watched them scurrying around the kitchen taking care of things. Timmy even thought about bringing the coffee pot over and filling up Tricia's cup while they were working.

When the children had finished cleaning up, Tricia said, "Why don't you guys go get out of your pajamas and into some clothes. And while you're doing that, think about what you would like to do together this morning. I have to make a phone call while you're doing that and then I'll be ready."

Tricia made her phone call and fortunately connected with the party that she was calling on the first try. The children changed into some clothes, combed their hair and brushed their teeth before meeting Tricia back out in the living room/dining room area.

"Did you decide what you wanted to do this morning," asked Tricia?

"What if we go for a walk in that wooded area like we used to when we first moved here," asked Timmy?

"Timmy, that sounds like a wonderful idea. Candy, what do you think?"

"It sounds like fun, but won't we get wet? It is raining outside," said Candy.

"It's not raining that much. We'll just put on our rain gear and our boots and pretend that we are ducks," said Tricia.

"Can we splash in puddles too," asked Candy?

"I don't see why not. You will have your boots on. We should be able to find some puddles. It sure has been raining a lot lately," said Tricia.

"Let's go then," said Timmy.

The three of them had a wonderful time exploring the trails through the wooded area, splashing in puddles and picking up little treasures along the way – treasures like an odd shaped rock, or a feather, or an interesting twig; the kind of treasures that spark a child's imagination and help them believe that the world is a wonderful place. By the time they headed back home their pockets were full of their finds and only slightly damp, but their spirits said that they could conquer the world, and that their mom was the best mom in the whole wide world because she had spent time doing something that they liked with them and they knew that she loved them. Tricia only had a little bit of time to fix some sandwiches and put them on a plate with a few chips for the children's lunches before the time that she had set to leave for the prison rolled around. She had decided that she wanted to give Mark the maximum amount of her time that she possibly could. She wanted to send him a message that he was important and that he was not just getting the time that she had left-over from something else, that he was getting prime time. He mattered. He was important to her.

When she got into the visitation room she was only a few minutes later than she had wanted to be, but it was much earlier than she usually had been. As Tricia saw Mark through the glass approaching the room she could see in his countenance that he was still in the same mood that he was in the last time that they were there and had thrown such a fit. Tricia, bowed her head slightly, and breathed a quick, silent prayer to herself asking God to help her, to give her the right words to say to Mark and to touch Mark and begin the work of that miracle that Candy had prayed for.

"Hi, Mark. You look good. How are you doing? The kids and I have been missing you," said Tricia.

Mark only grunted recognition of Tricia and her statements and plopped down in one of the chairs that was pulled up next to a table.

"Mark, I want to apologize for not treating you very nice the last time that we were here. I'm sorry. I know that it's not easy for you living in here. I do love you and care about you. Please hang on until you are released and we can be together again as a family. All of us miss you very much and want you back with us."

Mark's countenance began to soften as Tricia was telling him this and when she had finished he said, "I'm sorry for acting the way that I did. I was just having a pity party for myself."

"The last time we were here you were asking about your appeal and I told you that I had not heard anything. Well, this morning I called the lawyer that is in charge of your appeal and miracle of miracles, I reached him. I actually got to talk to him, not just some receptionist or some legal assistant, but the actual lawyer that is doing all of the work. He wouldn't tell what it is, but he said that there is something really big in the works on your case and that you shouldn't give up hope. I was really excited after I got off the phone with him. What do you think he meant?"

"I have no idea. I haven't heard anything in here. You know sometimes you hear lots of rumors about this or that and the next thing you know the rumor turns out to be true; but I haven't heard anything like that about my case."

"You have to hang on for us, Mark! Don't give up hope! No matter how long it takes."

"I'll try babe; I will try, but it is so hard, so very hard."

"Mark, BJ suggested something that sounded like a really good idea and I want to see what you think. I have been feeling like we have been drifting apart as a couple and as a family. When I shared this with BJ, she suggested that we pick a book and begin reading it together; I mean we each read the same chapters, but separately, and then the next time we get together, we can discuss what we have read."

"But Tricia, I know that you don't like to read very much."

"It's OK Mark. I will make myself do it; because I love you and I care about our commitment to each other and our family."

"Really? You would really do that for me?"

"Yes, Mark, I would really do that for you. I told you that I loved you and now I want to show you that I love you. There aren't too many ways that I am able to do that right now, but I thought that this suggestion just might fill the bill."

Mark could hardly believe what he was hearing. Tricia had always balked at reading anything together and now her she is suggesting it to him. One of his favorite activities and she was willing to sacrifice for him to be a part of it. He was speechless and one lone tear snuck out from the corner of his left eye. He pretended that he had something in his eye, but Tricia knew better, she had seen the tear make its way out of the eye and down his cheek. She didn't say anything, but it encouraged her that she had hit a nerve and she knew that she was on the right track. Now she just had to follow through.

"Mark, since you know more about books and you know what books you have access to, I want you to pick out the book that we will read together and I will go get the same one somewhere and we will start reading it."

"Tricia, I just checked out a book from the prison library this morning that I have been wanting to read for a long time and never have read it. I think you will like it once you start reading it."

"What is it?"

"It is '**The Grapes of Wrath**' written by John Steinbeck."

"I have heard of that book. OK. When I leave here I will go see if I can find a copy some place in town and start reading it."

"How many chapters should we read?"

"I was thinking 2 or 3. That way it should be enough for us to discuss and not too much that we won't be able to read it before we meet again – especially me as slow as I am at reading."

"Alright, that sounds fair enough."

About that time the warning buzzer sounded that indicated that there was only five minutes left in visiting hours. Tricia didn't know where the time had gone. It seemed like they had just started and now she has to leave.

Mark looked her in the eye and said, "Thank you! Today you have restored my hope. I know now that you still love me and care about me. Thank you!"

"You're welcome. I am sorry that it has taken me this long to learn this. I want to try to bring the children more often than I have been bringing them. I think that it's really important that they keep that connection between you and them just like we need to maintain our connection and relationship."

"I will be looking forward to your next visit, Tricia. I love you!"

Tricia couldn't believe that she heard that. Usually she was the one that initiated the 'I love you' sentiment and he merely repeated it because he knew she was expecting him to. Tricia left the prison knowing that the miracle that they had prayed for in Mark was beginning. And as she pulled out of the parking lot she breathed another prayer, only out loud, in thanksgiving of what God had already begun and prayed once again that the miracle would continue to develop and grow to complete that work that God had begun.

# Section 2

✠

# 26

❧

Stan was growing frustrated with the progress that he was making in securing a companion for his cabin. His efforts at obtaining any meaningful video from his cameras that he had inserted in Claudia's and Tricia's houses were a major setback and point of frustration for him. His mastery of the drones was going slower than he had hoped for. And working out the logistics of how this all would take place was proving to be a major nightmare. He was beginning to think that having two 'wives' may not be such a good idea after all.

For whatever reason the camera that he had placed in Tricia's house in the bathroom was not functioning and apparently that was the room where she did her changing. And because he didn't have his new high tech night vision cameras installed, he couldn't see much in her bedroom because she was not in there much with the light on. At Claudia's house the camera's appeared to be working just fine and he did get a small portion of video that he kept poring over, but he could not really see what he would have wanted to see because of that nosey, gun-toting, old dog-walking neighbor of hers. He was not sure what to do about him, but he was afraid to go back over there and attract his attention any more than he already had.

As for the drones, he had practiced and practiced using the things, but it was not as easy as the website where he had ordered them from had made it out to be. In fact he was almost ready to abandon the idea of using them and go for some less high tech method; one of the methods that he had used before and had been successful with. But then one day it had all worked, he had flown one of the drones that was about the size of a bumblebee on steroids and sounded like a couple of mosquitoes around the room, landed it on an orange and inserted its stinger into the orange's flesh. Now he was getting pretty good at doing that now, but when he had made the switch to 'nighttime' operations it was almost as if he was back to square one in his learning curve with the thing. He was having trouble adjusting to the night vision goggles and being able to follow the path of the drone quick enough to make flying adjustments, especially when he went to land the thing. He had gotten to where he could make it work 1 out of 10 times, but that was not satisfactory. He needed it to work 100% of the time, not just 10% of the time. He figured that he would only have one shot at it and then it would be all over. And he still did not know how the subjects would react when one of them landed on them while they were sleeping. He couldn't really test that out. He had landed one on himself, but that was not really the same. He did feel it when it landed, but he was awake and he was expecting it. He did not know if in their sleep they would hear it and be awakened by it or if they might swat it like a mosquito since it sounded like one. He figured that his best chance of success would be to do this when they were in the Slow Wave Non-REM sleep stage, the deepest sleep period a person goes into. Those sleep periods when you are less aware of your surroundings, are more focused inward and harder to arouse from sleep. But knowing when they had entered that stage would be difficult to know without having them connected to an EEG device and he did not think that was in the offing. He surmised since the Slow Wave Sleep stage was the 3rd and 4th stages of Non-REM sleep that if he could time it so they had been asleep for 2 or 3 hours he might be able to catch them in that optimal sleep period. The only way that he would know for sure would be to do it. He did not like the idea of not being in control of every single detail. He wanted no chance of error, no possibility of something going wrong and he could see that his plan was fraught with all sorts of those types of possibilities.

Stan's plan in its simplest form was for him to extract Tricia and then Claudia, take them to his house, unload them from his car parked in the garage, take them down to his boat in the cart, load them into the boat and take them to his cabin. It all sounded so simple, but each one of those steps had its own pitfalls and places where something could go haywire, totally haywire with no hope of recovery. He knew that if he were caught it would be all over. He would be exposed for who he really was and he could not have that. He had lived two lives for so long now that he needed both lives in order to function – at least that's what he thought.

Assuming that the drones did their work without being detected, Stan would have to get his new 'wife' out of bed, out the door of her house and into his car without attracting any suspicious attention from anyone. Stan had rationalized his abducting women for so long that he did not need to go through that exercise any more. In anyone else, he would have condemned the action or even the thought of them doing it, but for him it was perfectly fine and did not present any sort of moral dilemma whatsoever. He did not know why man had changed from his method of getting wives by the foraging, pillaging, taking any woman that he wanted to this modern method that was all mushy, gushy, win-their heart sort of arrangement. He could even understand the buy your wife plan, but not this romantic process. It took too long, one had to invest too much of one's time into it and after all that they might break your heart into a million pieces. No, that was not for him. He preferred the good old-fashioned way; see them, want them, take them.

But the taking part was the stickler. Society now days sort of frowned on that approach to obtaining a wife so he had to do this discreetly. And that would not be easy since they would basically be dead weight when he took them. His little drone bees would deliver a serum that would ensure that they remained asleep for four or five hours; which meant that from the time the drone injected it's serum into his first 'wife' he would only have that amount of time to get her in the car, go get his other 'wife' and get them both to his cabin before they woke up. He had decided that Tricia would be his first 'wife' because he had selected her first, and secondly he thought that she was prettier than Claudia, and lastly and more importantly, she went to bed first which meant that she would probably go into that Slow Wave Sleep stage before Claudia did. He was planning on having along a little extra serum just in case one or both started to wake up too early or things were taking a little longer than he had planned on.

The next question that he had to address was when. He needed to do this on the first day of his day off, which would mean that it would be that night so that he would have time to get back home on the next day, get some rest and be back to work on the third day just like a normal weekend. No one would know any different. No one would expect it to be Mr. Law Enforcement man; the squeaky clean guard from Pelican Bay. Life would go on as if nothing unusual had ever happened. Yes, there would be a few sad people for awhile, but they would soon enough forget about Tricia and Claudia and life would go on without them.

He figured that it would probably be quite awhile before anyone would miss Claudia, but not Tricia. Those two kids of hers would be the problem. He probably shouldn't have picked someone with kids. Kids only get in the way. He felt like they never contribute to anything anyway. Maybe he should do something to those two kids of hers to silence them. No, that would be murder and he despised murderers too. He would just have to take his chances that the trail would be cold enough by the time they discovered that their mom was gone and the time that the police started snooping around. He wanted – no needed – Tricia and nothing was going to get in the way of that happening.

So, looking at the calendar he kept saying, "When?" He wanted to do this before summer had completely slipped away. He looked at a three different dates, rejecting them all for one reason or another; too soon, something else happening on that date – like his social calendar was booked up with other engagements, fell on the wrong day of the week – like that mattered either, but Stan was also superstitious and he didn't want to jinx this thing from the very beginning. Finally, he selected a 'weekend,' which was not really a weekend at all as most people thought of it, but actually a Tuesday and a Wednesday – his 'weekend' – that was three weeks away from today. That would give him time to perfect his nighttime drone manipulation practice and to work out some of the other logistics and also soon enough to ease his anxiety about this phase of the plan. He always seemed to get anxious right before he would snatch his next 'wife' and then once that was over the anxiety would pass. So he needed to get past this phase as soon as possible for his own sanity if nothing else.

Stan put a big red circle on the calendar marking the date when this would take place. He would begin the countdown towards that date and all energies and efforts would now be focused in that direction. He started laying out what he needed to accomplish on each day leading up to the big date. Two new wives; it excited Stan all over just thinking about it. Of course he was a little bit nervous as well, but excited just the same. He had often wondered if this was how a groom felt those few days before his big wedding day. Well, he would never know that, he was not planning on going through all of that baloney. His method was much simpler, more effective and definitely more exciting. He thought that it was probably like big game hunting except that the catch was a real live woman; much better than some stuffed animal head or set of horns hanging on a wall.

On every day Stan put at the top of his "to-do list" practice night time drone flight and landings in big, bold letters that he underlined a couple of times to make sure that he noticed it every day. He also listed picking up supplies in there and the 'weekend' before the big day he planned on making another trip out to the cabin with more supplies and making sure that everything was in good working order and presentable for his new 'wives.' He also wrote on the day of the taking he would pick up some fresh food and run it out to the cabin. Next week he would take the boat into the marina and have them service the motor and go over the boat to make sure that everything on it was in good working order. That is all that he would need is to have the boat motor stop working when he was out in the ocean with a couple of abducted women onboard.

Pleased with his efforts and his plans, Stan retrieved the articles of clothing that he had taken from Claudia's and Tricia's houses and went through his ritual of caressing and smelling each item as he fantasized about the women until it was well past his bedtime.

# 27

Tricia was still in a very good mood. Everything was working out. She and the children were spending quality time together. All of them were visiting Mark regularly at the prison and they were beginning to reconnect as a family. Timmy and Candy were intent on sharing their lives with their dad. She and Mark had begun discussing the first few chapters of the Grapes of Wrath together. Mark was even slowly transforming back into his old self. He still didn't want to talk about or hear about God or Jesus, but everything else was open for discussion. Tricia had not heard any additional news on Mark's appeal and told him that every time that she saw him because she realized that was important to him.

Little did Tricia realize the tsunami that was now less than three weeks away from changing her and Claudia's lives forever. If she would have known, she probably would have run to a very high mountain to escape the destruction that was headed her way. But she didn't know and so she was feeling really good about everything in her life. That is the real danger in a tsunami; that it is so silent and so deadly. A tsunami can have you surrounded before you have any idea that anything is wrong. And what did Tricia know about tsunamis anyway. She was never in one; she only knew what other people, like BJ and Ralph, said about them and the devastation that they left behind.

So Sunday morning she was up early in anticipation of being in church once again. The children were a little less enthusiastic, at least at first, but once they woke up and started moving about their enthusiasm picked up and by the time it was time to leave they wanted to be there already not just leaving the house. Tricia stopped by Claudia's place to pick her up on the way. Claudia had really turned a corner with her relationship with Jesus since she had talked with Tricia and she also was excited about being in church and growing that relationship.

The music was lively and uplifting to start the service and everyone seemed to be getting into it. By the time Pastor Grime got up to preach everyone was all ears wanting to hear what he had to say. The bulletin said that he would be preaching from the life of Joseph and that the key verse was found in Genesis 45:8. Tricia couldn't remember what that verse said so she looked it up before Pastor Grime got up to preach. She thought to herself, "What a strange verse. I wonder how he is going to tie this verse into a lesson." The verse said, 'Therefore, it was not you who sent me here, but God.'

Pastor Grime got up to speak and read the verse out loud, "'So then, it was not you who sent me here, but God.'" He went on to say, "We have probably all been in a situation where we felt like we didn't belong there and wondered how and why we got there. Maybe we were there because of something that we did or some choice that we made or maybe we were there because of something someone else did. This morning I would like to share with you the story of Joseph. I know that many of you have heard this story before, but maybe you haven't seen it in quite this way before.

Joseph had eleven brothers and at least ten of the brothers hated Joseph because their father, Jacob loved Joseph more than any of his other sons. This made the other brothers jealous of Joseph. Because of their jealousy and because Joseph had told of his dream that they would bow down to him, they despised him. One day Jacob sent Joseph out to the fields where the other sons were tending the herds and when they saw him they plotted to get rid of him. When he got there they took his coat from him and threw him into a pit. When a caravan of traders came along they sold Joseph to them as a slave. Then they took his coat, put blood on it and took it back to their father and told him that a wild animal had killed and eaten Joseph.

The caravan of traders took Joseph to Egypt where they sold him to Potiphar as a slave. Everything that Joseph did in Potiphar's house was blessed and so Potiphar put Joseph in charge of everything in his household. Potiphar's wife wanted Joseph and kept after him to sleep with her, but Joseph continued to resist her telling her that it was wrong and that he could not do that. One day, when he went there the two of them were all alone, when she made her advance on Joseph, he ran away but left with her holding his coat. When Potiphar came home she accused Joseph of trying to rape her.

Potiphar had Joseph thrown into prison. God was there in prison with Joseph and blessed everything he did there so much that the warden put Joseph in charge of everything in the prison. Later the king's cupbearer and the king's baker were thrown into prison. Each of them had a dream on the same night. Joseph interpreted the dreams for them. To the cupbearer he said that in three days the king would restore him to his former position and to the baker he said that the king would take his head off and hang him from a tree. Each of their dreams came true just like Joseph said they would.

Two years later Pharaoh had a dream that none of the wise men of his kingdom could interpret. The cupbearer remembered Joseph from prison and told the king about him. Pharaoh sent for Joseph and told him his dream. Joseph told Pharaoh that he could not interpret the dream, but that God could give Pharaoh the answers that he needed. Joseph said that Pharaoh's dream meant that there was going to be seven very productive years followed by seven years of famine and drought. He also told him that he should select a wise man to store up some of the plenty in the good years and then to administer the distribution of it in the lean years. Pharaoh decided that Joseph was just such a man so he made him second in command in all of Egypt.

When the years of famine did come it affected Canaan where Joseph's father and brothers lived as well as in Egypt. When they learned that they could buy food in Egypt, Jacob sent all of the rest of his sons except Benjamin there to buy food so that they could eat. When they arrived in Egypt, they had to talk to Joseph to buy grain. Joseph recognized his brothers, but they did not recognize them. So he questioned them pointedly, accusing them of being spies. In order for them to get grain he had one of the brothers bound and put into prison. He told them that the only way they could get him released or buy any more grain was if they brought Benjamin back with them.

On their way home they discovered that all of the silver that they had given the Egyptians had been returned to them in their bags of grain. When they discovered that their silver had been returned to them, it really frightened them. Upon returning to Jacob, they told him everything that had happened in Egypt and that they could only go back and buy more grain if they took Benjamin with them. Jacob declared that this would not happen, that Benjamin would not be going to Egypt because if anything happened to him it would kill him.

When their grain had all been eaten and they were getting hungry, Jacob told his sons to go back to Egypt and buy some more grain. Judah told him that if Benjamin didn't go with them that the man in charge of the grain would not even see them if he was not there. Judah said that he would be responsible for Benjamin. Otherwise, all of them were going to starve to death. Jacob finally agreed to let him go.

Back in Egypt, as they were leaving with their load of grain, Joseph had his servant put all of their silver into their sacks of grain and Joseph's silver cup in Benjamin's sack. After they had left Egypt, Joseph had his servants chase them down and accuse Benjamin of stealing his cup. When they were all brought back to Egypt to face Joseph, Joseph wanted to throw Benjamin in prison and to let the other's leave. Judah pleaded for Benjamin's life and offered his life in place of Benjamin's life.

Finally, Joseph couldn't stand it any longer and had to reveal himself to his brothers. When his brothers realized that it was Joseph they became frightened and feared for their lives because of the way that they had treated him when he was younger. But Joseph tried to reassure them that he had no desire for revenge and that is where our key verse comes in. Joseph wanted them to know that it was God's plan that he be in Egypt. It was God who sent him there so that he could provide a way of salvation for their family.

We can't know God's plan for us and how everything that happens to us all fits together. But we need to remember that God uses the events in our lives for our good and for the good of others. And sometimes those events are hard to accept and live with. Sometimes we may never know the complete outcome of those things that we find ourselves caught up in. It is our jobs, our responsibility to trust God to work out his plan in those times.

In conclusion, I want you to remember that God knows where you are and what you are going through. And that God has you where you are for a reason even if you don't understand it right now."

When the service was finished and dismissed, Tricia, Claudia and BJ stood where they were discussing the message that they had just heard from Pastor Grime. Claudia said, "I am sure glad that you suggested that I read that story the other day when I talked to you Tricia. It really made a lot of sense when pastor was talking about Joseph and telling his story."

"I know I suggested that you read Joseph's story, but that was not the conclusion that I had in mind when I told you to read it. I wanted you to see that you can do the right thing and live a moral life even in the hardest of circumstances," said Tricia.

"I figured that was why you wanted me to read it," said Claudia.

"That is a good application that pastor made with this story though," said BJ.

"Yes, it really is. I have wondered that a lot lately in the situation that I am in right now. I just keep looking for God to reveal himself in my life and have everything work out," said Tricia.

"I don't know about a 'happily ever after' type of life," said Claudia. "Life just doesn't seem to work that way."

"I agree. Not all of life can be tied up in a nice neat little bundle like Joseph's life was, but I don't think that pastor was necessarily saying that. I think his point was that God put Joseph where he ended up for a reason and it just so happened that it turned out really good for him and his family. We can't expect the same, but we can believe that God puts us where he wants us for a reason no matter how things turn out," said BJ.

"Well said. Good summary of the pastor's point. Are you ready to go home Claudia? I have been encouraged and challenged today by what pastor has said," said Tricia.

"I am ready," said Claudia.

And with that Claudia and Tricia said their goodbyes to BJ, rounded up Timmy and Candy, who were playing outside with some of the other kids that were still there and headed for home.

# 28

The days marched on, one day after another, marching on towards the red circled dates on Stan's calendar, the Tuesday and Wednesday that he had selected three weeks earlier. And each day he checked off the items on his "to do list" that he had made up when he selected the date. And each item went off without a hitch. Stan had even perfected his night time flying ability with the drones and his night vision goggles to where he was comfortable at the controls and would miss 1 out of 50 attempts; a 2% failure rate — 98% success rate. He would have liked to have had a 100% success rate, but he did not think that he could achieve that in the amount of training time that he had had.

He awoke early on Tuesday, extraction day, wide awake and excited about the events of the day. He was also slightly nervous, but knew that would dissipate once he started and once his adrenaline had kicked in. Stan knew that he should be sleeping because it would be several hours before he would have a chance to get much sleep. He had planned to get a little nap later this evening, but it would not be long. He couldn't get back to sleep, sleep seemed to elude him as his mind raced from sequence to sequence of the day's events and back again. Round and round his thoughts went until he was certain that he had scrambled them all up or left out something important in the middle of it all.

Finally he decided it was no use. He was not going to get any more sleep. He might as well get up and get started on today's check list. Maybe there was a reason he woke up so early. Maybe all of those things on the list were going to take longer than he had anticipated. Or maybe, there was going to be some kind of interruption that would throw a wrench into the works. So Stan got up. Stan knew as he placed one foot on the floor and then the other that this day was going to be the beginning of an event that would change his life for eternity. And that thought electrified him. He wondered if any other great man felt the same way that he felt right now. His destiny was right there in his hands and he was not going to let it slip away. He could stop right where he was and life could go on just like it had for the last 20 plus years of his life. But Stan was not satisfied with the usual, with the normal; he wanted the unusual, the excitement that this change was going to bring to his life.

With that thought in mind, Stan was going to move forward with his plan and nothing was going to get in his way. Today was a new day. Today it was going to happen. And by getting out of bed, Stan had started the clock. A clock no one knew about except Stan and Stan's Creator. But Stan didn't recognize or believe in Stan's Creator, so as far as Stan was concerned it was only Stan who knew that the clock had started or even existed.

After showering and getting dressed, Stan made himself some breakfast. He was fastidious about eating healthy, always had been and if he had his way he always would be. This morning, like every other morning, it was oatmeal (rolled, organic oatmeal with no additives, a sprinkle of organic brown sugar and a half dozen raisins – again organic), dry whole wheat toast with a very thin layer of an organic raspberry spread (with no added sugar or preservatives), and a small glass of fresh squeezed orange juice from organic oranges. As he slowly ate his breakfast he glanced through the morning paper to see if anything had changed in the world while he was sleeping. He got most of his news online, but he still could not break himself of the paper habit.

Finishing that, he took out his "to do list" to double check which items he had put on the list for today. It was more out of habit than necessity. He had memorized the list on the second or third day after he had made it, but he still checked it every day, morning and night, to make sure that he had completed each task that had been assigned to that day. Looking it over, he decided that the first thing he should do would be to go to the store and pick up all of the fresh items that he needed to run out to the cabin; the eggs, milk, bread, a little bit of meat – he didn't think that eating meat, at least red meat, was very healthy for a person so he wasn't going to be feeding that to his new wives; he wondered how they felt about tofu – and some fresh vegetables and fruit. He couldn't take too many perishable items since the refrigerator at the cabin was not very big and it did not keep the temperature very low, especially if the door was opened often. He thought about maybe picking up some little mints that he could leave on the turned down bed, but figured that the sentiment would be lost in the moment.

He had jotted down a list earlier of all the items that he needed to purchase so he scooped that up along with his keys and headed out the door to the car. He didn't particularly care for shopping. He wanted to get in and get out. He only shopped at one grocery store so that he would know where everything was. He had memorized the layout on his first trip so that when he went there he already had his path through the store mapped out. That way he could get each item on his list in the most efficient manner possible. And if the store had moved a section since he had been there last, it was not a very pretty scene in that store. It had gotten so bad that the manager was now afraid to change locations of any of the items, even if the corporate office had sent out a mandate to that effect.

Today, would be no different; like a machine or a robot – to the store, into the store, run the predetermined route and gather the items on the list, check out, take the items to the car and home. Any impulse buying that they hoped that Stan would make from fancy displays or eye-catching gimmicks would be wasted on Stan. If it didn't appear on his list, it didn't get purchased and today would be no different in that respect. That is exactly how it happened and fortunately for Stan and the store, they had not moved any of the sections that Stan was gathering items from today.

It took Stan slightly less than an hour, fifty four minutes to be exact, to make his run to the store and get back to the house with all of the items on his list – nothing more, and nothing less. He was still on schedule. He had to constantly remind himself to slow down; to enjoy the day. After all, how many times in a guy's life does he get two wives in the same day?

He loaded all of the items directly from the car into the boat as well as a few other items that he already had at the house that he wanted to take to the cabin. When he had double checked that he had everything loaded into the boat, he locked up the house, started the engine, cast off the lines mooring the boat and headed out of the little bay where the boat had been docked. The seas were relatively calm and the weather forecast for the next 48 hours showed that it was supposed to remain that way. He was grateful for that. That is all that he would need is to have a small craft warning after he had the women in his possession. What would he do with them then? His place really wasn't suited for having women there. Some day that might have to happen, but it did not look like it would today.

The trip out and back went well for Stan; uneventful – just like he liked it; no surprises. He was pleased that everything was going so well. A good omen he thought. The cabin was now stocked with fresh food and there already was quite a large supply of canned goods, cereals and pastas in the pantry. Once he had returned to his home dock, Stan filled up the gas tank, made sure that enough life jackets were on board, that the pillows and blankets were all in the proper places and in good working order before heading back up to the house. He needed to catch a few hours of sleep before he went to collect his wives. As he made his way back up the path to his house, Stan whistled a little ditty – not really any recognizable tune, just a bunch notes that he strung together; some that went together and some that did not. He was whistling more as a way of releasing his nervous tension than for any other reason.

It was now 5:30 PM and he needed to be up no later than 10:30 PM. That would give him five hours of sleep and two and a half hours before he wanted to be inside Tricia's house or at least getting ready to go into her house. He had already put his equipment in the SUV that was parked in the garage, but when he had gotten back to the house he looked inside of it to make sure that it was still in there before he lay down for his nap.

He thought he might have trouble falling asleep since it was so early in the day and he was so wound up, but the day's activities and all of the nervous energy that he had expended had tired him out more than he had realized and he was asleep before he knew it. It was a fitful, troubling sleep however and when the alarm went off at 10:30 he was certainly not ready to get up. The most troubling aspect of his sleep was his dream. He dreamed that he was called in before this all powerful being and this book about his life was opened up before him; he had to stand there and watch as this being, whoever he was, pointed out every detail, every wrong that he had ever committed. He felt this intense, searing inquisition happening deep inside of him as these events were played back to him. When it was finished, the being, stood up, towering over him, and ordered other creatures that had been standing beside him to throw Stan into this pit where he could see huge tongues of fire shooting out of it. And all during this time he had been screaming, "NO! No! No!"

Stan couldn't think about anything else but that dream as he dressed and got ready to go on his mission. He kept telling himself that the dream was nothing. It was merely from his childhood upbringing when he had been made to go to church and they were always talking about a mean old God, who would throw you into hell if you did one little thing wrong. But since there was no God, Stan had nothing to fear. His personal belief on the matter was that this life was all that there was; no judgment, no afterlife, just this one go-round. And if this was all there is, then you needed to enjoy it while you could.

Stan ate a turkey sandwich that he had made earlier that day; one of the items that had been on his "to-do list" and had been done and checked off. He didn't know when the next time he would have a chance to get something to eat so he figured that he should eat something then. That would help him wake up and to collect his thoughts before leaving the house. It was already dark outside, but Stan had only turned on a minimal amount of light; one reason would be in case anyone had been noticing his house they would not think that he was up, and the other reason was that he wanted to keep his eyes dilated as much as possible so that his night vision would not be impaired.

He knew that it took him twelve minutes to reach Tricia's house from his house. So, at twenty minutes to 1:00 AM Stan eased his SUV out of the garage without any lights on and waited until he was away from his house before he turned them on. Stan didn't use his SUV much; only for special occasions such as this. In fact, most of his neighbors didn't even know that he owned an SUV. He drove his car most of the time and the car never was parked in the garage so that he didn't have to open the garage door on the rare chance that someone might see the SUV.

Stan was proud of his SUV. He had ordered and fixed it up special. He had a trick paint job put on it so that in different lighting conditions it would change colors. He had the windows tinted as dark and as black as he could possibly get them. The rear seat had been removed, and he had installed one of those mesh grates like the dog owners have in their cars from floor to ceiling and from side to side. The interior handles on the back doors had been disabled so that they were only pseudo handles; accomplishing nothing if you pulled on them.

Stan was keeping to his schedule when he backed slowly into her driveway as far as he could with the lights off. When he was in as far as he dared to go and still have room to open the rear lift gate and to maneuver at the back of his SUV, he quickly killed the engine. It was 12:54 AM and time to go to work. He made sure that the interior lights would not come on when he opened the door, put his night vision goggles on, grabbed his bag of equipment and opened the driver side door to go claim his first of two new wives.

# 29

At 12:54 AM Wednesday morning, BJ was awakened with a start. Not quite sure what had so abruptly interrupted her sleep she sat up in bed, looked at the clock to make sure that it was not time to get up and she listened. Straining harder, she listened some more. The only sounds that she heard were the usual night sounds that she had become accustomed to in the half century that she had lived there; the creaks and groans of the house expanding and contracting, breathing like an asthmatic needing his inhaler; the crickets and other insects that used the night for their play time; and of course Ralph with his rhythmic snoring - nothing unusual, nothing out of the ordinary, just the usual night sounds.

But BJ was wide awake now. And then she heard it. Not an audible sound that you could hear with your ears, but nonetheless, it was unmistakably a voice that she heard deep within her; a voice that she was all too familiar with. She had trained her ear and she knew enough that she knew that she needed to listen closely to what the voice was saying because it was important.

And what BJ heard the voice say was, *"Get up and pray for Tricia, she is in trouble and she needs your prayers. Pray! Pray! Pray!"*

BJ quietly slipped out of bed so that she wouldn't wake Ralph, put a robe on over her nightgown and went out to her chair in her sewing room where she read her Bible and prayed every day. She sat down and began to pray for Tricia. And as she was praying for her that same voice said, *"Pray for Claudia too, she is in trouble also!"*

Unbeknownst to either one, at the same time that BJ was being awakened, Pastor Grime was also awakened out of a deep sleep. But he did not hear the same voice, at least initially. What woke Pastor Grime was a sharp stabbing pain in his rib cage. He got up wondering if he was having a heart attack or kidney stones or gall stones or what was wrong with him. After getting up, going to the bathroom and getting a glass of water, the pain subsided so he decided that it was nothing and would go back to bed. When he started to get back into bed the pain returned, so he went back out into the other room. Again after the pain receded he tried once more to get back into bed; and again the pain returned. However, this time when he went into the other room he said, "OK Lord, what is that you want?"

Pastor Grime did not hear a voice like BJ, he had a vision and he knew that it was Tricia and she was pleading for him to help her. So in the moment, Pastor Grime dropped to his knees and began crying out to God to help Tricia. After he had prayed for her for awhile, then a vision of Claudia came to his mind and she too was begging him to help her. Then he would switch and he would see Tricia again and she would be asking for help. Back and forth all night long it went; first Tricia and then Claudia and back again. And whenever he started to get sleepy or think about going back to bed, the sharp pain in his ribs would return and he would start all over praying for one and then the other as the vision changed faces before him.

BJ did not have trouble staying awake or want to return to bed. She had an ache deep down inside of her for Tricia and Claudia and she kept hearing that same voice saying, *"Pray for Tricia! Pray for Claudia! They are in trouble! Pray! Pray! Pray!"*

Ralph got up at his usual early time to go to do the chores and noticed that BJ was not in the bed. He was not too overly concerned because she did that sort of thing quite often; going to the bathroom; up early to finish some project or another; getting ready to go into work early; or in her chair reading her Bible and praying. Ralph dressed quickly and quietly left the bedroom. As he went down the hall to go outside he noticed a dim light on in BJ's sewing room and figured that she must be reading her Bible and/or praying so he didn't disturb her and went on out to do his chores.

# 30

S tan opened Tricia's back door as effortlessly as he had when
he had entered her house to install the video cameras. Moving
slowly, being careful not to run into anything or knock anything off
onto the floor. Stan had all of his senses operating at peak capacity
making sure that nothing unusual escaped him that would put him
or his mission in jeopardy. He was already familiar with the house
so he went directly to Tricia's bedroom. Looking through his night
vision goggles he could tell that she was still sound asleep. Not only
could he tell visually, but she was making the sounds that a sleeping
person makes when they are deep in sleep.

Standing in the doorway to her bedroom, Stan took a drone
out of his pocket as well as the flight controller box. He started the
engine on the drone and released it into the air. In his many hours of
practicing flying his drones Stan had learned that if you flew them
into your target area in a circular pattern (starting from a large circle
and drawing in to an ever smaller circle as you flew into your target
– like a corkscrew) instead of flying straight into the target your
percentage of successful landings increased dramatically. So that
is what he did, he started with a large circle higher and away from
Tricia and began circling smaller, lower and closer to his target. He
could see that his primary landing zone was clear of any bedding
or nightclothes and he hoped that it would remain that way for a
few more minutes while he brought the drone in for a landing. He
preferred the neck for two reasons; one, the neck tissue was softer

and easier for the drone "stinger" to penetrate and be able to inject the serum and two, the blood supply to that part of the body was quite high which meant that the serum would be transported to her nervous system quicker.

By the time the drone was close to Tricia she had grown so accustomed to its sound that she didn't even seem to notice it when it was near her ear. As it settled gently on her neck, she flinched slightly, but didn't try to swat it away like Stan was afraid might happen. Once he was sure that it was firmly attached to her neck (it had little sticky pads on its feet that allowed it to land and stick to most any surface almost like a fly does) Stan pushed the button that inserted the "stinger" and the serum into Tricia's neck. Now all he had to do was wait a few moments to allow the serum to do its work and he could claim his prize.

As he was waiting, Stan opened up an empty duffle bag and filled it with a pair of shoes and some clothes that happened to be there handy. Once that was accomplished, he moved over next to the bed and gently moved Tricia's hand. She didn't respond at all. The serum had done its work quickly. There would be no need to tie or gag her as she wasn't going anywhere or saying anything for a few hours anyway. Besides it would be easier to move her if she wasn't all trussed up. Stan threw the covers off of her and moved her legs so that her feet were on the floor and she was sitting up.

This was as close to his new wife as he had ever been. He was even touching her. But he had to put all of those thoughts out of his mind for now. He needed to get her out of here and transported to his cabin before he could entertain any other notion. He picked her up in the fireman's carry and went slowly back the way that he had come in. He still had to be careful because he could not afford to wake the children.

Once outside he didn't bother to shut the back door but headed directly to his waiting SUV, looking around in all directions as he went to make sure that the coast was clear. He had left the lift gate on his SUV open so all that he had to do was lay her down in the back, put her legs inside, throw her bag of clothes in and close the door. He then hurried around to the driver side, got in and started the car. He pulled out, but he left the lights off until he was out of her driveway and around the corner from her house. Once he was out on the main street he took off his night vision goggles and turned on his headlights. The traffic was light just as he had expected. In fact he only saw one other car as he drove the short distance to Claudia's house.

As he drove, he couldn't help but be a little puffed up at his accomplishment. He had flown the drone perfectly and the injection system and serum had performed beautifully. He wondered why it had taken him this long to go high tech with his wife gathering procedure. He had one new wife and was about to take another one. He couldn't have planned it any better than it had worked.

Stan drove by Claudia's house and her gun-toting, dog-walking neighbor's house to make sure that they were all in bed and that they were not going to give him any trouble; especially that nosey neighbor guy. Stan would've liked to have used a drone on him, and instead of sleeping for a few hours maybe he could help him sleep for a very long time. Well, Stan didn't have time for him either. He circled back around the block, turned off his lights as he approached Claudia's driveway and backed into it like he had done at Tricia's. However, here he couldn't back in as far as he had at Tricia's place. Her car was only pulled half way into the driveway for some reason that Stan couldn't easily see. He did not like where he had to park, because he was more exposed, more vulnerable out here where he was.

Stan made sure that he still had a couple of drones in his pocket as well as the flight controller box. He grabbed another empty duffle bag and his small bag of tools and quietly slipped out his driver side door. However, this time he did not leave the lift gate open like he had done at Tricia's place. It would be more inconvenient when he returned carrying Claudia, but he couldn't chance leaving it open while he was in doing his work; not that Tricia would likely be going anyplace soon, but he didn't want prying eyes to possibly see her in there and start asking too many questions. Not that he had or would see anyone else; nevertheless Stan liked to play it on the cautious side of things.

Stan moved quickly to the rear of the house scanning right and left as he went not wanting to miss something that might be a danger. Claudia's rear door opened even easier than it had the last time that he was here. He reminded himself to be extra careful in here since Claudia was not as neat as Tricia and there could be all sorts of potential trip hazards and shin knockers all along the route he had to take to get to her room. As he crossed the back porch and headed into the kitchen this thought crossed his mind, *"What if she is not here? What if she went somewhere?"*

He quickly dismissed that thought and moved on through the house silently; stopping at each doorway that he came across to peer inside to see if she might be in there instead of in her bedroom. But she was not, she was sound asleep in her bed just like he had hoped and planned that she would be. Again standing in the doorway to her room he took a drone and a flight controller box out of his pocket and set the drone on its flight path towards his new target. And again he started with a large circle up and away from Claudia before circling in and down towards its target. Claudia's neck was not as exposed as Tricia's neck had been so this might be more of a challenge flying the drone into the target area than he was used to.

As he approached Claudia suddenly she swatted the drone with her right hand apparently believing that a mosquito was about to have lunch on her. The drone went skittering off somewhere, but Stan did not see where it went. It was not enough to wake her, but Stan stood there for a couple of minutes to make sure that it had not awakened her. He took the second drone from his pocket and started it up. Only one more chance and then he would have to do it the old fashioned way. Flying in again he decided that the slow circular route might not be the best method with Claudia so he made the decision to fly straight in to the target and perhaps he could out maneuver her swats. He knew that flying straight in would lower his chances of success, but he did not have many options right now. Getting closer to her Stan kept one eye on her right hand to see if he could see it move soon enough to move out of her way in time. She started to raise her arm one time and Stan zig zagged to the left, but she didn't follow through with her swat. He managed to weave his way past the cover and landed on her neck. As she started to raise her arm, Stan pushed the stinger button hard before he was certain that the drone had landed and attached itself to her. But it had, and the "stinger" found its mark.

Which clothes should he pick? There were so many clothes scattered all over the room that he had no trouble finding some to put in his bag. He was sure that no matter which ones he picked she would complain that they didn't go together, or that those were dirty or some other silly complaint. Too bad! Be thankful that I was thoughtful enough to grab some clothes at all. You could have been stuck in your nightclothes.

When he checked Claudia, she groaned a little bit, but showed no signs of waking up. Just as he had done at Tricia's, Stan picked Claudia up in a fireman's carry and started out of the bedroom and the house with her. This time he didn't have to be quiet as he left. There was no one else in the house to wake. And he didn't bother to shut the back door as he left either. He stopped at the edge of the house and looked all around in all directions to make sure that no one was out prowling around. He had no desire to tangle with Mr. gun-toting neighbor. Not seeing anyone, he moved quickly to his SUV and opened the lift gate (thank goodness for powered lift gates that pop open at the push of a button). After it had opened itself, Stan lay Claudia down on the floor next to Tricia and closed the door.

Just like he did when he left Tricia's, he did not turn the lights on until he had driven away from Claudia's house and had turned onto another street. He breathed a sigh of relief about then; actually he noticed that his breathing was heavy and that he felt tired all over. Again the thought that maybe he shouldn't be taking two wives at one time flashed through his mind and he noted that he entertained the thought longer this time than he had the last time it had come flitting through there.

Stan drove cautiously home making sure that he did not speed and that he obeyed all of the traffic laws. He had checked all of the lamps in the SUV two days ago to make sure that they were all in good working order so that he would not give a policeman an excuse to pull him over. He made it to his house without incident, pulled into the garage with the SUV and shut the garage door.

Instinctively he glanced at the clock and saw that he was only about 2 minutes behind the schedule that he had set up for himself.

He opened the lift gate to make sure that his new wives were resting comfortably and pulled the drones off of each of their necks since they had served their purpose and had helped him capture his prey. He took the two bags of clothes and put them in his garden cart in the bottom and he put the drones, the flight controller box and any other evidence that might be incriminating into a lead lined box and securely fastened the lid on it. He was going to send that to the bottom of the sea when they were out there a ways. It was amazing how much the ocean could hide for you if you wanted it to.

Next he loaded Tricia into the cart and wheeled her down to his waiting boat. Getting a dead weight into a boat that is bobbing up and down was a challenge that Stan had encountered before and had worked out a method that proved to work as well as could be expected. Once he had Tricia on board, a life jacket put on her and comfortably laying down in the bottom of the boat, he took the cart back up to the house to get Claudia. He loaded her up like he did Tricia and carted her down to the dock and to the boat. He got her into the boat and fitted with a life jacket as well before laying her down next to Tricia. Then he covered them up with a blanket and a tarp.

He took his cart back up to the house and locked it up. He had to be back here soon enough, but there was no use in tempting someone with an open door. Untying the lines from the dock, Stan pushed away from the dock and used a small trolling motor to ease out to the mouth of the small bay before starting the main motor. The trip up the coast was calm sailing like he had hoped it would be. He threw a fishing line into the water without putting any bait on it just so it appeared that he was fishing. He really didn't want to catch any fish right now. He had more important matters to take care of.

It was going just as he had planned it and he was right on time. Stan would check on his wives from time to time to make sure that they were still sleeping soundly. The last thing that he needed out here on the water was for one of them to wake up and to go crazy on him. It was better when they went all crazy in the controlled environment of his cabin. Stan was not looking forward to the next phase of his wife project – the training phase as he thought of it. Some women did not take to this lifestyle very easily, but with some persuasion all of them came around to see it his way. And the sooner that they did see it his way, the easier their life would be; as simple as that.

# 31

❧

When Ralph came back in from doing chores BJ was still in her sewing room. He poked his head in and asked, "BJ, are you OK? Is something wrong?"

"I don't know Ralph. I have been up since 12:54 AM with such a heavy weight for Tricia and Claudia that all that I have been able to do is to cry out to God for them. I don't know what they are facing right now or what they are going to face, but I do know that they need help."

Not knowing what else to say, Ralph said, "Shall I fix the breakfast?"

BJ replied, "I am not going to eat, but I will come fix your breakfast. You go get cleaned up and by the time you finish, breakfast should be on the table."

"You are fast, but you aren't that fast."

"If I have breakfast ready by the time you get to the table then you have to do the dishes, otherwise I will do them," said BJ.

"You have a deal," said Ralph as he started off down the hall to the bathroom.

"No fair! You had a head start," exclaimed BJ as she headed for the kitchen.

She was right. She was fast. Breakfast was on the table getting cold waiting for Ralph to get cleaned up and seated at the table. And it was not just a piece of toast or a muffin and coffee. It was breakfast like Ralph liked it. It did include toast, but it also had bacon and eggs and hash browns thrown in for good measure. Ralph was flabbergasted when he walked in and saw the spread before him.

"How did you do all this woman? I wasn't gone that long," said Ralph.

"It's all in the timing. The timing is everything," said BJ.

BJ sat down at the table with Ralph but didn't eat anything. She did have a cup of coffee, black, but that was all. She sat there silent with her head in her hands, looking up at Ralph occasionally as she took a sip from her cup.

"Are you still troubled about Tricia and Claudia," asked Ralph?

"I am," answered BJ.

"Maybe you should run over there to see if everything is OK," said Ralph.

"I was just thinking that I should do that."

"I have to clean the dishes anyway and someone should be here when Rod wakes up so unless you want me to go with you, why not head on over there?"

"I was thinking that it might be a little early since it is only 7:30, but I think Tricia had the early morning shift today which means that the kids should have already been here by now. Oh dear, I better get over there."

"Call me if you need some help," said Ralph as BJ scurried off down the hall to their bedroom to throw some clothes on and run a brush through her hair.

BJ pecked a kiss on Ralph's cheek on her way by and out the door. Fortunately for her there wasn't a policeman along her route to Tricia's house or she might have gotten a speeding ticket. She was still feeling distraught as she pulled into Tricia's driveway and as she did she noticed that her car was still there. She hurried up to the front door and rang the doorbell. No answer. She rang it again; still, no answer. She knocked loudly on the door and waited. No answer. She tried the doorknob and it was locked. Then she decided to go around the back to see if that door was unlocked or if someone would hear her knocking on that door. When she went around the corner of the house she saw that the back door was wide open and the weight that she had been feeling just got heavier. She shot up a quick prayer as she slowly entered the house.

As she walked in she didn't see anything amiss or anything that might indicate trouble. So she went a little farther into the house and down the hallway where the bedrooms were. The first room that she came to was Candy's room. BJ poked her head in and saw that she was sleeping soundly so she went on to the next room which was Timmy's room. Looking into his room she saw that he too was sleeping soundly without a care in the world. Then she went on down the hall towards Tricia's room. The closer she got to her room the more uneasiness BJ was feeling. What she saw when she got to the doorway to Tricia's room stopped her in her tracks. The bed covers were thrown back and the bed was empty. No Tricia! She quickly scanned the room from the doorway but saw nothing that would indicate a struggle or that she had really been there.

BJ went out into the other rooms and didn't see any sign of her anywhere. Tricia's purse was still sitting on the counter where she usually kept it when she was home. She decided to wake Timmy to see if he knew where his mother might be. Going back to Timmy's room and over to his bed BJ gently touched him and said, "Timmy, honey, you need to wake up, its grandma."

"Huh, what? Grandma? What are you doing here? Where's my mommy," asked Timmy?

"Honey, that's what I am trying to find out. Did your mom have to go somewhere this morning?"

"Yes, she said that she had to go to work. Is she here?"

"No dear, she is not here. I am going to call the restaurant to see if she made it in to work. Why don't you get up and put some clothes on while I do that. OK?"

"OK! Is Candy still here?"

"Yes dear, Candy is still here. Maybe you should get her up too and have her put some clothes on."

"All right, grandma."

BJ went out to the kitchen where the phone was and dialed the number for the restaurant. Steve, the manager answered the phone at the restaurant and BJ said, "Good morning Steve, this is BJ, is Tricia there?"

Steve said, "No she is not. I was just about to call her house to see if she had overslept. Do you know where she is?"

"I don't know. I am at Tricia's house and she isn't here. Her children are still here. Her car and purse are still here, but she isn't."

"That doesn't sound good," said Steve.

"No it doesn't. Look, call me if she shows up and I will do the same if we locate her. You have my cell phone number don't you," asked BJ.

"I do have your cell phone number and I'll call you if she shows up here," said Steve.

"Thanks Steve, bye!"

"Goodbye, BJ!"

"Was she at work grandma," asked Timmy?

"No honey, she wasn't. But the manager said that he would call me if she did show up. I think you and Candy should come home with me until we can locate your mother," said BJ.

BJ could see that he was trying to be tough and not cry so she said, "I know that we will locate her soon. She probably went to the store or out with a friend."

"What if she comes back while we are gone? She won't know where we are," said Timmy.

"I will leave her a note and tell her that I took the two of you to my house. Now, why don't you help Candy get ready and I will go write that note."

They each went separate directions to take care of the task that they were going to do; Timmy to his sister's room to help her get ready and BJ to the kitchen to write a note telling Tricia that she had taken the children to her house and for her to call when she returned home.

BJ rounded up the children and took them out to her car. As she was backing out of the driveway, the thought came to her that she should go by Claudia's house but she didn't know where she lived.

"Timmy, do you know where Claudia lives," asked BJ?

"Yes, grandma, I do. Do you want me to show you how to get there?"

"Please do, dear!"

Timmy directed her right to Claudia's place like he had been driving there himself for years. BJ pulled into her driveway and turned the engine off. She said, "Why don't you two stay here in the car? I am going to ask Claudia if she knows where your mother is."

"OK," said Timmy.

BJ went to Claudia's front door and after trying the doorbell and pounding on the door several times, she got no response. Then she went around to the back of the house and saw that her back door was wide open like Tricia's door had been earlier. "Not good. Not good at all," muttered BJ under her breath as she stepped into the back porch area of Claudia's house. Making her way slowly, into the main living area, she was struck by how opposite Claudia was compared to Tricia as far as housekeeping went. She couldn't tell if it always looked this way or if there had been some sort of tussle that went on here that made such a mess all over. She looked in all of the rooms until she came to the room that was probably her bedroom, but did not see any sign of Claudia. Looking into her bedroom from the doorway she saw a scene similar to the scene in Tricia's bedroom; the bedcovers were thrown back and the bed was empty. No Claudia. No sign of Claudia.

The rock in her stomach was growing larger by the minute. She decided that she needed to notify the authorities, but she needed to take the children home first.

Ralph and Rod greeted the three of them as they came in the door and Ralph was about ready to ask how things were when he got that look from BJ. That look that said, *"Don't you dare ask about Tricia or I will kill you!"* So instead Ralph said, "Are you kids hungry? I made some pancakes for Rod and there are still some left."

"I am not real hungry, but maybe I could eat some," said Timmy.

"I'm hungry," said Candy. Candy still had not grasped what was happening and did not understand that her mom was missing.

So Ralph busied himself fixing some pancakes for Timmy and Candy while BJ went to her sewing room. She said that she was going to make a few phone calls.

When the children had gotten enough to eat, he told Rod to take the kids out to play and he went down to BJ's sewing room to find out what was going on. He overheard BJ talking to someone and could only make out BJ's side of the conversation.

"Officer, I am telling you I think these two women, Tricia and Claudia, have been abducted. We don't have time to wait the 24 or 48 hours or whatever it is that you need to wait before filing a missing person report. You need to get on this right away. Don't you know how many young women have disappeared from our community in the last 10 to 12 years," asked BJ?

There was a pause as the officer responded...

"Sir, both of their cars were still in their driveways. Both of their purses were still there. Both of their bedcovers were thrown back. Tricia's kids were still there sleeping in their beds. Tricia wouldn't just go off and leave them. Tricia was scheduled for work this morning and she didn't show up. It is not like her to even be late let alone to miss work. You need to start looking for them right away before the trail gets any colder."

Another pause as the officer was obviously talking...

"Do you want my cell phone number in case you need to talk to me," asked BJ?

Another pause...

"It is 707-322-1623. Please have him call me."

Another pause...

"Goodbye"

"BJ, what is going on," asked Ralph?

"Oh Ralph, I think that someone has taken Tricia and Claudia. I went to both of their houses and they were not there. Both of their back doors were wide open. Their cars were still in their driveways and their purses were still sitting there. The covers on their beds were thrown back like they were leaving in a hurry. But I could find no sign of them; no sign of a struggle, nothing."

"And the police don't want to do anything?"

"No, the officer I spoke with said that he would take the information, but that they would not do a missing person search until after 48 hours. They could be dead or completely out of the country in that amount of time."

"Maybe you should call Pastor Grime and see if he could call the prayer warriors of the church to pray," said Ralph.

"Ralph that is a great idea! I don't know why I didn't think of that."

BJ picked the phone back up and dialed Pastor Grime's number from memory. "Good Morning, pastor, this is BJ."

"Good morning, BJ. I was just about to call you. Let me guess, you are calling about Tricia and Claudia," said Pastor Grime.

"How did you know pastor?"

"BJ when the Lord gets me up in the middle of the night with a sharp pain in my ribs and it will only go away when I pray for Tricia and Claudia. And when I try to go back to bed or start to nod off the pain comes back... I think there must be a reason. Are they in some sort of trouble?"

"I don't know for sure, pastor. I too have been awake most of the night praying for Tricia and Claudia. I had such a heavy weight on my heart for them that I finally went over to their houses this morning. When I got there, their cars were still there, their purses were still there, their bedcovers were thrown off the bed and they were nowhere to be found. In Tricia's case the children were still there in their beds sound asleep. Oh, and both of their back doors were wide open. It looks to me like someone has kidnapped them."

"Have you talked to the police," asked Pastor Grime?

"I tried. They took the information but they said that they would not do a missing person's search for 48 hours."

"BJ I am going to call all the prayer warriors in our church and a few that I know that go to other churches and ask them to pray for this situation; and maybe to even fast and pray. I believe that God is going to use this for his glory. I don't know how, but I had that assurance that he would as I struggled in prayer last night."

"Thank you, pastor! If I hear anything from anyone I will let you know."

"Thank you, BJ."

"Ralph, pastor is going to call the prayer warriors of the church and some others that he knows and ask them to pray and maybe even fast and pray for Tricia and Claudia," said BJ.

"I guess I shouldn't have had that breakfast," said Ralph.

"You can still start right now," said BJ.

"BJ, let's pray together about this for awhile," said Ralph.

"Tricia and Claudia need all of the prayers that we can give them right now."

# 32

S tan sat there in a chair in his cabin watching his two new wives, Tricia and Claudia, as they slept off the effects of the serum that his drones had injected into them last night. He had tied them to the bed next to each other so that when they did awake they couldn't do something stupid. One of the first of his many wives had tried to kill him with her bare hands when she woke up so after that he had always tied them up until he could get them conditioned to their new life with him. For some it took a little more persuasion than for others.

He had dozed off a few times himself while he was watching them sleep. It had been hard work moving two 'dead weights' 500 yards up from the beach, strapping them one at a time in the harness with him and hoisting them up to the platform, before he could finally drag them inside and lay them on the bed. He wasn't getting any younger and that certainly was a lot of work. But it would be worth it. And as he sat there he couldn't help but be pleased with himself and his accomplishments; two new wives in one night. He didn't know if that was a Guinness Book of Records effort, but he sure wasn't going to submit it to find out. That was the problem with this type of record, who was he going to tell?

He now had his work cut out for him. He had to 'train' two wives at one time. This had to be the worst part of this entire process for him. He wished that he had some sort of a machine that he could plug them into and they would be automatically programmed like he wanted them. It would make things so much easier; easier on him and easier on them. Then they could get down to the fun part of their relationship. But that would have to wait. He would have to bring them along the old fashioned way. He had developed some pretty good tactics over the years for getting them to the place where he wanted them to be. The only thing that bothered him about some of the methods was they used pain a little bit more than he really cared to administer. But he rationalized it as being OK since the end result justified the means in getting to where you wanted to go. So he would continue to use those methods that produced the results he wanted.

Tricia suddenly groaned and tried to turn to her side, but the restraints kept her from doing that and she strained a bit trying to free her arms and legs so that she could turn, but she eventually gave way to the sleep that was pulling at her and stopped fighting against the cable ties that held her. Stan knew that it would not be very long now before she would be completely awake. He had seen this process happen several times and it had always gone the same way. Then he would have a fight on his hands.

He got up to pour himself another cup of coffee. He wanted to be fully alert when it did happen. He took out his taser from the holster that was attached to his belt to have in the ready position. That particular little tool was very effective at making converts to his way of thinking. Most of the time it only took two or three hits by the electrical voltage that it produced to get them to do what he wanted them to merely by showing them the taser gun. He wasn't trying to do much training other than to let them know who the boss in this cabin was.

Just about then Tricia came to and when it dawned on her that she was not in her room, not her bed, she let out a blood curdling scream that would have put the fright in anyone's Halloween. Then she saw Stan and screamed even louder. All of the commotion caused Claudia to start stirring. Stan realized too late that he had forgotten to put his earplugs in his ears. Now he would have to endure the screaming of two crazed women.

When Tricia finally decided that her screams where getting her nowhere except hoarse, she decided to stop screaming. But when she stopped screaming she began to cry with huge sobs. She did get some of her wits about her and began firing questions at this man who apparently held them captive at the moment.

"Where are we? Who are you? Why are we here? What are you going to do with us? When are you going to let us go? We have no money for a ransom, why do you want us?" And the questions continued to pour out of her without giving Stan a moment in which to answer any of them.

About that time Claudia began to rouse and when she realized what kind of a predicament that she was in, she too began screaming at the top of her lungs. Except not only was she screaming she was thrashing around so much that the bed began to bang around on the floor. Stan was afraid that she was going to hurt herself against the cable ties that held her hands and feet tight to the bed. She would certainly know by tomorrow that she probably would have been better off if she hadn't done that. Those cable ties were going to leave a nasty abrasion where they had rubbed against the skin.

Claudia must have had stronger lungs than Tricia because she carried on with the screaming for a much longer time than Tricia had. She would have gone on longer, but Tricia had intervened to help calm and quiet her. When she had subsided to some low whimpering noises, Stan thought that he should explain to them their plight.

"Ladies, if I could have your attention for a few minutes I want to try to answer some of the questions that I have heard you asking since you have awakened. First off, you can call me Stan-daddy. The two of you are my new wives..." At that, both of them started screaming at the top of their lungs once again. Stan wasn't sure if it was the Stan-daddy name or the idea that they were now his new wives that upset them so much.

"Ladies! Ladies! We have a lot to go over here before I have to leave so can we get through this and then you can scream all that you want after that. If you continue to make this difficult I will have to bring out my friend the persuader and show you how it works and how good it feels when I use it on you. So, please be quiet. I said that you **will** call me Stan-daddy. I am now going to be your new husband. I will protect you and provide for you. I will be leaving soon, but I will be back in four days for a little fun. Try to use the water and the electricity as sparingly as possible. This cupboard here is your pantry. I have stocked it and the refrigerator with healthy food. When I return in four days I will bring more food to resupply you. I have brought a bag with some clothes in it for each of you. You won't have a big, huge wardrobe but where are you going to go and who are you going to impress? There are also some clothes in that closet right there that you are welcome to use if you find anything that sort of fits. They belonged to some of my previous wives and they won't need them anymore so help yourselves.

Now let me explain what you are living in. This is a sphere; a ball that has been suspended up in the air 25 to 30 ft. on a cable that has been strung between two trees. The sphere is almost indestructible so you might as well forget about breaking out of here. Right now the sphere is next to a platform, but when I leave I will push you and the sphere out into the middle of the cable span. And even if you did manage to escape, which no one yet has succeeded in accomplishing, you are 30 feet up off the ground and you are miles from any kind of civilization even if you knew which direction to go.

Your life is with me now. Forget about those loser husbands of yours rotting away in that cell. I can and will meet all of your needs from now on. The quicker you learn that little lesson the better everyone's life will be, including your own. When I return I want you to stand right here in front of the door where I can see you and you will hold your hands straight out in front of you so that I can see them at all times.

And if you become more of a pain than you are worth, we will take a little trip together and you will go swimming with my other ex-wives. So it does pay to get in line and stay in line. I am going to be leaving now but before I do I will cut you lose from the bed. Don't try anything stupid, I don't want to have to show you how my little taser friend works."

Tricia and Claudia were stunned speechless from what they had just heard this Stan-daddy guy just tell them. Neither one of them tried to do anything as he cut them loose. As he backed out the door, watching them all the way, Tricia and Claudia sat up in bed and when he had gone both of them simultaneously broke out in a sobbing fit. When they thought that they could cry no more, one of them would begin again and then the both of them would be sobbing as loudly as ever.

Stan untied the sphere from the dock and pushed it out into the middle of the suspension cable before he let himself down with the winch. He made his way back to the boat and out into the ocean to head back home. Fishing had been good. He had caught his limit and now he was headed home. No one needed to know that what he had caught was not fish at all, but two lovely ladies that he had just made his wives.

He didn't have to worry about Frank. Frank wasn't speaking to him anymore and he really didn't want to speak to Frank either. But he had decided that even if they were still speaking he wouldn't tell him about his wives. He might put two and two together and come up with the right answer and Stan couldn't have that happen.

A glance at his watch and a quick calculation told him that he would get back to his home dock at dusk. He would sleep well tonight. He was really tired. It was going to be very hard to stay awake and alert enough to pilot the boat back. He wondered if anyone had missed either of the girls yet. Those kids would certainly have missed their mommy by now, but probably no one has even checked to see if Claudia was still around or not. He then wondered if it had made the news yet or not. He would have to turn on the TV to see if it had made it on their news. That is if he can stay awake long enough to watch. He was getting very sleepy. He wished he would have brought that coffee along with him. Sleepy! So sleepy! He had to stay awake. His life depended on it. His two new wives depended on it.

# 33

After speaking with BJ, Pastor Grime knew what he had to do. He had to make a visit to Pelican Bay State Prison and try to talk to Mark and Ricardo, Tricia and Claudia's husbands. He did not know if Ricardo would receive him or not, but he did know that Mark had told Tricia in no uncertain terms that he did not want to talk to a minister. So his plan was to see the warden, tell him the disturbing news and offer his services if either man or both wanted to talk to him.

All during the drive to the prison a struggle went on inside of Pastor Grime. One side said, *"Why bother, these men are hard, they don't want to talk to you. They probably don't even care if their wives are missing. You would do more good staying home and praying."* And then there was the other side that would fight back with, *"These men are lost and searching too. They will be hurting when they find out that their wives have been abducted. They will want to talk to someone. You need to put some feet to your prayers. You can pray while you talk to them."* Back and forth it went. The closer he got to the prison the stronger the fight became.

Even as he sat in the waiting room waiting to be shown into the warden's office the war inside of him went on. The one side saying, *"It's not too late, get up and leave;"* and the other side saying,*"Stay, see this thing through. You are almost there."* As he sat there struggling and praying, praying and struggling, the guard had to call him twice to go into the warden's office he was so focused on the struggle within him.

"Pastor GRI-me, welcome. Please be seated. How can I help you today," asked the warden?

"Sir, my name is French and is pronounced, 'Gre-MAY,'" replied Pastor Grime.

"My apologies, sir. I was just reading off of your card and it looked like GRI-me to me. You know we specialize in grime around here," said the warden.

"Well sir, I too specialize in grime. My remedy for grime is a little bit different than your remedy for grime though," said Pastor Grime.

"Interesting! I would love to discuss this more with you some-time, but I doubt that you are here for that today. May I ask again, 'How can I help you?'" asked the warden?

"Sir, one of my parishioners and I were awakened early this morning with a strong sense that something was wrong with two other members of our church family. When she went over to their houses she discovered that both of them were missing. The one young lady has two small children that were still at their house. Both of their purses and their cars were still there and both of their back doors were wide open, but no ladies," said Pastor Grime.

"I am sorry to hear that, pastor. But what does that have to do with me other than when they catch that jerk, and believe me sooner or later they will catch him, he might be living here for the rest of his days," said the warden.

"Sir, both of the young ladies have husbands that are incarcer-ated here. And I thought that you should inform them that their wives are missing and I want to offer my services in whatever capacity you might need from me; counseling with the men, what-ever," said Pastor Grime.

"That changes the whole ballgame altogether. Who are the men whose wives are missing," said the warden.

"The one young lady is Tricia Noyes, Mark Noyes' wife. And the other is Claudia Sanchez, Ricardo's wife."

"I know both of those men personally. I will have them brought to my office and inform them right away," said the warden picking up the phone and punching in some numbers.

"Yes, can you bring Mark Noyes and Ricardo Sanchez to my office as soon as possible," said the warden into the phone.

"Pastor, I can't guarantee that they will want to talk to you, but I will tell them that you are available," said the warden.

"Thank you, sir! I don't know what your policy is on visiting hours, but I make myself available all hours of the day and night, especially for extreme situations such as these. Not that I have ever had to deal with a situation quite like this before in my ministry, and I hope that I never have another one like it, but it is usually a death or sickness that I have to deal with," said Pastor Grime.

"Like I said, I will tell the men that you are available. Normally we are pretty rigid on our visiting hours here, but I am human sometimes and I think that this would be reason enough to circumvent those rules if the men need to talk to you at some time other than the regular visiting hours," said the warden.

Pastor Grime stood to leave and extended his hand to the warden and said, "Thank you again sir!"

"I wish we were meeting under different circumstances, I like the way you think," said the warden.

"You have my card and number, the offer extends to you as well. Anytime, anyplace, any subject," said pastor.

"Goodbye, I hope this turns out for the good," said the warden.

"Sir, it will turn out for the good. God has already assured me of that. Have a good day," said pastor as he turned and went out the door to the warden's office.

*"Strange fellow, but I like him. I am going to have to look him up sometime and I would like to know his thinking on the remedy for grime,"* thought the warden.

As he was deep in thought about his conversation that he had just had with Pastor Grime, he was buzzed and informed that Mark Noyes and Ricardo Sanchez were here as requested. He had them shown in, but asked the two guards to remain in the office with them. He told Mark and Ricardo to be seated but he left their shackles on their hands and feet for security measures. Then he began to relay the conversation that he had just had with Pastor Grime to them.

When it finally dawned on Mark where the conversation was going he kept shaking his head saying, "NO! NO! NO!" The more the warden shared of the conversation the more agitated he became. Until the warden could see that he needed to get control of him and said, "Mark, you need to control yourself. It won't do any good to be all riled up. I am sure that there are good men out there looking for your wife right now and they will find her."

"Find her just like they have found all of those other women. All of them had connections to this prison and they haven't found them yet," said Mark.

"Well, you just need to calm down," said the warden. "Pastor Grime has offered to talk with you, pray with you or do anything he can for you. And he offered to do it at anytime of the day or night. I told him that we normally don't break the visiting hours that have been set, but this is an unusual circumstance and we will make an exception for this. So, if you want to talk to him at anytime just get word to me and I will contact him for you," said the warden.

"If he wants to do something, then tell him to go find them! I don't need to talk to NO pastor, I want my wife back," said Mark as he got up and started to throw a fit. Both guards were on him immediately and had him subdued before he could do anything.

"Mark, I told you to calm down. If you don't, I am going to have you put in solitary until you do and I don't think that you want that right now," said the warden.

Mark sat back down and managed to get his temper under control, somewhat. While all of this was happening, Ricardo just sat there dumbfounded, not saying a word, not showing any kind of emotion, just sitting there expressionless.

"If you have no other questions, then I am finished," said the warden. "You can take these men back to their cells and I want them put under a suicide watch."

The two guards pulled Mark and Ricardo to their feet and pushed them towards the door. Mark defiantly shook them off and went stomping out the door. Ricardo, listless, shuffled out the door behind him as if he were in a stupor.

Back in their respective cells, Mark paced his cell like a caged lion or tiger. Ricardo on the other hand lay on his bunk as if he were dead. In fact, if you would have asked him, he probably would have told you that something inside of him had just died. He now had no reason to live. His plan was to stop living; stop eating, stop everything that was his life now. He would simply lay here until they carried him out.

Pastor Grime had decided to stop eating, but for a different reason. He was going to fast until a conclusion to this matter was reached. He would not eat and spend that time in prayer. He also cut back all unnecessary appointments, errands and plans in order to spend the time in prayer. He was not the only one in the Living Waters Fellowship that had made just such a commitment to fast and pray. There was a core group of about seven people, including BJ and Ralph that had also made that same commitment. Others in the congregation had also made a commitment to pray when they could, but for one reason or another they could not commit to fast.

Wednesday afternoon BJ received a phone call from the FBI and said that they would like to meet with her at Tricia's house later that day. They explained that the chief of police in Crescent City had contacted them about two missing women from the town and that they were looking to get in on a case like this one early on since there had been so many disappearances of young women from the town in recent years. He said that they would be coming from the San Francisco office and would take them a couple of hours to get there by plane. They would be bringing a field office later by car, but they wanted an advance team of forensics to get started on this while the trail was still relatively warm. He told BJ that he would call when they got into town and then they could meet at Tricia's house.

BJ spent the time trying to console Timmy and Candy without much success. She tried to persuade them to pray for their mom and that seemed to help the most. Rod and Timmy wanted to strike out on their own looking for Timmy's mom and Claudia, but BJ talked them out of that. So along with several others they resigned themselves to the only option that they had; prayer.

Slightly less than two hours after BJ had talked to the FBI man, he called again and said that they were in town and would be heading over to Tricia's house directly. The local police department had sent a cruiser out to the airport to pick them up and would take them to Tricia's. BJ told him that she would head right over there and meet them there.

After the formalities of introductions in the front yard of Tricia's house, BJ began telling the FBI what she knew starting with how she had been awakened at 12:54 AM and the heaviness that had lasted through the night until she finally came over to check on Tricia and the children. Then she said, "And when I got here the car was still in the driveway which was odd because Tricia was supposed to be at work early this morning and she is never late and never misses work. I rang the doorbell a couple of times and no one answered so I knocked really loud a couple of times and still no one came to the door. Then I went around to the back and the back door was standing wide open. I knew something was wrong then, because Tricia is a little paranoid about keeping her doors locked at all times. Then I went inside but didn't see anything too unusual. I have not been inside this house too many times, but enough to have spotted something out of the ordinary I think. I went down this hall and poked my head into each of the children's rooms as I went and they were all still sleeping soundly. But when I got to Tricia's room I stopped in the doorway and saw that her bed covers had been flung back and the bed was empty. I searched the rest of the house and did not find any sign of her, but I did notice that her purse was still on the counter where she keeps it.

Then I went back to Timmy's room and woke him up to ask him if he knew where his mother was and he said that he didn't know. I had both of the children get up and get dressed so that I could take them home with me. And on my way home I decided to stop by Claudia's house to see if she was OK since I had the same feeling about her that I had had about Tricia. When I got to Claudia's, it was the same scenario. No answer at the front door, the back door swinging wildly open and her bed empty with the covers thrown back except her house is way messier than Tricia's house."

"Thank you, BJ! If you think of anything else here's my card with my number on it. Don't hesitate to call me whatever time it is. The FBI can't rest because the criminals don't rest. A couple of my men are going to start looking at the evidence here and a couple of them are going over to Claudia's house with me to start looking at the evidence there as well. Tomorrow all of our team will be here from San Francisco and we will attack this thing head on to get this solved. You reassure Tricia's children that we will find their mother. And I will keep you informed about our progress," said FBI agent Lonnie.

"Thank you, sir," said BJ.

"Your welcome," said Lonnie.

# 34

❦

Tricia and Claudia spent the rest of Wednesday after Stan left curled in the fetal position on the bed sobbing and whimpering. Sometime during the middle of the night Wednesday or early Thursday morning after she had sobbed until it seemed like she had no more sobs left in her, Tricia began hearing that familiar voice that kept saying over and over, *"Trust Me! Tricia, trust Me! I have a plan! Trust Me!"* The more Tricia tried to argue with the voice, the more it kept repeating to her, *"Trust Me! You need to trust Me!"* Tricia tried explaining their situation but to no avail. The voice just kept saying, *"Trust Me! Trust Me! Trust Me!"* At one point the voice reminded her to remember the lessons that Pastor Grime had given recently about Daniel in the lions' den and the other one about Joseph and the difficult times that he had endured.

Finally in the wee hours of the morning, Thursday morning, Tricia stopped fighting and said, "OK God, I give up. I will trust you like you have asked me to do." When she did that she fell fast asleep and slept like a baby for 3 hours. When she woke up she felt refreshed and ready to go. She looked over at Claudia lying next to her and saw that she was sleeping fitfully and crying out as if having nightmares. Tricia lay there praying for a half hour while Claudia slept before getting up to check out their new 'home.' She had explored all that there was to explore by the time Claudia decided to open her eyes and keep them open longer than 15 seconds.

When Claudia saw that Tricia was awake and up she said, "I thought that I was having a bad dream, a nightmare, about being held captive in some little cabin. Then I realize that it is not a dream; that it really is happening; that we really are being held against our wills in this godforsaken place."

"Claudia, this place is not forsaken by God; nor are we. God spoke to me all night long last night and kept reminding me to 'trust Him!' I don't know why or what we are supposed to do exactly, but that is not our job. Our job is to be obedient to do what he asks us to do and to do it when He asks us to do it," said Tricia.

"Tricia, you make it sound so easy. I don't think I could have that kind of faith," said Claudia.

"Claudia, do you remember Pastor Grime teaching us about Daniel when he was facing the lions in their dens for doing the right thing," asked Tricia?

"Yes, why," asked Claudia?

"God reminded me of that lesson this morning. Remember what the scripture says when they took Daniel out of the den the next morning? It says, 'no wound was found on him because he trusted his God.' Claudia, this is our lions' den and when they take us out of here they will find no wound on us either."

"I wish I could believe that. This Stan daddy guy gives me the creeps. Did he say that he had other wives? What happened to them? Won't the same thing happen to us?"

"Claudia, God also reminded me about Joseph and the lesson of his life. How many hard things did he have to endure and yet he trusted in God for a good outcome to his circumstances."

"Tricia, I don't want to have to live in this ball up in the trees for 20 or 30 years. What kind of a life is that?"

"Claudia, what if God was using this situation to work out something great in our lives and our families' lives? Wouldn't you want that?"

"What good could come out of this? This is a horrible thing that has happened to us? What did we do to deserve this?"

"Claudia, just because we have been forgiven by Jesus doesn't make us exempt from the bad things that happen in this world. The Bible tells us that we need to rejoice in all things. We might not understand how, but God will bring good out of the most evil of intentions. Just like Joseph's testimony to his brothers when he said, 'you did not send me here, God sent me here to save our families.' I don't know why we are here Claudia, but I do know that God is with us and He has a plan for us and He will bring good out of it."

"Maybe He will, but I still don't like it," said Claudia.

"I didn't say that I liked it. I said that God would bring good out of it. Who can know but Him what that good might turn out to be. Even if we die here, God can use that too."

"Tricia, I'm scared! I'm afraid what that creep is going to do to us when he returns."

"Claudia, we have a few days until he returns and until he does I think that there are some things that we can and should do until then. I think we need to make sure that we eat so that we can have enough strength to do whatever God wants us to do. I also think that we should try to find a way out of here. This is not like a maximum security prison like Pelican Bay or something. There has to be a way out. Sooner or later we should be able to get out of here. And I think we should find or make some weapons to have ready for when he does return. Maybe we will have a chance to overpower him and get out that way."

"Even if we do manage to get out, he said that we are 25 or 30 feet up in the air. What do we do about that? He also said that we are miles from nowhere. We don't even have a clue where we are; let alone know which way to go to get help."

"Claudia, let's take it one step at a time and see how God will help us to take the next step. When we get out we will trust him to show us how to get down. Then we will trust him to show us which direction to go."

"Let me go to the bathroom and get freshened up a bit. Do you want to find us something to eat? Then we can start checking this place out to see what weapons we can find; and maybe find a place where we can start attacking to try breaking out of here," said Claudia.

"It sounds like a deal," said Tricia.

So while Claudia was in the bathroom, Tricia whipped up some chicken noodle soup she found in the pantry and made some toasted cheese sandwiches. Not exactly breakfast food, but it was approaching lunch time and this sounded more like comfort food, at least to Tricia.

Claudia devoured her soup and sandwich like it had been a couple of days since she had eaten. As they were cleaning up and washing the dishes Claudia said, "Thank you, Tricia for everything; for lunch, it hit the spot; and for encouraging me and helping me get my eyes off of my situation and focused on where our help will come from. You have been the best friend to me that I have ever had in my life. No matter how this turns out, I want you to know that. Thank you so much."

"Claudia, I have not always been such a great friend to anyone. I can be pretty selfish at times, but God is working on changing me to be more like Jesus. He is the best friend ever. I can only hope to be a small fraction of the friend that he is. Come on! Let's see what we can find in this place. You want to start around here and I will start over there on the other side of the bed. Remember, we are looking for either some type of weapon or some way out of here."

"OK!"

It was Tricia looking on the other side of the bed that discovered something of interest first. "Claudia, come take a look at this! It looks like someone else tried to break out of here. Maybe we can finish the job that they have already started. What do you think?"

Claudia came to examine what Tricia had found and saw that someone had used something to scratch a small hole through the shell of the sphere to the outside. The hole was located underneath of the bed where it wouldn't be easily detected. They could see daylight through the hole so it gave them hope that maybe in time they could enlarge it enough to get out of it. Tricia grabbed a spoon and started digging at it to see how difficult it would be to make a larger hole. She dug for an hour and a half and couldn't tell if she had changed anything on the hole or not. Finally she said, "I am going to keep looking around here to see if there might be some other way out. We can keep this hole as an option, but it will take a long time at the rate that I am going."

Claudia's search didn't produce any results either. She had tried working on the door, but it had appeared to have some type of locking mechanism on the outside of the door that held it shut and in place, so she too abandoned that effort and sat down on the edge of the bed and began to cry softly.

Tricia came and sat down next to her and said, "It is getting late. We will try again tomorrow. Maybe tomorrow we will find the key. Let's fix some dinner. What would you like to have for supper tonight?"

# 35

❦

The FBI had found a small office in the police station that they could use as their temporary field office while they were working this case in Crescent City. It had ended up as a catch-all space for the department so even after they had spent a couple of hours cleaning it up there were still some boxes and odd pieces of furniture that no one knew what to do with and they couldn't just pitch out. So by the time they shoved a small desk that they had rounded up from somewhere and a couple of chairs the room was getting pretty crowded and then when you tried to stuff six FBI agents in as well, it was almost unbearable.

That's where agent Lonnie found himself Friday morning after his return trip to San Francisco and back since Wednesday afternoon. He had called for a debriefing meeting as soon as he had arrived to find out what, if anything the forensics team had discovered in the short time that they had been on the case.

"OK people, who wants to go first? Tell me what we have so far," said agent Lonnie.

"Sir, at Tricia's house we found a small transmitting camera in her bedroom and when we talked to her son, he said that they found one that looked just like it in the bathroom that had fallen off of the wall about 3 or 4 weeks ago and they didn't think much about it," said agent Raul.

"Did you run the manufacturer on it and then see if we can get any kind of distributor located and maybe a customer on that camera," asked agent Lonnie?

"We tried sir. The manufacturer has been out of business for 3 years now and no one we have contacted so far seems to be selling this brand anymore. So it seems that road is a dead-end," said agent Raul.

"What about prints? Any prints in either of those houses or on the cameras," asked agent Lonnie?

"Negative sir, we didn't find any prints except the ones that should have been there," said agent Nick.

"Any hair or anything else that we could do a DNA analysis on," asked agent Lonnie?

"No on that one too," said agent Jan.

"Come on people; tell me you found something that we can use. What about the neighbors? Anyone see anything unusual," asked agent Lonnie?

"We haven't contacted all of the neighbors yet sir but no one that we have talked to yet saw anything unusual that night," said agent Raul.

"Well, keep working the neighbor angle. Maybe you will find someone that saw something," said agent Lonnie.

"Sir, we did find a strange little contraption in Claudia's bedroom that appears to be some type of flying drone and it has a stinger on it with some type of liquid in it. We have sent the liquid to the lab to be analyzed. The drone we have traced down and we found out that a shipment of a dozen of them was sent here to Crescent City to a Walter Green at a mail stop box in town. And when we checked with them they had no other information on this Walter Green guy. Their application for the box shows that the guy that took it looked at his California driver's license for an ID, but he didn't write the number down. That was 15 years ago and that employee is long gone. We are trying to track him down, but haven't had much luck with that," said agent Maurice.

"That may turn into something we can use. Keep on it. Have you checked out the boats in the area? Maybe the guy used a boat to take them away," said agent Lonnie.

"No sir, we have not done that yet," said agent Jan.

"What else are we overlooking? Have you checked the two ladies phones for unusual phone calls? I assume that since their purses are still in their houses that their cell phones will be in the purses. What about our psychic? Has she had anymore revelations; a vision or whatever it was about them being in trouble," asked agent Lonnie?

"Sir, please don't call her a psychic. What that lady experienced is 180 degrees away from what a psychic does. If you want me to explain it further for you sometime I will be glad to do it, but just don't call her a psychic," said agent Maurice.

"OK, she is not a psychic. She seemed pretty dead on with what she saw though. Has she had any more of those types of revelations," asked agent Lonnie?

"She has not mentioned them to us sir and I would have to believe that if anything else like that were revealed to her she would let us know right away," said agent Maurice.

"Very well, I was hoping that we would have a little more concrete evidence to go on by now, but keep at it. This guy, whoever he or she is, is good. But no matter how good they are they always slip up sometime and when they do, we will catch them. All right, let's get back out there and turn a few stones over," said agent Lonnie.

The rest of Friday and Saturday went the same way. Not much evidence to go on and they couldn't find anyone that had seen anything on the night that Tricia and Claudia had disappeared. Agent Lonnie was starting to get frustrated with their results or should I say lack of results.

In the early morning hours on Saturday, Pastor Grime's phone rang. He was just in that dreamy state of sleep where you are not quite aware of what is happening when he heard the phone ringing. At first he thought that the ringing was part of the dream he was having and then he came to his senses and knew that it was indeed his phone. He doesn't know how many rings it had already rung, but he was sure that it was just about ready to go to the answering machine when he picked it up. He answered it with a groggy, "Helloooo."

"Pastor Gre-MAY, this is Pelican Bay prison calling and the warden instructed us to call you at any time if either Mark Noyes or Ricardo Sanchez wanted to talk to you. Mark has been asking for you; rather should I say he has been yelling and throwing a fit to have you come talk to him"

"All right, let me get some clothes on and I will be right down there. Should I ask for someone in particular or...?"

"Sir, all of the guards are very aware of the situation and can help you get to where you can talk to Mark."

"Very well, I will see you in about twenty or twenty-five minutes," said Pastor Grime.

When he got there Pastor Grime found Mark already waiting for him in the visitor's waiting room. After the security check, the pastor was ushered into the room where he sat down in a chair opposite Mark.

"Mark, I am Pastor Grime. If it is easier you can call me Tony. Actually my name is Anthony, but close friends call me Tony. So you can call me Tony. Let me say how sorry I am about Tricia's disappearance. She is a great gal. You are a lucky man to have a wife like her."

"I know, I don't know what I would do if anything happened to her. I think that it would kill me," said Mark.

"So, Mark, what is troubling you right now? How can I help you?"

"Tony, it is eating me up sitting in here not being out there searching for her. Are they making any progress in locating her?"

"Mark, I wish I could tell you that they are getting close to finding her, but I have tried to stay out of the way of the professionals that are doing the searching. I have been fasting and praying to God, believing that he has the solution right there ready to divulge."

"Pastor, my wife is a really good woman now. She didn't use to be, but something has changed in her and now she is a pleasure to be with. I find that I keep anticipating the day when she would come see me again. And now that she can't, I really miss her. What happened to her? What changed her? Is it something that I can get?"

"Mark, what makes your wife so beautiful and attractive is that she has asked Jesus to forgive her for living her old way of life and invited him to change her into a person more like him. And he has done just that. What you see, is Jesus shining through your wife's life and it is attractive to you. If you want it you can have it too; it's free, all you have to do is ask for it. Would you like to ask Jesus to forgive you and change you right now?"

"I think that I am too rotten. I have done some very bad things in my life. If I were Jesus I wouldn't want me either."

"Mark, none of us are good enough to come to Jesus. It is by his grace that anyone is forgiven and changed. He loved you enough to die for you no matter how evil you or I have been. We can't earn it; we can't be 'good' enough, that's why it's called grace."

"Pastor, I do want this in my life."

"Mark, I want to warn you. Just because you ask Jesus to forgive you and change you, it doesn't mean that your wife will automatically reappear. She may never turn up. But I can guarantee you that whatever happens, you can be at peace with it because you can know that Jesus has taken care of her."

"Somehow I knew that would be the case. But I still want this change to happen to me. There are times that I can hardly stand to live with myself. I don't know how my wife has put up with me sometimes."

"Like I said Mark, it is a pretty simple process. Just ask Jesus to forgive you and to change you into a new better person."

And Mark did just that. And that transformation began right then and there. When they got up Pastor Grime grabbed him and gave him a big hug. He was not aware of the visitor rules of no contact and he had Mark hugged before the guards knew what was happening. When they were finished, the guards warned Pastor Grime about the rules and told him that they would let it slip this time, but not to let it happen again.

Pastor Grime left Pelican Bay a little bit lighter that day than he had been the last few days. If only Tricia could be here to realize this same joy. And Mark went back to his cell a changed man. The anxiety was no longer eating his insides out and the anger that was burning him up was no longer there. Instead a peace that it would all be OK that he had never experienced before in his entire life had settled inside of him.

Sunday morning rolled around and no one from Living Waters Fellowship felt like going to church this morning. In fact they had not felt like doing much of anything since they had heard the news about Tricia and Claudia, but they went anyway because they were family and that is what families do; they stick together when times are tough. As they came in, soft, meditative music was playing over the sound system in the sanctuary. Everyone came in quietly and sat in the pew that they normally liked to sit in without saying much to each other. When it was time for the service to begin, Pastor Grime got up and said, "I think most of you already know that two members of our family were abducted last Wednesday morning. So far no clues have been found as to where they might be. We serve a mighty God who knows all things. He knows where they are and he can rescue them. Some of us have been fasting and praying and others have been praying that they will be returned to us safe and sound. I would like to have a little different type of service this morning. We are going to dispense with the regular music and with the preaching and I would like as many as can to spend this time in prayer for Tricia and Claudia. We will have no benediction, when you feel you must go, just leave quietly without disturbing those that are still praying."

And with that brief explanation of the service that morning, the church got down to the business of the church; praying that God's hand would be moved. It was almost dark when Pastor Grime finally looked around to see that he was the last one there and that he should probably close up the church and head for home. But somehow, he knew deep down inside of him that God's hand was about to move; how he was not sure, but he just felt like something was about to happen.

# 36

✠

Tricia and Claudia spent all day Friday, Saturday and Sunday looking for the weakness in their spherical tree house prison, but to no avail. Tricia had gone back to the small hole in the floor that was under the bed several times, but she could not make any progress on enlarging the hole. Likewise, they hadn't had much success in finding anything that might work as a weapon on Stan-daddy when he returned. Hopelessness and despair were beginning to gnaw at the edges of their consciousness and they were starting to snap at each other. They knew the longer that they were held captive there in that place the harder it would be to escape and get away from the monster that had taken them from their homes, their loved ones and their lives. And there was a very real possibility that they might never get back to those things. How could someone be so cruel, so selfish?

Knowing that they were running out of time, they finally took a couple of really dull knives from the kitchen and placed them by the door where Stan wouldn't be able to see them from outside the door. Their plan, as lame as it was, was to rush Stan when he entered the sphere, grab the knives on the way by and attack him with the knives at the same time. They thought that with two of them they might be able to overwhelm him and thus gain the upper hand.

They breathed a little prayer together asking for God's help and protection in their attempt and then they just sat there. Every little noise made them jump and listen closer to see if it might be him coming. They asked each other if it was going to be like this every time he was going to appear.

Meanwhile, Stan had been eagerly awaiting the end of his shift so that he could make a run to his cabin before dark set in. He had the boat already loaded with the non-perishable items that he was taking to the cabin, that way all he would have to do would be to load the fresh items in the boat and cast off. The day dragged on and on for Stan, but when the clock hit his clock out time he was gone. You couldn't have paid him any amount of money to work overtime on this night. He had a date with destiny and he aimed to keep it. His wives were calling. How could you keep your newly 'wed' wives waiting? He had already kept them waiting for 5 days as it was.

His mind was so filled with thinking about Tricia and Claudia that he couldn't even remember getting into his car in the prison employee parking lot let alone the actual mechanics of driving to his house. From the time he had clocked out at the prison until he started the motor on his boat was exactly 44 minutes and that included driving home, changing his clothes, loading the remainder of the items that he was taking to the cabin into the boat and closing up his house.

Stan couldn't be on autopilot steering the boat through the ocean to the bay where the dock for his cabin was like he was in the car on the drive home. The ocean was too rough and the wind was blowing at a pretty good clip so he had to pay attention at all times and continue to make course corrections to counteract the force of the current and the gusts of wind that wanted to send him off in another direction. Because of this it took Stan longer than usual to make the journey from the dock at his house to the dock at his cabin. It was so much longer that by the time he pulled up to the dock it was already quite dark out.

He had wanted to get here when it was still light, but this would have to do. He already had an idea of the type of reception that he would receive from the girls Why would they be any different from any of the other girls that he had taken, but he always had hope that they would welcome him with arms wide open and a big, long-lasting kiss that said, *"what took you so long, I have missed you."* But that only happened in the fairy tales, this wasn't a fantasy, this was reality; real life. Those kinds of things didn't happen in real life. So he steeled himself for the most likely of scenarios; that they would be lying in wait for him ready to kill him if there was any possible way to do that.

Since he had to work with a flashlight anyway, Stan took his time unloading the boat into the cart and then pushing the cart up to his tree where the cable hoist was. The sphere of the tree house was silhouetted by an almost full moon. He could also see the few small windows that the sphere had glowing yellow from the lights inside the sphere. His heart started to beat a little faster now thinking again about the two women up there in his cabin waiting for him to come home. He would take a few things (the perishable items) up with him on this first trip and let them know that he had arrived. When he reached the platform, he put his load down on the platform and reeled the sphere in from the middle of the suspended cable so that it was docked next to the platform.

There could be no surprise visits here. His arrival would have already been announced and they were probably waiting for him to come through the doorway. He looked through the small porthole in the door and couldn't see them anywhere so he told them over an intercom system to stand in front of the door with their hands held straight out. He could see them moving reluctantly into position and slowly raising their arms out in front of them. When Stan was satisfied that they didn't have any weapons on them he slowly opened the door looking cautiously all around and above him. He spotted the two knives on either side of the doorway and said to himself, *"so you want to play this game."*

When he had gotten far enough into the room the two women rushed at him trying to grab a knife on the way by. But Stan was prepared for their antics, Claudia was slightly ahead of Tricia so she received the brunt of the taser. Once she was down on the floor writhing in pain, Stan turned his attention on Tricia. What they didn't know was that Stan was an 8 Dang Thuong Dang (highest level of 'black belt' attainable in the Qwan Ki Do martial arts of Vietnam; but the belt was actually white with red and a yellow edge). Tricia was no match for a man trained like this. A couple of quick moves had sent the knife flying across the room and Tricia was smashed down onto the floor and gasping for breath.

Stan had moved over Tricia and was just about ready to deliver another blow to her when they all heard a low rumble that seemed to crescendo in pitch and intensity. Then they heard several loud cracking noises. That was followed by the sphere swinging wildly back and forth. It was so violent that Stan almost lost his balance and was sent falling across the room before he caught himself on the kitchen counter. After the oscillations of the sphere had slowed down and it stopped pretending that it was a pendulum, the three of them looked from one to the other asking the same question, "What was that?"

Stan said, "I am going out to find out what that was. Don't think that you have escaped the wrath of Stan. I will be back and when I return we will continue where I left off. It seems that I need to teach my wives that they need to respect their husband. I will not stand for a disrespectful wife. Think about that while I am out. Maybe I won't continue if you come begging me for mercy."

Stan went out the door, slamming it behind him as he went. Tricia went over to where Claudia was still lying on the floor curled in the fetal position whimpering. Tricia helped her up and over by the bed where they huddled together.

All that Stan could see was that it looked like one of the trees that was supporting the sphere might have been leaning a little bit more than it was earlier, but he couldn't tell for sure. He decided to go down and check the tree out and bring another load back up with him. This way it would give his wives more time to think about their actions and whether they wanted to continue down the road that they were going.

Stan hooked himself up to the winch cable and started lowering himself down like he had hundreds of times before. However, this time, the only time that it has ever done this in all of those hundreds of times going up and down, Stan got down to where he was about 12 feet off the ground and the cable jammed and he stopped descending. He tried going back up and it wouldn't budge. He was stuck there and stuck good; he couldn't go up or down, stuck.

He was fiddling with the harness and the connector and failed to notice the wall of water that was moving quickly ashore and up to meet him. What they had heard and felt was an earthquake centered about 10 miles offshore due west of the cabin. That earthquake had spawned a tsunami that was now bearing down on a helpless Stan fighting with the hoisting cable that had somehow jammed and had left him dangling 12 feet off the ground. When the full force of the water hit Stan he didn't even see it coming. In a matter of seconds he was 10 feet under water and the waves treated him like he was a tetherball on a rope; it took him and wrapped him around and around the tree pinning him underwater with no hope of swimming to the surface or of clinging to the tree until the water surge had retreated. Justice was meted out to Stan Wosniak in the same manner that he had snuffed out the lives, hopes and dreams of a dozen other young women. Justice served without chance of appeal or pardon. The ocean had claimed him like he had forced it to claim the lives of his victims, but the ocean dwellers wouldn't have the same opportunity to dine on him as they did his victims.

Tricia and Claudia heard the rush of the water and swayed back and forth as the tsunami buffeted the trees. The water didn't get as high as the sphere so they weren't in any danger from that, but when the waters had receded back into the oceans' confines, the one tree was leaning precariously. However, Tricia and Claudia couldn't know that from the inside because the sphere hung level once the swinging had stopped.

They had no idea what had happened to Stan. They expected him to come bursting through the doorway at any minute and take up where he had left off with his beatings. All night long they huddled together comforting and protecting each other, dozing off a few times only to be abruptly brought back to wakefulness by some noise or some nightmare or just from being in one position too long.

After it had been light for about an hour, Tricia couldn't take it any longer. She needed to move; she needed to find out what had happened. She slowly got up, stretching as she stood and gingerly made her way across the room to the door. In the moving, Tricia realized that every muscle in her body screamed out in pain. She couldn't tell if there was one single place on her body that didn't ache. She didn't think that anything was broken, but it sure did hurt. She couldn't remember ever hurting this much in her entire life; and she had had some very major injuries in the past.

When she got to the door and tried it, she discovered that Stan had failed to lock it from the outside when he left last night. Cautiously she opened the door half expecting Stan to be on the other side just waiting for them to come out so that he would have an excuse to beat the tar out of them again. But he was not there; in fact the platform was now sitting at an angle to the sphere. Not a steep angle, but nonetheless it was not level and it took all that Tricia had to stand on it and maintain her balance.

As she began sweeping her eyes across the landscape she saw the devastation that the water from the tsunami had caused. It looked like all of the trees and shrubs that were still standing had been run through one of those stripping machines that took all of the branches and leaves off the trunk; but only up to a certain level and then the foliage was just like it was before. Of course, Tricia didn't know what the before picture was other than what she could she from the tiny little windows in the sphere.

Tricia went and stood in the doorway to the sphere and said, "Claudia, come look at this. You will never believe this landscape."

Claudia came outside reluctantly, but when she did, she was as flabbergasted as Tricia had been and maybe more so. Claudia began scanning the landscape just like Tricia had done, except that she also looked down and that is when she saw him; their captor. He was wound around the tree like a ribbon attached to the top of a May pole on May Day after the celebration is finished. Claudia said, "Look Tricia, there he is! And it doesn't look like he is moving!"

"I think you are right. The Lord has rescued us," said Tricia.

Claudia was just about ready to say something about how were they ever going to get down from there when they heard it; the distinctive chop chop chop of helicopter blades slicing through the air. When they finally spotted where the sound was coming from they could see it following the coastline and approaching their location. Tricia hurried as fast as she could back inside and grabbed a couple of white dish towels from the kitchen. Coming back outside, she gave Claudia one and the both of them began waving them frantically back and forth over their heads hoping that whoever was on board would notice two women up in a tree waving white towels; they waved them like their lives depended on it.

# 37

✠

When the residents of Crescent City awoke Monday morning, they were greeted with the aftermath of the tsunami that had struck the coast late Sunday night. Initial reports were that no major structural damage had been sustained by the surge of water that had swept into town. There was going to be some major work that would be needed in cleaning up the mess that the water left behind when it receded back into the ocean. Everywhere you looked you could see flotsam, seaweed, dead fish and crabs as well as other debris the ocean had collected from someplace and had redistributed. Several of the places that were close to the shoreline had water still standing inside of them and they were going to need some major drying out and cleaning before they would be able to be used again.

But it was not like Crescent City had never been here before; they had. Many of the residents had been here during the last major tsunami in 1964. Although there had been many new residents added to the city since that time, there were enough of the 'old-timers' around that knew what to do and how to do it, that it didn't take the town very long to organize and get busy doing the things that needed to be done right away. They also knew which things could be put off for a few days without causing any additional problems that were worse than what they would have to deal with at that later date.

Since there had been very little warning of the impending disaster, the city council, at the mayor's request, began looking at ways to improve the warning response time for the future. But it was going to be an exercise in futility. The speed at which the tsunami had formed and had surged ashore would be difficult to detect and sound the warning, let alone give people time enough to evacuate to higher ground. But it would satiate the people that were clamoring for something more to be done to protect lives and property.

The police department had some minor flooding, but not enough to force them to move elsewhere to conduct their business. Agent Lonnie was in his tight little office behind his child-size desk early Monday morning. He was sitting there shuffling papers when agent Raul burst into his office with the latest news, "Sir, we made contact with one of Claudia Sanchez's neighbors, an older gentleman, that has been out of town since we started talking to all of them. He said that he noted a strange car in the neighborhood with a guy just sitting there working on a laptop about 3 or 4 weeks ago. He thought that it was strange at the time since it was about 10:30 or 11:00 at night so he jotted down the make and model of the car and the license plate number. When we ran the number with the state it came back registered to a Stan Wozniak. Stan is a prison guard here at Pelican Bay. In checking with the prison this morning they said that he was off today and tomorrow. We went by his house after that, but no one came to the door. He must have gone out of town or something. When we went out to the prison we were able to talk to another guard that used to be his friend but they had a falling out not to long ago so he didn't know what he was doing now. He did say that he had a cabin somewhere that he went to quite often. He didn't even have a general direction where the cabin might be. He really didn't know much else."

"It is probably nothing, but keep on pursuing that lead. We don't have much else right now to go on. And I guess we will have to wait until this guard returns from wherever he went to, to be able to question him on his activities," said agent Lonnie.

"Did we get anything on that serum that was in that drone thing," asked agent Lonnie?

"Not definitive sir. Preliminary results are that it is some type of a sedative or sleeping potion similar to the date rape drug, rohypnol," said agent Raul.

"Very well, keep me informed if you have any further developments," said agent Lonnie.

Because of the tsunami the Coast Guard had sent out helicopters and boats to patrol the coastline looking to see if anyone had been stranded by the surge water. One of the helicopters flying along the coast was approaching the spherical tree-house from the South when the spotter on the craft called out to the pilot over the intercom, "Looks like two people up in that tree waving white rags."

"Where," asked the pilot?

"At two o'clock up in the tops of the trees. They are standing on a platform next to a big round ball of some type. It almost looks like it might be some sort of living quarters," said the spotter.

"You're right! I see it! I am going to get a little closer and circle it to see if they need some help," said the pilot.

"From the looks of the tree that is holding up that ball, I would say yes they need some help," said the spotter.

"There is no place that I can land this thing. Do you want to ride the cable down to them or should we send someone back for them," asked the pilot?

"Let's try the cable, the wind isn't blowing very hard so we should be able to drop right down there on them without much trouble," said the spotter.

"OK! Let me know when to lower you," said the pilot.

"That is looking really good right there. I am in the harness and ready to go. Start the winch," said the spotter.

Tricia and Claudia were overjoyed that their prayers had been answered when it dawned on them that the helicopter had spotted them and was sending down someone to rescue them from their predicament. The spotter landed perfectly on the platform and hooked up Claudia into the harness with him. He relayed up to the helicopter to bring them up. After Claudia and the spotter had lifted off and was almost up to the helicopter, Tricia began having a mild attack of anxiety thinking that she was going to be left here all alone. But in that quick span of time she heard it again; that quiet voice within her that said, *"Trust Me! Trust Me! I am still here with you. I will never leave you!"* And as quickly as the anxiety and panic had set in, so too the peace and assurance that comes from trusting in Jesus flooded in like the surge waters of a tsunami and dispelled all of the fear and anxiety that had just as suddenly threatened her security.

It was not much longer afterwards that the spotter came back down to put her in the harness and hoist her up into the safety of the helicopter. Up in the helicopter they were each given a set of headphones with a microphone attached so that they could communicate with the helicopter crew. The pilot asked, "Is there anymore down there?"

Tricia replied, "Only that monster that kidnapped us and he is wrapped around the tree. I think that he must be dead."

None of the crew had seen Stan yet because of the direction that they had approached the scene and the side of the tree that he was pinned to, but when they moved the helicopter and looked closer, then they could see him held tightly against the tree by the cable that he had used to lift himself up and down to the tree house. The spotter looking through binoculars said, "I think you are right. He is not moving at all."

"Let's get you two to the hospital! We can send someone back here on land to see about him," said the pilot.

"I don't think we need to go to the hospital, do you Claudia? I want to get home to my family," said Tricia.

"I don't want to go to the hospital either," said Claudia.

"Very well! You gals are the boss! I will take you to Crescent City," said the pilot.

About 5 minutes into the 20 minute flight to Crescent City, both Tricia and Claudia were sleeping like babies. The tension from the past 5 days, the security of being in a safe environment, the sound and vibration of the helicopter, and the comfortable seats all combined into a womb like state that the women succumbed to without much effort. And before they were ready, they had arrived at the airport in Crescent City. As much as they wanted to see family and friends and to be back home, they really wouldn't have minded if the helicopter would have taken a long detour to get there. The pilot of the helicopter had radioed on ahead that he had picked up a couple of passengers named Tricia Noyes and Claudia Sanchez and he was in route to the airport in Crescent City.

When the news that Tricia and Claudia had been found and rescued, it went like a wildfire throughout the town sending waves of hope to all who heard it. Where the mood of the town had been dark and gloomy because of the recent kidnappings and the flooding that had just been caused by the tsunami, that mood was now joyous and celebratory even though the sky and weather was still the dark gloomy gray that it is much of the time. And before the helicopter reached the airfield, a small group of 125 to 150 people had dropped everything and hurried to the airport to greet them.

Some of the notables that made the welcoming party were the mayor, the police chief, FBI agent Lonnie and 4 of his field agents, Pastor Grime, Steve the manager of the Chart Room Restaurant, and of course Ralph, BJ, Rod, Timmy and Candy. Timmy and Candy could hardly contain themselves as they waited for the helicopter to arrive. They had missed their mommy so very much in those 5 days that she was missing. They had tried to keep their hopes up that she would return safe and sound, but each passing day that hope was being eroded away little by little, but now they were just ecstatic.

When Pastor Grime had told them about their dad and how he had begun a relationship with Jesus, they made him take them out to see him the next time he could have visitors. Their meeting had been bittersweet; they were happy that their father had become a new, changed person, but they were also sad by the fact that Tricia was missing. Timmy and Candy begged (actually they didn't have to beg very hard at all) Pastor Grime to take them to the prison every day during visiting hours to see their father. For some reason they seemed to get some consolation by being with him.

Timmy was the first one to spot the helicopter coming and he started yelling, "There it is! There it is! Here comes my mommy!"

At that, the crowd began clapping and cheering, partly out of a release of tension and partly because of their joy and excitement that the women were returning home safe. As the helicopter settled to the ground, the noise of the crowd almost drowned the engine and the whirring blades of the helicopter. Timmy and Candy pushed their way to the front of the crowd to get a better view and to get closer to their mom. The side door of the helicopter opened and a Coast Guard crewman got out first. To the disappointment of Timmy and Candy, the next one out of the helicopter was Claudia and the crowd erupted in clapping and cheering all over again. But their disappointment was short-lived; as soon as Claudia was out, the next one out the door was Tricia. With the trained ear of a mother to her children she heard it loud and clear even above the clapping and cheering and the noise of the helicopter; she heard, "MOM!" and "MOMMY!" coming from her two beautiful children Timmy and Candy.

There has never been a sweeter reunion than what took place that day on the little airstrip in Crescent City between a mother that had been missing for 5 days and her two young children. The hugs and kisses and tears of joy were going to be a memorial stone for all of them for the rest of their lives. No one present that day would ever be able to forget the pent up emotion that was released in that reuniting.

Claudia was almost feeling a little jealous, a little left out when BJ came over to her and threw her arms around her and welcomed her back. And there wasn't a dry eye anywhere; even Ralph, emotionless, stoic Ralph, had watery eyes.

In all of the commotion, the helicopter had lifted off and was headed back to their base a little prouder that they had helped make that joyous occasion happen. It made all of their efforts worth it to see the reunion that had just taken place, but it was especially heart-warming to see those two young children getting their mother back. That crew would sleep well tonight knowing that those two children had their mother with them again.

One by one, the crowd slowly left and went back to whatever they were doing when the call reached them telling them of the good news. Before he left, Steve, Tricia's manager at the restaurant, came over to her and said, "Don't worry, I'm still holding your job for you. Take your time in coming back. Just give me a call when you're ready and I will put you back on the schedule."

"Thanks, Steve I appreciate that. I would like a day or two with my kids," said Tricia.

"Like I said, take all the time you need," said Steve.

When most of the people had gone, agent Lonnie, came over to where Tricia and Claudia were and said, "I really would like to talk to the both of you about what you have been through if you are up to it; maybe tomorrow?"

"What do you think Claudia, can you handle talking about this tomorrow," asked Tricia?

"Not really, but I know that we need to. Not too early though," said Claudia.

"Is 10 o'clock too early," asked agent Lonnie?

"I think that will work," said Claudia.

"That will work for me too," said Tricia.

"All right, I will see both of you tomorrow. My office is in the police department. Here is my card, just ask for me at the front desk and they will show you back," said agent Lonnie.

As he was walking away, BJ said, "Do you two want to come over to my house for a bite of lunch?"

Tricia hesitantly said, "I...huh...really wanted to get cleaned up and go out to see my husband during visiting hours this afternoon."

"You don't need to stay long. It won't take me very long to fix it and then you can leave as soon as you've eaten. Besides, you need to eat something," said BJ.

"All right, but someone will have to give me a ride home," said Tricia.

"That can be arranged. Pastor, you are invited too," said BJ.

"I can't stay very long either, but I will take you up on your offer. I haven't had a decent meal in 5 days," said Pastor Grime.

"What do you mean pastor? You haven't had any meal for 5 days," said BJ.

"You didn't eat for 5 days! Were you sick," asked Tricia?

"Pastor and several others have been fasting and praying for you and Claudia ever since you turned up missing," said BJ.

At that news, both Tricia and Claudia started crying all over again.

"I can't believe that you would do that for me; for us," said Claudia.

"Both of you are part of our family and when you turned up missing, it was like part of me that was gone and it hurt. It hurt real bad. And the only thing that I knew to do was to fast and to cry out to God to have mercy on you. And he did, Praise his name forever," said Pastor Grime.

"Come on, we can share our side of the story while we eat and if you want to you can share your side, but you don't have to," said BJ.

"I don't think that I am ready to do that," said Claudia. "I am not even sure that I am ready to go back to my house."

BJ had been thinking about this already and she said, "Claudia, and you too Tricia if you want to, are more than welcome to stay at my house until you are ready to go back there or until you get another place to live."

"I appreciate the offer BJ, but my children need to be in their own home with their mother," said Tricia.

"But I'm going to take you up on your offer," said Claudia.

"OK everyone over to my house," said BJ.

"Pastor, can we ride with you? It looks like Ralph and BJ have a car full," said Tricia.

"We want to go with you, mommy," said Candy.

"You can come with us," said Pastor Grime.

They all made it to BJ's house where she had lunch whipped up in no time. BJ and pastor shared their stories, particularly their visions and then the rest of the night that they had spent praying for God's help that fateful night when Tricia and Claudia had been kidnapped. Neither Tricia nor Claudia said much the entire time that they were telling it. Nor did they tell their story. It was still too painful; still too fresh. They needed to distance themselves from it a little more and be in a more secure environment; they needed a place where it was more intimate, fewer ears, less distraction, a lower chance of condemnation. And they didn't feel that it was here now.

Finishing lunch BJ said, "Tricia you run along now and go see that husband of yours. He has been worried sick about you. And he has something special he wants to tell you."

"Tell me what," asked Tricia?

"I'm not going to spoil it. You go find out from him," said BJ.

"I know mommy. I know," exclaimed Candy.

"Shhhhh. Remember, let daddy tell her," said BJ.

"I will," said Candy.

"Timmy, Candy why don't you stay here until your mom comes back from the prison," said BJ.

"That's a wonderful idea, BJ. I will be right back kids. Don't worry," said Tricia.

"We didn't worry mom," said Timmy trying to sound brave and confident.

Tricia kissed them both again and then went out the door to get in the car with Pastor Grime. When they got to Tricia's house, pastor asked, "Do you want me to go in with you?"

"Would you mind? I know that it is all taken care of and all, but it might freak me out going in there for the first time since..."

"It's OK, I understand. Come on I'll go with you," said pastor.

It was not as bad as Tricia had expected it to be. In fact, because she could not recall any of the events surrounding the actual abduction, it was like coming home from being on a vacation for a few days. Once she discovered that, she told the pastor that she would be alright and said her goodbyes and thanks' to him. One of the first things that she did was to check her phone for messages. She saw that the lawyer that had been handling Mark's case and appeal had called 7 times and said that it was urgent that he talk to her about the new developments in Mark's case.

Tricia wanted to get cleaned up and head out to the prison, but she decided that this must be very important and that she should probably call the lawyer before going out to the prison. When she called the lawyer's office and identified herself, the receptionist said that it was urgent that the lawyer talk to her and please hold on while she got him on the line. While she was waiting for him to pick up, her cell phone started beeping the low battery song. It had been over 5 days since it had been recharged and she kept praying that it would last until she could talk to the lawyer. It was going to be hard enough to hear what he had to say without having to hear over that incessant beeping sound.

"Hello Tricia! So glad you called. Have you been out of cell phone range or something," asked the lawyer?

"Yeah, something like that," said Tricia. If he hadn't seen it in the papers, she didn't want to tell him all about it, at least not now.

"I have some good news for you and Mark. They have arrested another man that has confessed to the crime that Mark was accused and convicted of. They caught him in a robbery that had the same MO as the one Mark was accused of committing. He also confessed that they set Mark up to take the heat for the robbery that they committed. It is going to take the state a few more days to process the paperwork and then they will release Mark," said the lawyer.

After a long silence the lawyer finally spoke up again and said, "Tricia, are you OK?"

"Yes, I'm just speechless. I don't know what to say. This is the most wonderful news. I am going right out and tell Mark."

"You do just that," said the lawyer. "Goodbye, I'll keep in touch."

"Goodbye, and thank you for everything," said Tricia.

Tricia flew around getting a shower and clean clothes on before heading out to the prison. Her reunion with her husband was almost as wonderful as it was with her children in the morning except that they couldn't hug or kiss or even hold hands. But it was wonderful just the same. You couldn't tell which one was the happier, Mark or Tricia. And when they started to tell each other the wonderful news that they wanted to share with each other they fought over who would tell the other their news first.

Once they had both told the other, the joy and the tears started and they wouldn't stop. The guards finally had to tell them that the visiting hours were over and they had to break it up. The difference this time was there wasn't the sadness and heaviness of parting that went with them back to their respective places; he to his cell and she to her house without a spouse. No, this time a joy and an expectancy of what the future held for them as a couple and a family burned inside them.

# 38

❧

Tricia and Claudia's Tuesday morning meeting with agent Lonnie of the FBI in his small cubby hole of an office at the police station confirmed the FBI's mounting suspicion of Pelican Bay prison guard Stan Wozniak of being the perpetrator behind the disappearance of close to a dozen women or maybe more over the course of that many years. After questioning the two women the FBI obtained a search warrant for Stan's house and a team was sent out to the location of the spherical tree house cabin to obtain evidence and retrieve Stan's body that had been adhered to the tree by the winch cable that he was fastened to and couldn't free himself from when the tsunami hit.

Searching Stan's house they found all of his video surveillance equipment, the video's of several of the women and the houses they had been abducted from, the drones like the one that they had found on the floor at Claudia's house, vials of liquid that was presumably the sedative that he used, several notebooks filled with notes on the women that had been missing and a final entry that merely read, *"FISH FOOD."* They also found stacks of printed photos and on one of his hard drives the digital copies of all the women that had been missing in various states of undress.

The warden and the other guards thought at first that there must be a case of mistaken identity; there was no way that the Stan that worked there could have done all of those horrible things, but as the story kept unfolding and the evidence kept coming in that pointed the finger directly at him they couldn't continue in their denial. The question that everyone kept coming back to was always, *"How did we miss it? How did he fool us for so long?"* And no one had an answer. It hit Frank, his fellow guard and 'friend', particularly hard. He started meeting with Pastor Grime to help him sort out all of his mixed up thoughts and emotions encompassing the whole business.

There were some in the state legislature in Sacramento that were pushing to have Stan's medal revoked and his name removed from the Medal of Valor plaque, but there were others that were resisting that sentiment. Their reasoning was that the act that earned him the medal was still a valid historic happening and should be recognized as such. So the debate goes on about what to do with a fallen hero.

### Six Months Later

Mark was released from prison once the state had completed its' paperwork to a homecoming that Crescent City was going to be talking about for a very long time. Tricia, Timmy and Candy gave him a royal welcome home and then the Living Waters Fellowship had a huge open house party that they invited the whole town to. And because of Tricia's status as a heroine it seemed like more than half the town turned out to wish him well.

Steve, the manager at the Chart Room Restaurant, couldn't have been more pleased at how things turned out; again because of Tricia's status, the business at the restaurant had doubled and Tricia's tips increased as well.

Two weeks after Mark was released from prison and came home, Rod had to return home so BJ offered Tricia the money that Rod's parents had sent to take him to Klamath Falls to catch the train if they wanted a couple of days by themselves after putting Rod on the train. She was a little disappointed that she would not get to visit Crater Lake again, but she also knew how important it would be for Tricia and Mark to reconnect after being apart for so long without having the children around. She offered to watch Timmy and Candy while they were away and the children were okay with that; they had started to get over their phobia of not being right there with mom all of the time since she had gone missing. The only thing that BJ had made them do was promise to visit Crater Lake for her. It was one of the best gifts that anyone could have given them and their marriage.

Timmy and Candy were now back in school and doing so much better than they had ever done. The teachers that knew them from before and Tricia were all amazed at the difference in their school-work from just last year.

At first Mark talked about moving back to Southern California to the big city where the jobs and the action was, but after spending time there in Crescent City and time with Ralph and BJ and time with Pastor Grime and the rest of the folks at the Living Waters Fellowship, he wouldn't think about moving now. He had never been around a farm before in his life, but since he was having a hard time finding work, he started hanging around Ralph and helping him with the chores and it was beginning to grow on him. Also, in talking to Pastor Grime, they had decided to begin a prison ministry and Mark would be in charge of that. Mark had joined a small group that Pastor Grime had started for new believers studying the Bible. He was thinking about maybe starting his studies at home to become a prison chaplain and Pastor Grime was encouraging him to go for it. He was also doing odd jobs around the church; cleaning, painting, repairing some broken chairs, etc. – whatever needed to be done that he could do. It gave him real pleasure to be used and to help others. He even went with some of the other men of the church to a widow lady's place to repair some of the broken things there and do some painting.

The new Mark and the new Tricia were growing by leaps and bounds and not without their growing pains. But as each one came up, they learned how to work them through. So different from how they used to handle those difficult issues of life. There were a few times when one or the other or both would need to take advantage of the wisdom of an older, more mature Christian like BJ or Pastor Grime, but they were learning and they were growing -together. Happily ever after only happens in the fairy tales, but if you had asked Mark or Tricia about their marriage and their family they would have told you that it was 'happily ever after.'

Claudia stayed at BJ and Ralph's place for two weeks after she was rescued because she was afraid to spend the night alone in her house. BJ had suggested that she either find another place to live or take in a roommate to live with her. That would help alleviate her fear of being alone and it would also help her pay the rent. She thought the roommate idea was a good one. A young woman who was a new Christian and had just been released from prison had started to attend the Living Waters Fellowship and when Claudia approached her about moving in with her she was ecstatic. She had been praying for an arrangement just like that and God was now in the process of answering that prayer. Both her and Claudia were in the new believers' group with Mark.

Ricardo had snapped out of his depression when Claudia was rescued, but had still not begun his own personal relationship with Jesus. However Mark has been meeting with him and just being his friend; all the while praying that he would make that all important decision and first step. And Claudia took a page out of Tricia's book and was making a reconnection with Ricardo around his interest in older airplanes. Both Mark and Claudia were expecting that Ricardo would one day soon make that change.

Crescent City cleaned up after the flood waters of the tsunami just like they had for the previous tsunami's in their history and business was soon back to normal. What was going to take longer was the scar that a prison guard named Stan and inflicted on the community, but they were working through that as well. Pelican Bay was becoming more open and responsive to the suggestions of the community. They still had a long way to go, but progress was happening and relationships were being restored.

As Tricia lay her head down on the pillow she couldn't help but think of that verse in Genesis following Jacob, Joseph's father's death where Joseph was talking to his brothers. They were fearful that Joseph would exact retribution for how they had mistreated him and Joseph told them, "you intended to harm me, but God intended it for good to accomplish what is now being done, the saving of many lives." Tricia had to say, "God you asked me to trust you. I would not have chosen this method to save my family and others, but you knew best. Thank you for everything you have done in my life and my family's lives." And with that prayer breathed, she fell fast asleep next to a husband that had been recreated into a new man; and having a restored relationship and marriage.

# References

1. Lyrics from single "Come Home" on the album *Come Home* by Luminate (c) January 2011 by Sparrow/EMI/CMG records.

LaVergne, TN USA
30 March 2011
222089LV00002B/7/P